Once Burned
(Morelli Family, #3)

SAM MARIANO

This is a work of fiction. Names, characters, businesses, places, events and incidents are either the products of the author's imagination, or used fictitiously. Any resemblance to actual persons, living or dead, or actual events is purely coincidental.

Once Burned (Morelli Family, #3) Copyright © 2017 by Sam Mariano
A brief passage of *Fantomina; Or Love in a Maze by Eliza Haywood (1725)* is quoted in chapter two

ISBN: 9781090268211

DEDICATION

For you, dear reader.

Thank you for enjoying my stories and enabling me to have the best job ever!

20 years ago

IT STILL feels like I'm on fire.

I can't move. Even if not for the damage done to my body, they've wrapped me up in so much gauze I look more dead than alive.

I think of the time a couple Halloweens ago when I dressed up like a mummy. I bet I'd get more candy in this get-up than that one.

Someone's sniffling. I can't move my head, but I shift my eyes left and see my best friend standing there, dark head bowed. The sniffling is coming from him. I've never seen Mateo cry before.

I try to speak, but I can't move my mouth.

I have to wait for him to look at me again, to see my eyes are open now. It takes a few minutes, then his brown eyes, bloodshot and red-rimmed finally meet mine and all of a sudden my insides feel hollow, like a juicy watermelon after Mom finished scooping out its insides for a picnic over the summer.

Seeing I'm awake, he swipes a hand across his nose and stands a little straighter. "Hey."

I can't speak, but he might not know that. Either way, I'm not sure I'd answer him.

"Lucy brought me," he explains, his eyes moving over my face, taking in all the gauze. "I had to see if you were okay."

Luciana's old enough to drive, but I'm surprised she put her neck out, bringing him here like this.

I try to speak again, forgetting I can't. Just the slight movement of my facial muscles sends a shudder through me, and searing pain is my reward for the attempt.

"They said they gave you medicine, so it shouldn't hurt so much. They... they said you're gonna be okay."

A new kind of pain sears me, not physical, but emotional. The memory of my father begging. My desperate mother sobbing, screaming, pleading, reaching for me.

I try to speak again. A sound comes out, but it's not a word, and it hurts like hell.

Mateo shifts, attempting to anticipate whatever I'm trying to get out, but his face registers no comprehension. Not sure why it would, I guess, but I'm flustered all the same.

I try again, and manage a "Muh..."

I want to cry with how much it hurts, but I can't even cry.

I watch Mateo's face fall and he goes to step back, but stops, realizing I can't follow him. Pushing closer to the bed, he reaches out a hand, but mine isn't there to take; it's wrapped up in all the gauze.

"Your mom?" he asks.

I can't nod, but I try to convey with my eyes that yeah, I want to know about my mom.

He looks at the bed instead of me, and that's when I know.

Mateo whispers, "I'm sorry, Adrian."

My eyes burn with tears I can't shed. My face burns with pain. *Everything* hurts, and here stands my best friend, telling me he's sorry like it counts. Like it means *anything*. Like it *helps*.

The heart monitor I'm hooked up to starts to go haywire and Mateo backs up, startled, scared. A nurse comes hustling in to check on me and frowns at the sight of an eight-year-old in here by himself.

"You're not supposed to be in here without an adult, honey."

"He's my friend," Mateo explains, like that should be good enough.

"I understand that, honey, but you can't be in here by yourself. Why don't you go find your mom or dad, and you can come back in with one of them."

"But…"

Mateo just stands there, looking a little lost. Of course the nurse can't know that his mom's dead and his dad's the one who put me here.

But I do.

With one last long look, my best friend, Mateo Morelli, swears, "It's gonna be okay, Adrian. I'll come back for you."

This time I'm glad I can't speak. As much as everything hurts, as much as I've lost this night, I don't think I could bear looking at my best friend and telling him to stay the hell away from me.

PROLOGUE

"I'M GLAD you came, Adrian."

Shifting the clear glass of amber liquid in my hand, I take a sip, then look up at Mateo Morelli, perched on the edge of his father's desk, in his father's study.

Memories creep up on me, of us as kids, sneaking in here to see what was so important. We both had our first taste of gin, pilfered from one of Matt's decanters. Neither of us found the taste or the burn very much to get excited about back then.

Now I tip back my glass, welcoming the burn.

"Not every day you get invited to a Morelli family dinner," I say, lightly.

"Aw, come on. You know you could come anytime you like."

Mateo's lackey speaks up now, pointing in my direction to get my attention. "You used to live here, didn't you?"

"Lifetime ago," I acknowledge.

Shaking his head, the man says, "Man, I don't know how you leave all this. Way above my pay grade, but a man sure could get used to it, you know?"

I assume he's talking about the house, but his creepy gaze is locked on something behind me—the alcohol cart?

I turn to look and see the maid by the cart, wiping up a little spill, flashing Mateo an apologetic look, like she's just cost him thousands of dollars. Which I guess she might've; Mateo doesn't go cheap on his liquor.

"It's fine," Mateo murmurs, taking the glass she just refilled for him.

"I'm so sorry," she whispers.

He smiles at how nervous she is, shaking his head. "Spills happen, Elise." Nodding in my direction, he adds, "Try not to spill any on Adrian, huh?"

I want to tell him I'm fine, I don't need any more—I'm not as comfortable with people serving me as he is—but the little blonde girl is already bringing the decanter my way. I watch as she pours it without looking at me, at her pretty face, flushed with embarrassment. Her blonde hair, escaping the neat bun she has it pulled back into. Her blue eyes briefly land on mine, but apparently intimidated by me, she quickly flits away to refill this Rick guy's drink.

"How old are you, honey?" he asks, his gaze moving over her body.

"Me? Um, 16."

Rick lifts his eyebrows, glancing back at Mateo, then back to her. "Wow. Young."

"Yeah," I agree, since he's still looking at her like a piece a meat. "Real young."

"Haven't seen you in here before."

"Maria's sick today, so Elise is filling in," Mateo explains.

Elise moves away from Rick and back toward Mateo. She seems less tense around him, which is pretty much the opposite of what you'd expect. He doesn't scare me, but Mateo's generally considered a pretty intimidating guy. Elise moves closer to him like he's the sun, and she's stranded in a snowstorm.

The conversation turns to the neighborhood, the changes, the new talent. Mateo tries to bring me into his fold again, which shouldn't surprise me since he thinks that's why I'm here.

We keep drinking, and drinking, and drinking, and drinking. We're all trashed by the time we have to go to dinner, and Mateo doesn't usually let that happen, so he really must be pleased to see me.

A stab of guilt gets me, but I ignore it.

I'm good at ignoring pain.

One more night and I can get out of Chicago. I can make it through one more night.

Some people get more outgoing when they're drunk, but not me. I withdraw even further into myself, which is saying something.

Rick, he's the obnoxious type. Boisterous and loud—I can't believe he's Mateo's main hit guy. I wouldn't trust this asshole to take out an elephant with a fucking cannon launcher.

No subtlety.

I sort of wish he did have some, because then I wouldn't be boiling over here with anger by the time the ladies bring out dessert. Beth serves Mateo and takes a seat to his left. She looks tired. I'm surprised he didn't even mention her when we were drinking in the study, since they apparently had a kid together since I last saw him.

Francesca puts a plate in front of me, then Rick, before taking her own seat beside him.

"Where's that pretty little maid?" Rick asks Francesca.

"Elise?" she asks, frowning at him. "Cleaning up in the kitchen."

Please don't.

I know I can't say it, but as Mr. Fucking Subtlety eyeballs the door leading to the kitchen, I get a bad feeling about tonight. A real bad feeling.

A few minutes later, he needs to use the restroom. The nearest one is in the hall, but of course he doesn't head that way—

he heads for the kitchen.

Placing my fork down on the table, I look at the chocolate lava cake I haven't touched. I try to convince myself he just didn't remember about the bathroom in the hall, or he's drunk and went for the wrong door.

Only I don't believe any of that.

I look to Mateo, wishing he would've noticed, but he doesn't pay nearly as much attention to the maid as she does to him, and he doesn't seem to find anything amiss about Rick going to the kitchen instead of the bathroom. I look around at the other faces, and no one else seems to either.

Goddammit.

Finally, I push back from the table and stand, drawing Mateo's attention.

"Be right back," I mutter, heading for the kitchen doors.

I don't see Elise when I enter. It's a massive room, like all the rooms, but she's not by the sink cleaning up, or storing leftovers in the fridge. She's nowhere.

Something slams into the pantry door, grabbing my attention. The pantry's pulled shut, but something rattles from inside.

Clenching my fists at my side, I storm to the pantry and rip it open.

Face down on the ground with Rick on top of her, Elise's teary blue eyes look up at me, as if expecting a savior. The light dims slightly at seeing me, but she's not exactly in a position to be picky.

"Get the fuck off her," I tell Rick.

I look at the state of his clothes—his belt's undone, his pants tugged down, but I can't tell if he had time to finish the job.

He's not moving urgently enough and rage courses through my body. I grab him like he's nothing, throwing him against a shelf of canned food. "I said get the fuck off her."

Elise yanks her dress down, scurrying into the corner. I can't tell if she's still traumatized from his attack, or if she's scared of me. Either would be reasonable.

"Hey, man, what the fuck," Rick objects, his eyes wide with belligerence.

"Get out of here before I break your fucking neck," I tell him calmly.

"Mateo's gonna hear about this," he tells me, clearly thinking it's a threat.

Meeting his gaze with a smile, I reply, "Oh, you bet he fucking will."

Turns out, we don't have to wait long for that. The crash must've been loud enough that he heard it in the other room; before Rick can even make it halfway across the kitchen, Mateo's storming in with a scowl on his face.

"What the fuck is going on in here?"

Elise jumps up, seeing Mateo, and runs over to him. He catches her in his arms naturally, burying her face in his chest, and I can't help feeling a little rejected. Obviously I didn't do it for the glory, but *I'm* the one who paid enough attention to know something was up, I'm the one who came to make sure she was okay, and he's the one she runs to for comfort.

I also don't feel even remotely comfortable with the doubts it raises about their relationship. Mateo and I are the same age—28. This girl is *16*. I know he likes them younger than him, but that's too young.

Beth stands off to the side, watching. I search her face for any trace of jealousy, but come up empty—Beth doesn't seem to give a damn if some pretty young thing runs to Mateo for comfort.

"Did he hurt you?" Mateo murmurs.

Elise shakes her head no, and some of the tension eases out of me. Then she pulls back and adds, "Your friend stopped him."

She doesn't know my name. I don't know why that feels disappointing, but it doesn't matter. I'm just relieved I got here in time.

Mateo meets my gaze, and he looks a bit troubled. I guess he should be—an important member of his crew just fucked up in a major way, and now he has to deal with it.

I want him to pull his gun out right now. Put Rick on the floor, execution style, and put a bullet right through his sleazy brain.

That doesn't happen.

"I think we all need to... Dinner's over," he finally says. Glancing at me, he says, "You guys have had too much to drink."

I don't understand at first. What does that have to do with anything?

Then Rick smirks at me from across the kitchen, and I realize... that's it. That's all. Mateo isn't going to *do* anything about this, he's just going to shrug off the behavior by saying we've had too much to drink.

"You kidding me?" I say, unable to stop myself.

His eyebrows rise and he gives me a look that tells me how close he is to pulling rank. "Sleep it off, Adrian."

Wow.

My eyes fall to Elise, still snug against him like he's her fucking savior. Then to Rick, smug, thinking he's off the hook.

Finally I nod. "Fine. I'll sleep it off."

Without another word, and without waiting to be shown to guest rooms I already know how to find, I turn and leave the kitchen.

Leaning forward in the armchair beside Mateo's bed, I gaze at the face of a man I once called a friend. Even after his father murdered mine, even after the scars and the pain he inflicted on me to hurt them, I still considered Mateo a friend.

Not at first.

At first I was angry, hurt, alone in the world every way a kid can be. But Mateo never gave up, and Mateo's not the kind of friend who never gives up on you. Mateo's the kind of friend who's there when he wants something from you, and not so much when there's nothing you can do for him.

Me, I never had anything Mateo could've wanted, but he still stuck by me. Even when I didn't want him to.

But we're not those kids anymore. I grew up to be more ruthless than he ever could've expected, and him? Well, he grew up and took his father's place.

Staring at the gun in my lap, I finger the long, cold silencer screwed onto the end of it.

My gaze moves back to the bed, at Beth lying there beside him. She's turned the other way, with her back to him, but he still has an arm thrown over her, trying to get close.

I'm surprised he's still asleep. Mateo's a notoriously light sleeper—look at him and he'll wake up. Must be the alcohol.

Figuring I may as well get down to it, I inhale and push out a sigh so loud, I'm surprised I don't wake Beth.

Mateo's eyes open, and it only takes him a second to register a presence in the room. He pushes up, reaches for the nightstand.

"It's me," I say quietly.

He stops. Stares at me, then at the gun in my lap. Back to my face, a look of betrayal quickly moving in place of his alarm.

"Rick's dead," I tell him.

Something like relief flickers across his features as he mistakenly concludes that's why I brought the gun, that I didn't come here to hurt him, after all. He leans back, sighing and staring up at the ceiling. "Goddamn it, Adrian," he says, lowly. "I talked to him. He wasn't going to touch her again."

"Not good enough," I explain.

"Well, thank you for that. I needed him."

"He's an asshole, you didn't need him. Guys like him are

10

easy to find. You need someone better."

"You volunteering?" he asks, pushing up to look at me.

I shake my head no, looking down at the gun again, then back at him. "I didn't come here tonight to join your crew."

He holds my gaze, doubtful, but wanting to believe the best of me. "Then why'd you come?"

"Baryshnikov sent me."

His face falls. "The Russians? They don't even have a foothold in this city."

I merely shrug. I'm not here to explain. I don't expect to leave. Just figured I'd tell him.

Scoffing, shaking his head a little at the absurdity, he says, "You won't work for me, but you'll work for Baryshnikov."

"He knew I had an in with you. Offered me a lot of money."

"To kill me," Mateo states, this time coldly.

"Yes."

"So what are you fucking waiting for?" he asks.

It's a good question. One I've been asking myself since I managed to get in his room without waking him up. If I wanted to go through with it, I gave up my window of opportunity.

Instead of committing one way or another, I ask the question that's been weighing on me since dinner. "You fucking your maid?"

"What?" He pulls a face of disgust, like he can't believe I'd even ask. "No."

"Good. Don't." Nodding to the nightstand beside his bed, I tell him, "I wrote down the address where you can find Baryshnikov. His operation's small right now, you have more than enough clout to get rid of him."

Scowling, his gaze mistrustful, Mateo asks, "Why are you telling me this?"

"I know you have to kill me now," I say, reasonably.

He looks over at Beth, sleeping in the bed next to him. Then at the door to the adjoining bedroom, where their baby daughter sleeps. Finally, his gaze moves back to me.

Tiredly passing a hand over his face, he hauls himself out of bed. He crosses in front of me, clearly unafraid, and grabs a pair of jogging pants.

"What the fuck am I supposed to do with this, Adrian?" he asks, irritably, as if I've inconvenienced him by showing up but not finishing the job. I guess I have.

Once he's dressed, I follow him out of the bedroom. I guess it's not much of a loss, my life. His father stole my family, my face—half my fucking body is a mess, and that's not even taking into account the shape my insides are in. Matt Morelli stole what I had, and I haven't built much since. Nobody will miss me when I'm gone.

I'm surprised when he opens the door and leads me down to the basement. The wine cellar's the only part I've ever known him to go to, and that's nowhere near this part.

The basement is where his dad used to keep his mom when she pissed him off, so Mateo's never liked coming down here.

Dread courses through me when we stop outside the cell. Nestled beneath the beautiful Morelli homestead like a true dungeon is a small, self-contained prison. There's no guard, just a dirty cement slab with metal bars and an exposed toilet in the corner, like a jail cell. It's open, since there's no one inside, but Mateo grabs the key from a hook against the dirty wall.

Holding out his hand for my gun, he says, "Come on."

"Why?" I ask.

"I have to figure out what to do with you."

I sigh, my head lolling back. I don't want to do this. I don't want the dog and pony show. He has to kill me now—he should just do it. I'm not interested in the trial, in stalling for more time. Let's just do what has to be done. But since I'm maybe the only person alive who Mateo considers a real friend, he doesn't *want* to kill me. Maybe it'll take him a few days to realize he has no choice. I'll let him try to figure a way around it first. He won't, but

I'll let him try. I hand him my gun and step inside the cell.

Mateo closes the barred door, turning the lock and letting his hand fall to his side. Looking at me through the bars, he says, "If this was the only way, I wish you wouldn't have come back."

Then he heads back the way he came, leaving me alone in the dark.

It feels like I've been down here a year, but I'm sure it's only been a few days. Mateo brought me a few bottles of water the morning after he brought me down, but he hasn't been back since and they're long gone.

Sitting on the cold, hard floor in the corner, I wait. And I wait. And I wait.

But finally someone comes.

I expect Mateo, but I certainly *don't* expect the little blonde maid to come down to this dank, dirty secret beneath Mateo's home. I didn't even expect she would know about it.

"Hi," she says, offering me a tentative smile.

At first I remain where I am, on the floor in the corner, with my back against the wall. As she comes closer, I realize I should probably stand.

There's a little basket on her arm, but she puts it down and fishes out the key, awkwardly shoving it in the lock. "Sorry about all this," she says, as she turns the lock and opens the door.

Warily eyeing the key, I tell her, "He shouldn't send you down here."

"Oh, he didn't. I mean, I asked if I could come."

"Well, that's not smart. You shouldn't come down here alone," I revise, watching as she goes back out to grab the basket. "I could be dangerous."

"You won't hurt me," she says, rolling her eyes like it's a ridiculous thing to even suggest.

Of course she's right, but she shouldn't be so sure of that. "You never know what people will do."

Not accepting my advice, she peels back the little cloth over her basket and tells me, "I brought you some breakfast. Do you like muffins? I made some chocolate chip and banana. I didn't know what kind you'd like best, so I brought both."

I'm still a little uneasy as I take the first muffin she hands me, but my mouth waters at the sight of it.

She places a few bottles of water on the ground near the front of the cell. "I'll try to bring some dinner later, after everyone upstairs eats."

I'm not sure what to say, so I stick with silence.

Once the food has been dispersed, she gets a little more bashful. "I brought you something else. I thought… it probably drives you crazy how quiet it is down here," she tells me, drawing out a small, silver, circular object. A walkman? "It plays music," she tells me. "I just brought the one CD, but it's a greatest hits, so it's just the one case, but there are actually lots of songs to listen to."

She offers it to me, and she looks so damn hopeful, I take it. I've never been a big music fan, preferring the quiet, but I don't say so.

"It's my favorite," she tells me, bouncing forward on her toes, kind of excited to be sharing it with someone. "My dad loved Bowie. After I came here, I asked Mateo for these so I could listen, and… I don't know, it got me through some rough nights. I thought you could borrow it, to get through yours."

Smiling slightly, I finally say, "That's nice, Elise. Thank you."

She nods her head, glancing down at the empty basket. "I should probably get back upstairs before Maria has a cow, but… if you're still here Sunday, it's my day off. I could come down and keep you company, if you'd like."

"You don't want to spend your day off down here," I tell her.

"You're only down here because of me," she states.

"That's not true," I tell her. Of course, I can't tell her why I *am* down here, so I don't have anything to back that up.

"Well, I'm coming back Sunday," she states, adorably stubborn. "If you don't like it, you can just put on the headphones and ignore me."

I crack a smile, doubting I could ignore her if I tried.

"Okay," I relent, since it's not even a fight I want to win.

Nodding with satisfaction, she backs out of the cell and closes the door, securing the lock. "Make sure you listen to that whole thing. When I come back, I wanna hear your favorites."

"I will," I promise.

"Good." With one last bright smile, Elise gives me a little wave, and then she leaves me alone in Mateo's dungeon with only David Bowie for company.

CHAPTER ONE
Five years later

I DIDN'T expect my last day at the Morelli homestead to be a celebration, but the solemn non-event it turns out to be isn't what I expected either.

Of course, I didn't expect yet another of Mateo's lovers to betray him.

I didn't expect Mateo to be locked away in his surveillance room, too busy to even say goodbye, let alone attend my last Morelli family dinner.

The mood in the whole house is solemn. Mia and Vince showed up, none of us thinking to tell them dinner had been canceled. Joey shows up, but upon hearing there's no mandatory dinner tonight, he heads to Mateo's study for a liquid dinner by himself.

Elise looks at the cassata cake Mia picked up from the bakery for dessert—my favorite. With Mateo in the state he's in, there's just no joy in the house.

Approaching Elise, I touch her shoulder. She jumps, spinning around as if she doesn't know who to expect. I drop my hand, ducking my head.

"We should probably just go," I tell her.

Mia grabs a knife, spinning around to slice into the cake. "Well, wait. You have to at least have some cake. We brought this specifically for you."

"It was a nice thought," I tell her. "This isn't how any of us expected tonight to be, so we might as well just call it."

Mia's shoulders sag with defeat. "At least let me wrap some up for you to take."

Elise goes to a cupboard near the pantry and digs out two paper plates, then she grabs aluminum foil and comes to help Mia pack the cake.

"I like cassata cake," she says, glancing at me over her shoulder.

A ghost of a smile tugs at my lips. "Fine. We'll take some cake."

Mia cuts off two enormous slices and Elise wraps them. Dropping the knife into the sink, Mia turns back to me, bracing her hands behind her on the counter. "You're not even going to go say goodbye to him?"

"He's busy," I point out.

She rolls her eyes, unimpressed. "He's not too busy to say goodbye."

I don't like goodbyes anyway, but I don't bother further defending my decision. It's weird to think about, but I'll probably never even see Mia after tonight.

"I'll say goodbye to *you*," I tell her.

"I still think you should say goodbye to him. He's going to feel abandoned."

Normally Mateo wouldn't give in to the feeling of abandonment mere mortals succumb to, but in light of all this happening with Meg, and because it's me, she's probably right. Of course, I don't think he'll feel any less abandoned because of meaningless words like "goodbye" or "I guess it hasn't been so bad keeping you alive these past five years," so what's the point?

Elise grabs the cake, but she's watching Mia with a look I

can't quite peg. Like she's trying to understand her, maybe? Trying to relate.

Glancing at me, Elise points out, "I didn't really say goodbye to him either."

"Do you want to?"

This question makes her uncomfortable. Her gaze moves from my shoes to Mia's arm, then drops back to the expensive Tuscan tile covering the kitchen floor. "I don't know." Almost apologetically, she glances at me. "I have lived here a long time."

I stifle a sigh, nodding my head. "Fine. We'll say goodbye."

"I don't know," she says again, fidgeting with the foil wrapping edge of the plate. "Maybe we should just go."

I don't understand Elise's feelings for Mateo. I know it's something she's struggled with for years—more so since Mia forced her eyes open. She doesn't confide in me anymore though, least of all about him, so I can't be sure what she's feeling now, knowing she's really leaving, and she'll really never see him again. One would think that would be a good thing—finally leaving the home of a man who has *enslaved* you for six years. While on a rational level it's hard for me to swallow her conflicted feelings, psychologically I understand it's not so simple. I'm committed to accepting it, even if it annoys the hell out of me.

Not to mention, Mateo has a primal effect on women that no textbook need explain. One look at Mia provides solid evidence of that—she should hate Mateo, but here she is, worried about him feeling abandoned. It's like they can't help but care about him, no matter what he does.

I don't normally envy Mateo, but I wish I could have that effect—just on Elise, no one else.

Since I don't and he does, I find myself following Elise to Mateo's goddamn surveillance room.

Never having been inside the small room before, Elise's eyes widen slightly, taking in the many screens. Mateo is parked at a desk behind the largest one, a pair of black headphones on as he

18

listens to accompanying audio.

Upon seeing us enter the room, he presses pause and removes the headphones.

"You taking off?" he asks, rising.

I nod. "Yeah. Thought we'd say goodbye."

Elise fidgets again, toying with her own hands since she's not holding anything now.

Nodding, he comes out from behind his spy station, brushing past us to let us all out of the cramped space. The door opens up into his study. He pushes it shut behind him, and it just looks like a panel. Joey glances up from his wing chair, where he's drinking and playing on his phone, but Mateo dismisses him with a flicker of a glance as he heads to his desk. Retrieving a small rectangular package wrapped in glossy silver paper, he hands it to Elise.

"I got you a going away present."

I manage to remain blank as her whole face lights up the way it used to when he was around. "You didn't have to get me a gift," she says, taking it, her grin barely lessening as she bites her bottom lip.

"It's just something small, nothing to get excited over," he says lightly.

I watch her tear into it, all aglow, and think about how *this* is yet another thing I'm not going to miss.

She's delighted as she looks at the Disney movie, *Aladdin.* "My favorite," she says.

"I know," he says, with an affable wink.

She blushes with pleasure as she thanks him, impulsively stepping forward and giving him a hug that makes me want to die.

He turns to me once she lets go. I know he doesn't have a gift for me, because he already gave it to me. An envelope with enough cash to get us situated in a small apartment. He wouldn't give me that in front of Elise, because he wouldn't want to embarrass me.

"You'll be missed," he tells me simply.

With a gruff nod, I mumble, "Yeah, you too."

It sounds stupid once it's out there, but all I want to do now is get the hell out of this house. For Elise, this place is home, but for me these past five years, it was never more than a sentence I needed to serve.

Not really knowing what else to do, I go for a handshake. It feels even stranger than my last utterance, but he shakes it anyway as I say, "Take care of yourself."

"I will. If you change your mind, you know there's a spot for you."

"I won't," I assure him, meeting his gaze, "but thanks."

As we turn to leave, Elise glances back over her shoulder. I keep my gaze straight ahead and lead her back to the kitchen to retrieve the cake and say goodbye to Mia.

I'm not expecting her to hug me, but she does anyway. "You're sure you don't wanna say goodbye to Meg?" she asks.

I shake my head. I just want to leave, to get to our new home and see what Elise thinks of it. I'm also still disappointed in Meg. Right from the start I thought she might suit Mateo, and while there had certainly been lies I caught her in, I didn't think she was capable of pulling *this* off.

"Well, I'll give her the package when I take her the cake."

She ran this plan by me earlier. I'm not sure how Mateo will like it, but while I still have a few remnants of power in the house, I told Mia she could visit Meg and give her a break.

Once I walk out those doors, it's not my problem anymore.

It feels a little weird, I'll admit. I've imagined it so many times, but now that the moment's here, I somehow don't know what to expect. The rest of my life is on the other side of that door for once, and I have to start all over.

So does Elise. I hope *that's* why she looks so anxious as we approach the front door. I hope the dread on her face is because she's afraid of the uncertainty of this new beginning, because the mansion has been home to her since she was 15 years old, and now she's 21, but without having ever had the freedom to grow up. Elise is sheltered and innocent in so many ways, but she's resilient; I know eventually she'll catch up. Eventually she'll be okay.

She takes a deep breath and pushes it out as I open the door for her. My new car is silver and nondescript, nothing like I'm used to driving. Elise, she's not used to leaving the house at all. She's gone out on occasion, very rare occasion, but to be honest, aside from a trip to the grocery store, I don't know when she was actually out in the world last.

"You ready?" I ask, since she's just staring at the car, clutching the movie in her hands, unmoving.

She nods, but still doesn't move.

So I wait.

And wait.

And wait.

Eventually she pushes out another breath, like she's diving into a pool 50 feet beneath her, and drops into the passenger seat.

It's not the overwhelming relief I've daydreamed about, but it'll do.

I shut the door and go around to the driver's seat. I glance over at her as I fire up the engine, putting the car in drive and making my way out of Mateo's driveway. I feel like I should say something to her, assure her that everything will be all right, but she looks fragile, like one wrong word might completely disintegrate her composure.

So I say nothing.

The only person who vocalizes during the long ride is David Bowie, my constant companion. I hope it gives her some measure of comfort, even if she doesn't acknowledge it.

At one point I hear her sniffling, and I steal a subtle look at her. My stomach sinks at the realization that she's wiping away tears, turning her head to watch out the window so I won't see.

By the time we pull up to the parking lot of our new apartment, I'm convinced she's going to hate it. Ordinarily a person would have something to show for five years of crucial work for Mateo Morelli, but me, I only have Elise. I don't know precisely what he told her about the deal we struck—only that she initially said thanks, but no thanks, and then changed her mind after Mia outed Mateo's dark side. I don't know what she expects. We haven't talked about it at all. Honestly, it's seemed like she's wanted to completely avoid the reality as *her* sentence came to an end.

Elise looks around the parking area, at the waist-high wrought iron fence surrounding the miniscule courtyard. Red brick columns off to the left house the cluster of mailboxes, but I don't imagine we'll be getting much mail, so I don't bother to show her which one's ours.

Ours.

That's going to be weird for a while.

I open the door, letting her step inside first. Worn indoor outdoor carpet covers the ground in the hall, and Elise glances down at it, around at the dirty taupe walls. She is thus far unimpressed, and I can't say I blame her. She's used to Mateo's gleaming mansion, and I bring her to this.

"The inside's nicer," I offer.

It's sort of true. I made sure the apartment was virtually spotless. I can't do anything about the size of it, or the enormous silver pipe exposed in the kitchen, but at least I could make sure it was clean.

Our apartment is the last one at the end of the hall, right here on the bottom floor. I like that it feels more cloistered off by itself, but I don't know if she will.

Pushing the key into the lock, I glance at the cracked 104 painted on the brown door.

The first thing you can see as I push it open is the ugly seafoam green bathroom. It's cramped and has shitty water pressure. I close the door behind us, sliding the lock on the knob, the deadbolt, and the chain lock for good measure. Elise watches in a kind of fascinated horror as I secure all of them.

"Is this a safe neighborhood?" she asks.

"Yeah, it'll be okay," I tell her.

It's safe *enough*, but we probably have different safety standards, so I don't bother expanding on that.

The "hall" is all but nonexistent. The living room is two steps away, furnished with a secondhand black leather couch and a small, old television on a stand with wheels. Off to the right is our very small kitchen, with a tiny stretch of counter and dark, depressing wood paneling. There's just enough room for one person to move around between the counter and the side where the stove and refrigerator stand, and just beyond that is the tiniest laundry nook in the world. It's dark and there's only a pull-string light, so I decide not to show it to her right now.

Next to the kitchen there is a narrow hall, leading to the single white door—our bedroom. I head down that hall, and she follows behind slowly.

"I put your boxes over here," I tell her, pointing to them stacked in the corner. "There's no dresser or anything yet, but there's a closet and I grabbed some hangers, so you can hang up your clothes tomorrow if you want."

She nods absently, but her gaze is on the bed. It's a queen-sized bed with plain white sheets and the ugliest green and white floral blanket imaginable. It's not even an actual bedspread, just a damn blanket.

"Um, I'll get new stuff eventually," I point out, since she's probably unimpressed. "I mean, this is all new, but... Once I get—"

"It's fine," she interrupts. "Before I moved into the mansion, I slept on a twin with one of those short throws that doesn't cover your whole body. Not super warm in the winter."

Luckily it's summer right now, which is why I didn't bother with a whole bedding set. "I only signed a six-month lease for this place. I just need a little time to establish myself and get a little saved, then I'll move us someplace nicer. This is very temporary."

"It's fine," she assures me again, but she still doesn't look at me.

"Obviously I'll sleep on the couch," I tell her.

She shakes her head, rolling her eyes. For the first time since we left the mansion, she nearly smiles. "Don't be ridiculous. This is *your* apartment."

"It's your apartment, too. And I don't want to make you uncomfortable."

"I'll be extremely uncomfortable if I'm sleeping in this bed and you're stuck on the couch," she states. "It's fine. There's enough room for both of us."

The matter apparently settled, she heads back out to the hall, stepping into the kitchen. She puts the two paper plates down on the counter and begins opening cupboards.

I bought a set of dishes and a 6-pack of blue plastic cups. In the drawer she finds a cheap new set of silverware in a plain white tray, some essential kitchen utensils in the one beside it.

"There's not much in the fridge," I tell her, as she reaches for the handle to open it. "I figured we could go grocery shopping tomorrow."

Faintly smiling, she says, "At least that I'm familiar with." Reopening the drawer with the silverware, she extracts two forks. Grabbing the plates, she heads back over to me.

I take a plate and fork, watching as she peels the foil off hers. "Cake for dinner?"

She shrugs. "There's just bottled water in the fridge, so unless you'd prefer to eat air…"

"We could go out and get something to eat," I tell her. "Plenty of places to eat around here. I saw some kind of hot dog restaurant back there, there's a pizza place just behind us, I could walk over and grab one in like two minutes."

Her lips curve up as she digs in. "You can get whatever you'd like. I'm going to eat cake."

CHAPTER TWO

IT'S A long first night.

There's plenty we probably could do after dinner—explore our corner of the city, unpack our few belongings, address our situation.

Instead we watch *Aladdin*.

It's only 9:30 when the movie ends and I don't know what we'll do with the rest of the night. Elise sits on the couch in silence with me for a few minutes, then she pushes up and heads to the bedroom.

I don't know whether or not to follow her, but when she doesn't return after a few minutes, I head down the hall to see what she's up to. Leaning against the doorframe, I watch her sit down on the bed, curling a leg beneath her, and lovingly caress a worn, bent literature book, the pages slightly curled, the laminate on the cover peeling off. I recognize it, and even though she didn't invite me to, I step inside, moving closer to the bed.

Glancing up at me with a mercifully pleasant smile, she asks, "Remember how I used to read to you? And we'd talk about all these stories, and you'd tell me about the women who wrote them."

I nod. I doubt I've forgotten even a minute of that time.

"I loved that," she says simply, opening the book and flipping through various marked pages. "You always knew so much. It should've made me feel hopelessly unintelligent, but it didn't. You always treated me like I was far more interesting than I actually am."

"That's not true," I tell her.

She rolls her eyes, but she's still smiling. "Sit down, I'll read to you."

It's the lightest I've felt all day. Climbing on the bed, I make my way toward the head to relax on the pillows, while Elise remains at the foot. She begins reading without telling me which story she's chosen, but I recognize it by the end of the first (admittedly long) sentence.

Years ago, this was my favorite part of every day. It took Elise one week of faithful visitation to my cell before she had my allegiance. I can't say why—despite the burns and my general disinterest in people, it wasn't as if I'd never been around women. I've been with my fair share, though rarely for more than a few weeks. Two months, tops. It was never serious. I was never trying to connect, and neither were they.

But then Elise popped up, innocent and kind, thinking I landed in Mateo's jail cell for killing the man who tried to hurt her. I wasn't sure what it said about her that she was so comfortable with a man she fully realized was a killer, but I liked it, because it was me. Elise made me *feel* something—not sexually, not then. She was 16 at the time, after all. But when Mateo finally came back down, I had to know how she came to be there. I had to know if he'd ever let her leave.

He didn't want to kill me anyway, I know he didn't. What he wanted, what he had always wanted, was to bring me into his family the only way he knew how—by having me work for him. Realizing he had something I wanted, he offered me a bargain— he'd pardon me for my crimes against him and give me Elise, provided I give him five solid years of dedicated service.

Prior to that, there had been no end date on Elise's position. Much like Maria, Elise was simply there, and she would remain there. He never said so, but knowing him as I do, especially now, I assume if I hadn't come along, she would've ended up in his bed as she grew older. I don't think she would've stayed there. Mateo needs more of a challenge than Elise would've ever represented to hold his interest, but after Beth was gone, I'm sure Elise would've jumped at the chance to comfort the bastard.

Elise had always been pretty, but when I first met her, it was a girlish pretty. As I lived under Mateo's roof, serving him faithfully in a capacity I always swore I never would, she grew up. Elise hadn't been to an actual school since arriving at the mansion, so I offered to step in. I was no teacher, certainly, but I was knowledgeable enough to fill in the blanks of her education, to catch her up and introduce her to subjects she may not have delved into as deeply otherwise. Technically I was her tutor, but I lived for those moments. After she was finished cleaning, after I was finished doing whatever Mateo needed from me that day, after I'd washed the blood off my hands, it was the sweet sound of Elise's voice, the sparkle in her blue eyes, the glow in her cheeks… those were the things that helped blot the stains from my soul.

It's been a long, long time since I last sat with her like this, letting her read passages from classical literature, or debating the varying levels of atrociousness different historical figures managed to reach in their lifetimes. I knew I'd missed it, but I didn't realize how much until now. The stress of today, of this week, of *everything* melts away as I listen to the comforting sound of Elise reading to me.

"'He now took the liberty of kissing away her tears, and catching the sighs as they issued from her lips; telling her if grief was infectious, he was resolved to have his share; protesting he would gladly exchange passions with her, and be content to bear her load of *sorrow*, if she would as willingly ease the burden of his *love.'*"

She stops, sighing, and glances at me. "It's too bad. That could be so romantic."

"You and your terrible heroes," I say, shaking my head.

Her nose wrinkles up adorably. "I still think Beauplaisir's an idiot," she states.

I smile. "He's quite unimpressive."

"Maybe if the book was longer I'd understand the appeal," she states.

"Beyond money, I don't think he has any," I say.

She shakes her head, caressing the page. "It sounds so romantic."

"A rapey, unfaithful wastrel with money and station?" I ask lightly.

Elise rolls her eyes at me. "No, that passage. It should be about someone better than him."

"Agreed," I say, wondering if she sees the irony in this conversation.

Replacing the yellow bookmark, she says, "I know I didn't even finish the scene, but I'm going to stop here so I can reread it again tomorrow."

"Fine by me."

Flashing me a warm smile as she closes the book, she says, "This was nice."

"Yeah, it was," I agree.

She stands, placing the book on the floor in the corner. I guess I need to get a nightstand. Elise retrieves some pajamas from the box. I should probably leave so she can change, but I'm too comfortable, so she goes to the bathroom to change.

I *have* imagined Elise in my bed many times over, but now that we're here, I *can't* imagine it.

Normally I sleep without a shirt on, but that's when I'm alone. Considering the burn scars all down my left side, I decide to slip into sweatpants and a thin, long-sleeved gray shirt instead. I'm already warm, so I go out to turn the air down a notch. I don't want to freeze Elise, but damn.

When she steps out of the bathroom in a little pair of sleep shorts with a moon and stars print and a matching navy tank top with "sweet dreams" stretched across her clearly free-roaming breasts, I immediately rethink everything.

Averting my gaze so she doesn't feel awkward, I stare instead at… well, the wall. That's normal, right?

Elise's long blonde hair is pulled up in a perky pony tail and she flashes me a smile as she heads back to the bedroom.

Shit, I'm not ready for this.

She didn't turn off any of the lights, probably not sure if I was going to bed yet or not. It feels incredibly strange to realize I don't have to meet Mateo at the gym in the morning, so I'll be able to sleep in a bit.

Then the real work begins. I scheduled a haircut first thing, figuring I should clean up a bit since I'll be going to conventional interviews. I haven't worked a regular job in a little over ten years, but I falsified some recent work experience to get the apartment, so I'm using that on applications, too. Somehow I don't think my *actual* work experience will land me any ordinary gigs.

I want to give Elise a normal life.

Once I've turned off all the lights, I return to the bedroom. Elise is already curled up on her side of the bed, so I take the side that's left and settle in. Given she's been with Mateo since she was 15, I know this is the first time she's ever shared a bed with a man, and I'm hoping she doesn't feel too weird about it.

"What do you want me to do tomorrow?" she asks, once I've stopped moving around.

Her question catches me off guard. "Whatever you want. I have to go out for a little while in the morning, but I'll come back around late afternoon and we can go grocery shopping."

She nods, but still looks a little uncertain. "Well, good night, Adrian."

"Good night, Elise."

It's only been two days, and Elise already seems miserable when I leave. Apparently she's an early riser, or she's just still in the habit of rising before the sun from working at the mansion, but here, there's nothing to occupy her time.

The first day I went out, she had her clothes and mine all put away in the closets when I came back from job hunting. The second day, I came home to a dozen of three different kinds of muffins crammed onto the tiny counter and Elise throwing together a salad. She bought dried cranberries out of habit, and neither of us eats them. When she realized her mistake, she added them to her salad, but I caught the strange look on her face when she chewed them, and she pushed them off to the side after that.

The third morning I leave, she sits on the couch despondently, nursing a cup of coffee and staring at the television. It's not even on.

While I'm out I come across a book store, so I run in and grab a few things I think she might like.

She still reads to me every night. It does seem like she at least looks forward to my coming home, but probably only because she's bored out of her mind by herself. I told her she could go out during the day, but she doesn't feel safe going out alone.

Today I come home to Elise mixing a big bowl of pasta salad. She still hasn't adjusted to only cooking for two, so we end up with much more than we need, even to last the week.

"I brought you something," I tell her, offering the bag.

Her face lights up and she plants the spoon in the bowl, grabbing the bag and peering inside. "Oh, thank you, Adrian."

"It seemed like you were getting bored during the day. I

figured I'd give you something to do."

"I'm going to start offering to clean for the neighbors here soon," she states, nodding.

"You can do more than clean," I point out.

"But I like it," she says, looking at me.

I nod, but don't say anything. It's not like my disapproval of the good majority of Mateo's life is a secret, but right now I'm feeling particularly disenchanted with him. Elise was in her formative years when he took her, and now she's brainwashed into this indentured servant. It's not like I expected her to unlearn it in less than a week, but it still baffles me how she misses it.

Who *misses* housework?

"Do you have to leave every day?" she asks.

"Well, I have to find work. I thought I'd have time to line something up before I left, but then Mateo's world went to hell and I got too busy."

"Yeah," she says, her mouth turning down. "I wonder how Meg's doing."

"I'm sure she's hanging in there."

"Maria said he killed his first wife."

I hesitate, not wanting to discuss Mateo. "Yeah," I say, because it's simplest.

"Do you think he'll kill Meg?"

"No. He would've already." I glance at her, wishing she'd look bored enough that I could justify dropping it, but of course now I'm holding her attention. "Mateo's pretty even-tempered, but the Morelli men as a general rule can get sort of... malicious when they're enraged. I don't think he *meant* to kill Beth. He was a mess afterward. He just got so angry and..." I shrug, indicating that was that.

"So, it wasn't like they make it sound? Cold- blooded?"

"Do we have to talk about him?"

Shaking her head, she places the books down on the counter and goes back to stirring the already combined pasta salad. "No, of course not. I'm sorry."

I hate that she apologizes to me—she does that every time she thinks I'm slightly inconvenienced. Sorry when she realized she bought Mateo's dried cranberries. Sorry when she realized two people didn't need 36 muffins. Sorry when she stole the blanket in the middle of the night, sorry when she accidentally ran the hot water out because she didn't realize the tank here was so small, sorry, sorry, sorry.

"You don't have to keep apologizing to me," I say, because I can't help it.

"I'm sor—" She stops herself, flushing.

I bet she wants to apologize for *that*, too.

CHAPTER THREE

ON THE ninth day, I get to see Elise's temper.

I finally get a call-back for a second interview, so I leave in the morning to do that. It goes pretty well, but when I come home in the evening, expecting dinner (not because I'm an ass, but just because there's always dinner) I find Elise sitting on the couch staring at the blank television again. The last of her new books beside her, apparently finished.

I glance briefly at the kitchen, seeing there's no food, so I ask, "Should we go out to dinner?"

"No." She turns to glance at me over her shoulder, then she pats the couch, inviting me to sit.

A little uncertainly, I take a seat on the couch beside her. I do a double take when I realize she's wearing lingerie. I don't know why she *owns* lingerie at all, but she's wearing this slip of powder blue satin, lace trim, and it's damn distracting. I want to double check the time. Elise typically doesn't change into pajamas until right before bed, and right now I'm dreading going to bed if that's what she's going to wear.

Jesus, did the air stop working? Why is it so hot in here?

I tug at the collar of my shirt, shifting uncomfortably. I don't look at her, because... well, she's not wearing enough clothing to be looked at.

"Everything okay?" I ask, glancing at the blank television, since that seems safest.

She scoots forward, inching a little closer to me. Her book is still between us, thank God, but I have to physically force myself not to move away as she advances. What is she doing?

"How was your interview?" she asks.

"Uh, good. It went well."

"Good," she says pleasantly.

I nod, still staring at the television. "So, you didn't cook today. Do you want to put some—Uh, change clothes and we could go grab something? I'm kind of hungry." And also desperate to get clothing on her body, which will be necessary if we leave. "We could make a whole night of it," I add, since she doesn't immediately respond. "We could grab a drink, maybe catch a show. There's a comedy show thing—I saw a flyer. Do you like comedy shows?"

"If that's what you want," she replies.

I finally force myself to look at her, but I focus only on her face, no matter how tempted my eyes are to drop lower. "Do *you* want to?"

"I just said I did," she says.

"You said if it's what *I* want. That's not the same thing."

"Well, fine, then it's what I want. Will you wear one of your suits?"

I can't hold back a faint smile. "Do you like when I wear my suits?"

Blushing a little as she smiles, she nods her head. "I miss those."

Since we're living in the real world again, I haven't been dressing the way I did when I worked for Mateo. "I can wear more suits," I tell her.

"We should dress up for dinner."

34

"To go out? Yeah, sure."

"No, every night."

My pleasure wilts, just a bit. She wants to establish yet another Morelli tradition—the stupid formal dinners.

My hand moves to the back of my neck, rubbing it. I try to reclaim the pleasant smile I had a moment ago, but it's strained. "Sure, if you want to, I guess we could."

"I mean, I don't have a lot of pretty dresses, but Mateo bought me a few before we left."

Of course he did.

I'm losing enthusiasm about going out tonight.

"We could just stay in, if you'd rather," I say, watching her reaction to see if she actually *wants* to go out or she's just going along with whatever I say.

The expression on her face doesn't change—not even a little. It's like she literally has no preference. Nodding, she says, "Sure, we could do that."

Pushing up off the couch, I look around this tiny ass apartment, suddenly feeling caged. "I don't want to stay in."

She misses a beat—not because she's disappointed, but because I've just changed my mind so many times she doesn't know what to get behind. "Okay, we can go out."

"Goddammit, Elise." I go to run a hand through my hair, but it's all gone. Dammit, I regret that haircut.

She stands, frowning at me. "What did I do now?"

"Stop agreeing with everything I say," I say, even hearing how ridiculous I sound.

She stares at me for a second, blinking several times, then she glares at me. "I'm trying to make you happy!"

"I *am* happy," I all but scream.

Eyes bulging, she says, "Clearly! All happy people scream at their... their... *whatever the fuck I am.*"

I rear back, never having heard Elise swear. The sound of that word falling from her lips suddenly drains the aggravation right out of me, but apparently hers is just picking up.

Her arm flies off to the left, like she's angrily pointing at some invisible thing. "You tell me *nothing*. You drag me out of my home, out of my *life*, you drag me to this strange new place and you give me *no direction*. I have no idea what you want from me! I don't know why I'm here. I try to do the things I'm accustomed to, but it doesn't please you—you don't *like* when I cook and clean, you *hate* that I have the audacity to enjoy it. I have no routine. I have *no* purpose in this life, Adrian. I have no *place* in your life, and every day I wait for you to give me one, or for me to somehow figure it out, but I don't *know*. I don't know, and you won't tell me. I try everything I can think of to please you, and I'm out of ideas. I don't know how to make you happy, so if you know what you want, maybe you should clue me in, because I *do not know*."

"I don't want you to try to *please me*, Elise. I just want you to be yourself. I just want you to... be happy."

Tears glisten in her eyes as she screams, "I don't know how!" She angrily dashes away a tear that falls, visibly shaking with emotion. "I need *direction*. I need to know what I'm supposed to be doing with myself in order to know if I'm doing it well. Right now, I'm *empty*. I am *lost*. I have never felt so *useless* in my life."

I have no idea what to say to her. I have no idea how to *help*. My mind is blank, but I struggle to come up with something. "You're not an object, Elise, you don't have to be *useful*. If you're looking for purpose, I'm more than happy to help you find that, but... I don't know how, either. Maybe would you like to look for a job?"

"Like a cleaning job?"

"No." I shake my head, frowning. "No, Elise. Just a job, a normal job, where you could interact with other people, maybe make some friends."

"I'm not good at making friends," she tells me, sitting back down, her shoulders sagging.

"You're very nice, I'm sure it'll be easy," I tell her, taking a seat on the couch.

This time the tears that gather in her eyes appear to be tears of frustration. "Why did you make me leave?"

White hot anger courses through me, but I leash it this time. "I didn't *make* you leave. Mateo asked you, and you agreed to it."

"I didn't have a choice."

I roll my shoulders, cracking my neck. I clear my throat, trying to keep my cool. "Yes, you did. You know you did, because at first you said no, and then you changed your mind."

Her teary eyes dim when she remembers why. "If you wanted me to be yours, you could've kept me there. You didn't have to leave. We didn't have to come *here*." She says 'here' like we're literally in the worst place in the world. "You could've just told him. They could've moved me like we moved Meg. I could've kept my position."

I wish we did live at the mansion right now, so I could go to the gym and take my aggressions out on a punching bag. Because every single word out of Elise's mouth fills me with more rage.

"It wasn't a *position*," I barely manage to get out through my locked jaw. "It was *slavery*. He didn't pay you. He took you from your home when you were little more than a child, he took you out of school, he isolated you in his house. Mateo isn't your goddamn savior, Elise."

"I know that," she snaps. "I get it, okay? He's bad. I *get* it."

"I did all of this *for* you," I state.

"I didn't ask you to."

"I didn't expect a thank you," I shoot back. "But you're acting like I've *wronged* you in some way, and I haven't."

"And you're telling me you want me to be myself, but then when I am, it's not good enough. So if you want some alternate version, you're going to have to specify what fucking features I need to add."

"Oh my god, Elise. I don't want you to customize yourself for me."

"But you don't want me to do what I've been doing for the past six years of my life."

"Clean if you want to clean. Cook if you want to cook—I don't *care*. Make 50 fucking muffins every morning if that makes you happy. I don't hate that you do it, I just… I don't want you to feel like you have to. Or it's all you *can* do. I don't want you to feel like you're still…"

I don't know how to finish that sentence without further pissing her off, and she does not swoop in with a nod of understanding to save me.

"I wasn't unhappy there," she states.

"But you're unhappy here," I say, because it's not a question.

Her gaze falls back to the dark television screen, and she looks drained. "I just need a purpose. It's not that I can't be happy with you, I just… I don't have any idea what you want from me. I *need* to know what you want from me. I don't care if it doesn't make sense to you—you want me to be myself, you want me to be honest, that's what I need. I need structure. I need… someone to tell me what I'm supposed to do."

I feel like I'm trying to walk up the side of a steep mountain with no rope. Despair sweeps over me and I'm so *tired*. I'm tired of this, and it's only been nine days.

It's just not enough time. She just needs more time. She'll normalize eventually, but I need to take it slow. I need to take baby steps.

I need to give her a fucking task.

I feel dirty just thinking about it, but if it's what she needs, is it any better if I refuse to give it to her just because I think it's fucked up?

I want to rake my hands through my hair again, but I stop myself this time before I try. "Okay. I… I'll try," I tell her.

"I only want to make you happy," she states, and her voice is so small that I *do* feel like a monster. "I'm not trying to be an inconvenience."

"You're not an inconvenience, Elise. As you pointed out, you're only here because I wanted you to be."

Responding to the flatness in my voice, she stands, placing a reassuring hand on my arm. "I didn't mean it like that."

I don't feel right about her touching me right now, but I don't know how to pull away without making her feel rejected. "I'll try to be more supportive," I state. Dropping my arm so she has to pull hers back, I say, "Right now I think I need to get some air, if that's okay with you."

Elise sighs, but nods her head.

Retrieving my keys from the hook where I left them, I lock the door behind me and head for the nearest bar.

CHAPTER FOUR

I DON'T make it all the way to the bar. I prowl the city for a bit first, trying to think what the hell I can give Elise to do that will give her some direction. I wind up going in and out of shops, searching for something. I pick up a journal with pink and white watercolor on the front. Maybe a journal's a good idea. Even the 16-year-old girl I'd talked to in that jail cell had more self-direction than Elise does now, but that was also when she'd only been there for a year. I remember at one point she told me she wanted to write the story of her life, not necessarily for anyone else to read, but just for her, just so she had some tangible evidence that it all had really happened.

Reflecting on that, I go back and pick out a second one. I have an idea to meet her needs and force her to reflect on herself, but I'm not sure if it will work, mainly because I don't know if she'll welcome it. I'm supposed to assign her tasks like I'm her fucking boss, but does she just mean chores? My inner teacher has different ideas, tasks with more depth, tasks that might help her discover things about herself.

I should've realized this would be more work than I was expecting. I should've expected there to be a rocky adjustment period. Whether or not it was just, she's right—I *did* rip her away from her life (and perhaps more importantly, a lifestyle) and leave her stranded in a new one with no idea what was expected of her. I'm a 33-year-old fucking man, so I just figured she would be able to figure that out without me telling her, but that was my fault. I need to be less defensive and more compassionate.

Goddamn Mateo.

Finally, I go to the bar. I order a double straight up, and before the bartender can leave I slam it back and order another.

I need to not be sober.

I really didn't drink that much before working for Mateo, but for the past five years, it's been a part of my routine, and now that Elise is turning out to be more damaged than I realized, I just need something to clear my aching head.

I'm *finally* starting to feel less sober when someone hops up on the stool beside me. I turn to glare at them, since there's a whole empty bar, but I recognize the guy.

Colin McGregor. He's a freelancer, but he did some work for Mateo a while back.

With a jarring slap on the back, he says, "Adrian fecking Palmetto. How the hell are ye?"

I close my eyes at the sound of his Irish brogue. "I didn't come here to socialize, McGregor."

"No? What'd ye come for, then?"

"To get drunk."

He laughs at that, signaling for the bartender to come over. I guess he isn't going to move. That sucks. While the bartender's here, I raise my hand to tell him I need another, too.

"Celebratin'?" Colin asks.

"Celebrating?" I ask, wondering what the hell I have to be celebrating right now.

"Ye sure got out at the right time," he says, tipping back his beer and taking a big gulp.

"What are you talking about?" I ask, grabbing the new drink

the bartender sits down and wondering how much I should worry about paying this tab.

"Mateo Morelli," he says.

That makes me surly. "I don't wanna talk about him. I'm— He's an asshole. Elise thinks I'm a bigger asshole than he is, and that's… that's stupid."

He raises his dark eyebrows, and I can't blame him, since I'm not making much sense.

Waving him off, I say, "Forget it."

"Lady problems?"

"I'm not domineering enough for her," I state. "I think. I don't know."

"Then be more domineerin'," he says good-naturedly, with a wink. "It's fun."

"I don't wanna be an asshole."

"Ladies like assholes, Adrian, don't ye know anything?"

I roll my eyes, reaching for my drink. "Whatever."

He goes back to drinking his beer and I go back to my whiskey. He keeps up essentially all of the conversation, because all I want to do is enjoy my drink in peace and I keep hoping he'll leave.

It takes a lot longer than it should, because I'm distracted by my own problems, but my mind finally circles back around to what Colin said when he first sat down.

"Why did you say that?" I ask.

He spares me an uncertain look, since he hadn't been speaking at all.

"Earlier," I specify. "You said I got out at just the right time?"

"Oh," he says, nodding with his whole body. "Oh, I meant the shootin'."

I sit up a little straighter, scowling. "*What* shooting?"

"Ye haven't heard?" he questions, eyebrows rising like he's shocked. "Little John tried to take him out last night. Missed, hit

42

his bird instead. Right after he popped the question, if ye can believe it."

I feel like I've just entered an alternate reality. I look at the glass of alcohol, wondering if it's possible I'm drunker than I realized and I'm imagining all of this.

"Colin, what the *fuck* are you talking about? Mateo *proposed* to—I'm assuming Meg? Not Mia, because... no, it couldn't be— there's no.... But Meg.... Salvatore..."

"I think maybe ye've had enough," he tells me, eyes dancing with amusement. "Ye're not making any sense, lad."

"Someone tried to kill Mateo?"

Colin nods.

Just like that, I'm not mad at him anymore.

I mean, I *am*, but... I'm not.

"Is she okay?"

"I don't know. I'm stayin' the feck outta that one. Thinkin' about spendin' some time back east, head back to Boston until the dust settles here."

My head is spinning, and now I'm really regretting the alcohol. Shit. I need to get my head on straight. I need... I need coffee.

Fumbling for my phone, I find Elise's number in my contacts. I got her a phone, assuming she might actually leave the house on occasion, and that I'd need to reach her.

Widening my eyes to try and focus, I manage to type out, "Heading home now. Make me coffee."

A moment later she types back "ok!" with a little smiley face.

I shake my head, slipping my phone back into my pocket. "Didn't even say please."

"What's that now?" Colin asked.

"Nothing." I look at the liquor still in the glass, debating whether or not to finish it. I need to get my shit together so I can call Mateo, don't I?

Then again, Mateo's not my responsibility anymore and I *do* have to pay for it.

On a whim, I throw back the rest of it. Slamming it down with a thud, I gesture for the bartender. "I need to leave."

"Are ye okay?" Colin asks, watching me stand.

"Yep, I'm… I'm good," I tell him, nodding a bit unsteadily as I reach for the bill. I reach into my wallet for a depressing sum of cash and slap it down on the counter. "I need to sleep and Elise is wearing—anyway, it's good. I need to go sleep."

"Wait," Colin calls, hopping off the stool.

I turn back and see he's holding up the little plastic bag I'd forgotten about.

"Oh, yes," I say, falling back to grab it. "Can't forget those."

By the time I get home, I've completely forgotten I asked Elise to make me coffee. All I can think about are the soft pillows on our bed.

As soon as she hears me stumble through the door, Elise heads to the kitchen to get me coffee. "We don't have any mugs," she tells me, pulling out a blue plastic cup and looking at it a tad uncertainly.

"It's okay, I want to go to bed. Thank you for making me coffee."

"You're welcome," she says, replacing the cup and coming over to me, frowning. "You're really drunk, aren't you?"

"Yep," I verify, handing her the plastic bag. "These are yours. I'm going to give you assignments."

"Assignments?" she asks, her eyes wide with interest.

I nod again. "One of the journals is for you, one is for me. You can write whatever you want in yours, but in mine I'm going to give you tasks, things to write for me every day."

"Homework," she says, brightly, smiling.

She's so weird. And so pretty. I want to kiss her.

Nope, no drunk kissing.

I turn to head for the bedroom, where I can sleep and ignore all the shit I need to be figuring out right now.

"Should I...?" Elise trails off when she sees I've vanished.

I'm already in the bedroom, tugging my shirt off and dropping into the bed, yanking the blanket up around me and closing my eyes.

She quickly turns out the lights in the living room, then she comes into the bedroom and climbs in beside me.

"Do you feel okay?" she whispers.

Her concern makes me smile. "Mmhmm."

"What's my first assignment?"

Eyes closed, I murmur, "Ask me when I'm sober."

She laughs lightly. "Okay."

Opening my eyes, I indicate the powder blue satin thing she's still scantily clad in. "I like this."

"Yeah?" she asks, with interest.

"Mmhmm," I verify, closing them again.

"You should drink more often," she informs me.

I snort, then I really push my luck, draping my arm across her waist. I open my eyes to watch first, and while she does appear startled, she doesn't seem displeased.

After a moment, she looks up at me and smiles. "I had a crush on you, you know."

I did *not* know, and that almost sobers me. "What? When?"

She blushes adorably, averting her gaze. "When you used to tutor me. I think the authority figure thing..." She doesn't finish, but she bites her lip, all but explaining the rest.

Elise is attracted to authority.

Go figure.

I ripped her away from Mateo, literally *Mister* Authority, and I gave her absolutely none, because I didn't want her to feel oppressed. Because I *wanted* to be the opposite of him, the opposite of what she's drawn to, and I wanted her to like it anyway.

"I did everything wrong this week, didn't I?" I ask.

"Of course not," she says, and it even sounds like she means it. "We're just adjusting to each other, that's all. It's a learning process." She smiles softly. "That's kind of our thing, though, isn't it?"

Trying something new, likely because of the alcohol, I tug her across the bed until she's snug against me.

She gasps at first, taken off-guard, but then she settles into the embrace and snuggles up against me.

Heaven. I've found heaven. It's real and it exists, in my bed, with Elise in my arms.

Snuggling me.

I can't help but grin. I tuck her head under my chin so she can't see it, and she experimentally drapes an arm around my torso, like she's waiting to see if I'll allow it.

In the moment, I can't imagine for the life of me why I wouldn't.

CHAPTER FIVE

REALITY GREETS me with a vengeance the following morning.

My head is pounding. My mouth is dry. Elise remains snuggled up against me, her body warm, her face peaceful. Her soft skin is pressed against the ruined, puckered skin on my side.

"Fuck," I mutter to myself, carefully lifting her arm and climbing out of her embrace.

As soon as I'm standing, I regret leaving her, but I've got shit to do.

Of course I didn't bother charging my phone last night, so I fish it out of my pocket and grimace at the low battery. I plug it in to charge up a bit while I shower.

Once I'm out, even though I don't have to anymore, I put on a damn suit. Now that I know Elise likes it, it's an easy enough concession to make.

I dump out the pot of coffee she made me last night, rinsing it out, but I leave it for her to clean.

Then I take her journals out of the bag, looking between them. Ideally I would've liked for her to pick which one was hers and which one was mine, but she's asleep and something tells me she won't object to me making the decision for her.

Drawing out the first one I picked out, I grab a pen and jot down today's assignment at the top of the first page.

"While I'm out today, write about something you want to do someday. Something you want to experience, whether you want to do it with someone or alone, and why."

I don't fucking know. I'll throw shit at the wall and see what sticks.

That task complete, I take my phone off charge, sparing Elise a passing glance before heading back to the living room and calling Alec Morelli. He doesn't answer, so I call Joey.

He picks up. Sounds surprised to hear from me, but I don't know why. Of *course* I'm going to call and check in when something like this happens.

"What the hell happened?" I ask him.

"I don't know, man. Castellanos made a move."

I don't understand how *any* of it happened though—when I left the mansion, Meg was locked in Mateo's basement and he was locked away in his surveillance room, searching for evidence of her sins. Now they're going out on the town and he's proposing?

Joey spends the next few minutes catching me up, explaining how Meg wasn't guilty and Francesca's disappeared. I have questions about this, since I had verifiable evidence of Meg's link to Castellanos, but there's too much to absorb right now to bother arguing.

"Well, is he home? I wanna stop by and say hi."

"No, he's staying at the hospital with her."

That surprises me. "The hospital?"

We never go to the hospital. Too complicated, leaves you too vulnerable, open to investigation. I'm shocked Mateo, of all people, would go to the hospital.

"I guess she was bleeding pretty bad," Joey explains. "The bullet didn't come out, so they had to go in and get it. I guess... I guess she's pregnant."

My stomach turns over at that piece of news, especially in

light of him just telling me she was shot in the stomach. "Still?"

"I don't know. I haven't got an update yet today. Vince and Mia are heading up there to check in, so I'll hear more then."

I get the information from him, and even though the thought of going makes me feel like a lost, vulnerable eight-year-old again, I grab my keys and head for the hospital.

I'm glad I wore the suit today.

I didn't expect to offer to come back when I walked into the hospital, but seeing him there, looking so lost as he waited by Meg's bedside, I knew I had to.

This all happened on my watch, after all. Maybe it came to a head when I left, but it was all building under my fucking nose when I was preparing to leave.

I pay the cop a visit first, since that's the more immediate danger.

Then I stop by the bakery to grab security tapes.

Finally, I head to Mateo's house.

Maria comes to the door, but she doesn't even look surprised to see me. She glances past me to see if I'm alone, then she lets me in and closes the door, walking away without so much as a throwaway greeting.

I wonder if she's happy here, like Elise was. I didn't think about it too much when I lived here, I just assumed none of them wanted to be here, but now that Elise has yelled at me for rescuing her when apparently she wasn't in distress, I wonder.

Maria's pretty brusque, though, so I don't follow her to ask.

I also have a lot of shit to do, and I need to get started.

Once I'm in Mateo's security room, the first thing I do is text Colin McGregor.

"Don't go to Boston yet. I might have something for you."

He doesn't respond right away, so I pop in the tapes from the bakery and start looking into what Francesca's been up to. Going over security footage is one the most boring, tedious jobs in the world, but if you know what you're looking for, it can be useful. I'm not sure exactly what I'm looking for. If Francesca really was the leak, there's no way after growing up with Mateo she would allow anyone connected to Castellanos to walk into his family's bakery. I need to check her phone records. She was probably too smart to use her regular phone, but it's worth a quick perusal.

Time slips away from me and before I know it, Elise is texting me, asking if she should make dinner. Colin responded, too, asking "what kind of something?" so I answer him first, telling him to meet me where we met last night around 9pm.

Exiting the surveillance room, I stop at Mateo's desk. I know he keeps some petty cash here, and I blew most of mine at the bar last night. Peeling off $100, I shove it in my pocket and text Elise to tell her to go ahead and make dinner.

To be honest, I'd rather just grab something to take home, but I assume she wants to cook.

I stop to buy her a dress on the way home. I don't know exactly what she likes, but I grab one that's navy blue with lace and sequins—looks like something Mia would wear to dinner. Everything in me revolts as I take it to the register, in my damn suit, prepared to do what I can to emulate the one man I don't want to be anything like. I can't even recreate a shadow of Morelli family dinners, because we don't have a table. We usually just eat on the couch, but I'm gonna have to get one. There's a little space between the kitchen and the door for one, I just didn't have the extra money and it didn't seem essential.

I'll have to get her one, though. Maybe some decorative shit to put on it—a tablecloth, some kind of centerpiece.

Now that I'm actually working for Mateo for a little while, I'll have more money to work with. His lucrative offer to come work for him comes to mind, but I shove it away.

No. I'm not getting sucked back into Mateo's bullshit. I'll never get out again if I do. This is just temporary, I'm just going to help him get shit settled with Castellanos and make sure he's reasonably safe, then I'll find a normal job, like I intended.

Elise is in the kitchen when I get back home, but when she turns to greet me, a series of progressively happier expressions play out across her face as she notices first, I'm wearing a suit, and second, I brought her something pretty.

I'm not sure how to tell her I'm working for Mateo again. I don't know if she'll be pleased or disappointed, and I'm not even sure which I prefer.

"What's this?" she asks, smiling at me before her gaze moves to the white plastic covering the hanger dangling from my hand.

I hand it to her, and she wastes no time peeling it off. I'm rewarded with a little gasp of pleasure when she sees it, and I'm relieved she seems to like it.

"It's beautiful, Adrian; thank you," she says, surprising me by moving in to hug me.

I wrap my arms around her, hugging her back, but it only makes me think about last night. I'm tempted to apologize, but I stop myself. I probably shouldn't have had so much to drink, or pulled her against me in bed like that, and I definitely shouldn't have done it without a shirt on. But I did, and it's done, and she's in better spirits today, so I'll ignore my own reservations.

Pulling back, she tells me, "I did my assignment."

I'd honestly forgotten about it. Nodding as if I didn't, I say, "Good. I'll read it after dinner."

"I wrote a little in mine, too," she tells me, finally releasing me and taking a step back. "It's very pretty, thank you for thinking of it."

"I'm glad you like it."

I already feel tired, and I'm not looking forward to meeting up with Colin later. Actually, he hasn't even verified he'll show up, and he better, because if I haul my ass to the bar and sit there by myself, I'm gonna be pissed.

"I gotta go out later," I tell her.

"Oh, okay. Do you want me to go?" she asks as she heads for the bedroom to change.

"Nah, it's a... work thing." I grimace, scratching the back of my neck, figuring there's not going to be a better opening. "I have to help Mateo out for a little bit longer."

There's silence, and then her head pops out into the hall, the dress clutched to her chest. "What?"

"There was an assassination attempt. Another one. A more... effective one."

Her entire face goes white, and my stomach drops. "Is he...?"

"No," I say quickly, shaking my head. "They hit Meg instead."

Her jaw drops and she moves into the hallway, slowly releasing a breath.

"She's okay," I add, still watching her more closely than I should. I already *know* she has a fascination with Mateo; I shouldn't make it worse for myself by trying to find evidence of it.

Elise nods, but *I'm* relieved to see she looks pleased to hear that. "People really need to stop trying to kill him," she states.

"Maybe if he'd stop giving them reasons," I say, rolling my eyes.

A little smile tugs at her lips and she pops back into the bedroom to change.

Actually the funny thing is, as many people as there are with actual motives *to* kill Mateo, I don't know why Antonio Castellanos has such a hard-on for him. He's always been cold, since there aren't a lot of kind-hearted mobsters heading families, but it seems to me he's getting old and starting to lose his foothold within his own crew. There have been rumblings for a few months now that his family has started eyeing up his eldest son as a replacement—ruthless but charismatic, like Mateo, and more importantly, an ally to Mateo. Content to split territories like we've been doing with Castellanos for years, until he started getting increasingly greedy.

Of course, Salvatore Castellanos, heir apparent to the Castellanos family, isn't exactly on Mateo's good side these days. As of right now, we're not even sure where he is. The old man and the son have both been lying low since the attack on Mateo, in the event there's retribution.

Which of course there will be.

My phone buzzes and I look down to see a text from Colin. "See you then."

I drop the phone in my pocket, wandering in the kitchen to see what Elise is cooking.

I don't know if *this* is a good idea, either. Colin tends to be a bit of a charmer where ladies are concerned, so he'll probably get on Mateo's nerves being around Meg all the time. At the end of the day, McGregor's a professional though, so I think it'll be okay. I can't really spare anyone in our family until I make sure they can all be trusted.

It's a sad day when you have to bring in a freelancer because you don't trust your own people.

Mateo needs to get his shit together. Or, I guess *I* need to get his shit together, since I went and offered to come back until I get things resolved.

Right now my priority is wrapping things up as quickly as possible.

Elise emerges from the bedroom with a smile on her face, doing a little spin to show me her new dress. "Like it?"

"I do," I say. "Do you?"

"It's beautiful," she says, and I hate that even with something this simple, I can't be sure she's being genuine. Would she tell me if she hated it? I doubt she does, but I hate not knowing.

As she heads into the bathroom, I ask, "What were dinners like for you growing up?"

The question seems to take her by surprise. She grabs a loaf of freshly baked bread and starts slicing it, eyes on her task as she talks. "They were nothing special. We had fast food a lot of the time, or frozen food that someone threw in the oven. We only really ate at the table on holidays. When I first went to Mateo's," she says, glancing at me cautiously, but continuing, "I thought it was really nice the way they always ate dinner together. They dressed nice and sat at the table and were actually present with one another." She shrugs one shoulder. "It's nice. Growing up we usually just watched TV while we ate. There were a lot of times I sort of craved that togetherness like Mateo creates, and it just... I just never had that."

"You were an only child, right?"

She nods, arranging the bread slices on a plate. Too many slices for just the two of us, but I don't remark upon it. "My dad didn't want more kids. I think my mom might've, but I'm not really sure."

"What was their relationship like? Was it a good one?"

"I guess. I mean, they were still together. They had their issues like most couples, but it wasn't *bad*." Glancing up at me, she asks, "What about you? What was it like for you growing up? You never told me anything about your family."

I shrug, leaning against the counter and watching her work. "I don't really like to talk about them."

"How come?"

I shrug one shoulder, fighting the urge to retreat into myself. "Doesn't do me any good to think about it, I guess. To dwell on memories of things I can't change, can't get back."

"Is it painful?" she asks softly.

"Used to be. I don't feel it anymore."

Turning to face me, she says, "It's my turn to ask *you* a

question. A homework question."

The corner of my mouth tugs up slightly, but I nod, giving her permission to ask.

"Who do you miss? You've obviously lost people over the years… who *does* still make you feel, even now, when you consider having lost them?"

I stare at her for a moment, unsure how to answer that. I'm not exaggerating when I tell her I don't feel the losses anymore— I've numbed myself to them over the years. I can lie awake in bed and vividly recall Matt's wrath upon my family, the screams, the pain, the fire. It replays in my memory like I'm there, but I can't *feel* anything.

It's not that I don't have attachments to anyone anymore. I'd like to think that sometimes, but obviously I haven't turned off completely, or I wouldn't be here with her, I wouldn't have gone back to Mateo when he needed me.

But the truth is, she's the only person who really makes me feel anything. I don't know if she came into my life, a bright spot in my darkest day, at just the right time, or if it's something more, but whatever the reason….

I don't intend to tell her that, but I do. "Only you."

Quiet shock graces her lovely features, then she frowns a little. Finally, she gives me a shy little smile. "Cheater. You haven't lost *me*."

I shrug. "Then what have I got to complain about?"

She doesn't light up much around me, but she does now. I feel a little rush as she bites down on that lower lip of hers and looks at me like *I'm* something special.

I can't help smiling back.

Elise finally turns, grabbing the plates she set out for us and handing me one. "Let's eat."

I glance at the couch, recalling how unenthusiastic she was about having eaten that way with her family. Glancing at the open floor where I need to put a table, I get an idea.

Putting my plate down, I head to the bedroom, grabbing a couple of boxes and a spare bed sheet from the closet. I put them down on the floor and drape the sheet across it like a table cloth.

"Until I get a real one," I tell her.

She grins, putting her plate down gently and sitting down on the floor, curling her legs up to the side. "It'll do just fine," she tells me.

It's been a hard stretch, a rough adjustment, but here in the floor at our makeshift table, I finally start to feel a little bit of hope.

Maybe everything will work out, after all.

CHAPTER SIX

I END up at the bar with Colin for far too long. By the time I get home, Elise is in bed. I'm not drunk, but I've had enough to drink that I consider wrapping an arm around her again once I get in bed.

I don't.

The following morning I wake up before her. I realize I forgot to check her assignment yesterday, so I go ahead and look it over.

While I'm out today, write about something you want to do someday. Something you want to experience, whether you want to do it with someone or alone, and why.
I want to go see my mom and dad.
I don't want to go alone, because I wouldn't feel secure, but I want to see if they managed to turn things around. If giving me up was worth it.

Huh.

That wasn't what I was expecting.

Makes me a bit uncomfortable, actually. Elise never told me the story of how she came to be Mateo's, and I never asked him for the specifics, so I decide to make that today's homework.

I don't know if I'm *ready* for that story. He told me her father gave her to him in exchange for a debt, but for the sake of having to coexist with him for the next five years, I didn't dig much deeper. I head to the shower, already anxious at the prospect of having to read about Mateo from Elise's perspective. Not only that, but opening up the possibility of reading things about him that will make me less keen on protecting him, which is my job right now.

Mateo's transactional treatment of human beings is one of the harder things to handle—and it's not like he's an easy package to begin with. Women might be drawn to him, but as a human being, he leaves a lot to be desired.

I'm tempted to wake her up and make her get the story over with now, but I have to go to his house next, so I should probably wait.

It's a long day. A long, boring day full of fruitless perusal of surveillance tapes and talking to people with nothing useful to tell me. I end up staying later than I intend, and running late getting home. Elise is curled up on her couch with her journal when I get back, but she puts it aside and heads to the kitchen when I walk in.

"You should've told me you were on your way," she says, turning on the oven. "I'll just warm it up, it'll be a few minutes."

I don't even feel that hungry anyway, but it may be the anxiety I've had gnawing away at me all day. I pick up her journal, glancing down at the cover, dreading opening it.

"Oh," she says, approaching me with trepidation. "I did the homework, but I was very detailed. I didn't mean to be, I just started writing and got carried away."

"You can be as detailed as you want," I assure her.

"I didn't want to—I know you can be..." She trails off, her big blue eyes trailing down the arm of my sleeve. "I didn't want to make you feel weird."

"I don't want you to worry about that. Especially not when you're journaling. I'm not going to judge you."

She raises an eyebrow as if to say, "Come on, now."

I scowl. "I don't judge you."

The eyebrow climbs even higher, and she adds in a pair of pursed lips.

I open the journal, clearing any emotion from my face, and begin reading.

Tell me about the night you were sold to Mateo.

I was upstairs in my room when Mateo and his men showed up. I could hear my mom yelling at my dad downstairs, and he was telling her to shut up, that he would handle it. I was in bed, but I climbed out and crept to the edge of the stairwell. Mateo himself was downstairs, and I'd heard of him, but all bad things. I was expecting a monster. I was expecting some old, ugly gangster-looking guy with slicked back hair and a puffy, sour face. When I finally worked up the nerve to sneak down to the edge where I could sneak a peek, what I saw instead was Mateo. He seemed at ease, untroubled, despite my father's evident fear. One of his men had a baseball bat, and he kept twisting it, waiting for Mateo to tell him to use it.

My father spotted me on the stairs. Mateo turned to see what he was looking at. My dad told me to come down, and I was so scared, but I did.

Mateo's gaze must have lingered on me long enough for my father to notice. He didn't say anything, didn't even address my coming into the room, just turned back to look at my father.

"You like her?" my father asked.

It made me feel cold all over. I was inexperienced from a

59

practical perspective, but I wasn't so young that I didn't understand what he meant.

Mateo stared at my father, but his whole face was empty. He still didn't speak, and he'd been talking plenty before I came down, so it made me uneasy.

"Elise, come here, honey," my dad said.

I stared at him for a moment, then I took a few steps closer. Mateo seemed vaguely irritated then, and I wondered if I should go back upstairs, but I was afraid the men would come get me if I tried.

My dad wasn't perfect, but I knew he must be terrified to be bringing me into it.

Mateo looked me over one more time, his eyes landing on my face. "How old are you?"

I swallowed. I couldn't look him in the eye. "Fifteen."

My voice cracked in the middle of telling him my age, and I could feel my face heating with embarrassment.

Mateo nodded, looking back at my dad. "You think I'm attracted to your 15-year-old daughter, so you call her closer?"

My dad obviously didn't know how to respond. He was desperate and scared, and he wasn't thinking clearly. I'm sure he thought Mateo would have him killed, or he never would've done it.

Finally Mateo said, "I'll take her."

I didn't understand at first. Take me? Take me where? Take me how? What did that mean?

My father seemed confused, too. "Take her?"

"If you're willing to trade your daughter for what you owe me, I'll take her," Mateo specifies.

"Like... you'll keep her?" my dad asked, looking a little floored.

The corner of Mateo's mouth tugged up, but he did not look amused. Looking away from my father, he turned his attention to me. "What do you say, Elise?"

Just hearing him say my name made me shiver. You know that scene from Beauty and the Beast, where Belle offers to take her father's place? In my mind, it was like that. In my mind, it was so brave.

"You won't hurt my dad?" I asked him.

Mateo shook his head no.

I looked past him at my dad, and my stomach was aching so bad. Mateo wasn't what I pictured, but it was still utterly terrifying to imagine actually leaving my home and going with this dangerous stranger. Especially because I still thought he was going to hurt me—I still believed he had some sick interest in me, and still I told him I'd go with him.

My father didn't look comfortable with it, but he didn't even try to stop it from happening. He didn't panic at the last minute and try to change his mind, he didn't tell Mateo he'd give him the money instead. I don't even know why he owed him the money. My dad owned a small business, and while it wasn't extremely profitable, I wasn't aware of any money problems severe enough that he would take mob money, knowing what a stupid thing that is to do.

My mother was in tears, and she came forward to object. Before she kept back, even when my father was saying those things to Mateo, almost encouraging his interest in me. That was hard to swallow, but I told myself they had no other choice. She hugged me then, clutched me, saying "no, no, no," over and over again. I couldn't feel anything though. My mind seemed to have shut down and I couldn't even be in the moment with her, my last moment with her. I couldn't even wrap my head around what I'd just agreed to, what they'd just agreed to. All I could think about was what came next. What would happen to me? How long would I even amuse him, and what would happen to me if I stopped?

Everything was kind of a blur after that. Mateo accompanied me to his car, but two of his men stayed behind.

Mateo didn't wait for them. His driver pulled away, and I

looked back, confused. "Why did they stay?" I asked.

I didn't even really expect him to answer me. I expected him to be mean to me, to treat me less than human, but he said simply, "To conclude the transaction."

I wasn't sure what that meant. It wasn't a legal transaction in any regard, so what did they need to do, sign paperwork? But I didn't ask again.

I waited the whole car ride for him to do something. To pounce on me? To say something about his intentions? To act on them?

But he never did. He didn't even speak to me most of the trip, and then when we pulled up to his house, I was in shock. I'd never seen a house so big or so beautiful.

He got out of the car and headed inside, while his driver hung back and walked with me. (His house only further reinforced the Beauty and the Beast thing in my head. It was like a modern castle!) And then his man took me inside, took me to the servants' quarters, and gave me a lovely bedroom, nicer than the one I had at home. (Again, BEAUTY AND THE BEAST.) I sat on the bed, waiting for him to come, but he didn't. I couldn't even sleep that night, still waiting. But he never came, and he was NEVER mean to me, not even a little bit. He was a perfect gentleman, and... well, you know the rest.

She watches me read it, and fidgets when I finish.

"Well?" she asks, awaiting some kind of reaction.

"Well... I can never watch *Beauty and the Beast* again," I say dryly.

"I love that movie," she says, smiling faintly.

Since I have to, I ask, "So, you had feelings for him right from the start."

Her smile drops, and I know I've made her uncomfortable. She doesn't want to talk about this with me, because she doesn't want to upset me. "He was good to me."

I want to say *he bought you*, but I restrain myself. There's no reason to be mean to her, and this journal thing has to be a safe space for her to say anything to me, otherwise it's useless.

"It's not that I wanted to *be* with him," she adds, since I'm still listening. "I mean, I'm sure I would've, but... I admired him. He meant something to me. He was *important* to me. At a time when the people I expected to protect me... gave me away, the person I expected to hurt me... didn't. I know you like to say he wasn't my savior, and he certainly wasn't the traditional sort, but I did feel protected by him. I always did. And I liked that feeling. I thought he was a better man than people believed him to be. Even when Beth disappeared, I just thought... I don't know what I thought, but I never thought he was truly bad. I always thought he was nobler than he pretended to be. Until he hurt Mia. Then I realized... maybe it wasn't that he was better, it was just that he hadn't really wanted me."

I don't know how to respond to that. There are things I could say that would probably make her feel better about Mateo, but is that what I want? It's probably what *she* wants. I probably should.

Instead I ask, "It doesn't bother you that you're a human being and he bought your freedom?"

She meets my gaze, not hostile, just honest. "It doesn't bother me that you did, either."

I lean back, a little floored. "Excuse me? I didn't *buy* you."

Her eyebrows rise. "Sure you did, you just paid with your time and effort instead of money. I'm pretty sure my market value went up, though—or you way overpaid," she adds lightly.

I am not amused. "I didn't buy you, Elise. I don't *own* you. No one owns you. I logged my time and effort for you, yes, but not to *buy* you. It was to free you."

"You bought my freedom from the man who owned it, Adrian. The whole exchange happened between you two, and no one even consulted me until it was nearly time to cash in and take me with you. You *bought* me."

I shake my head, rejecting that. "No. No."

"It's okay."

"No, it isn't," I snap. "You are not trapped here, Elise. If you don't want to be here, if you don't want to be with me, you're free to leave. I don't *want* you to leave, of course, but you aren't my property. You don't belong to me, and you sure as hell don't owe me anything. I did what I did because I wanted to, not to *buy* you; I did it because I liked you and it was the right thing to do. That's it. Not to bind you to me. Definitely not to take Mateo's place as your goddamn master."

"I don't know why you have to say it like that," she mutters, rolling her eyes at me like *I'm* the ridiculous one in this conversation.

"Because that's what it is," I state.

"And then you say you're not judging me."

"I'm not judging *you*, I'm judging *him*," I say, struggling to rein in my frustration. "None of this was your fault. You were just a kid."

"Of course you don't judge me for *that,* but why is it my responsibility to hate him? Why is it only acceptable that I was miserable? I wasn't. I don't know why you're so determined to see me as some damsel who needed saving, Adrian. Why is it so important that I reject everything Mateo? Why does it *mean* so much to you?"

I feel myself closing down. It's not an unfair question, and I could throw back, "because I gave up five years of my life to save you!" but she didn't ask me to; or "because I want you to be all mine!" but that would split me open, and I can't.

I want to leave again. This apartment is too small; I'm used to Mateo's house now, and here in this tiny-ass apartment, there's nowhere to go to get away from her.

I don't understand how she can defend him. I don't understand why she has to make excuses. Why can't this one thing be black and white? Why can't she just agree with me that what he did to her was wrong? That what he *does* to *people* is wrong?

But then she speaks, her voice soft, "Why don't you ask about the night I met *you*? Or the crush I admitted to having on you back when you used to be my tutor? Why do we have to focus on him at all? Did I, at one time, have a crush on Mateo? Yes. But he never touched me. I was never his. If that's what you're worried about, you can just ask. I've never been with anyone."

Whoa, that was not what I was after.

I mean, I thought that might be the case, since she was cloistered away at his house so young, but I wasn't going to ask.

She has successfully sidetracked my train of thought. Now instead of Mateo, I'm thinking about Elise's body, about the formative years she spent isolated, about the experiences she hasn't had.

"Were you ever lonely?" I ask.

She nods, catching a strand of blond hair and twisting it around her finger. "Sure, sometimes. But I was lonely before I lived at the mansion, too. I was never good at making friends."

"No, me neither," I tell her.

I can feel her watching me, but I don't look up.

"Actually, that's not true. I was good at making friends until I was eight. I had lots of friends." Indicating the left side of my face, I say, "And then this happened. Then I had lots of sympathizers for a little while. Then I had one friend, and sometimes I didn't even want that one. I wasn't the same after that. I lost everything, and I got lost in it."

"You were only eight when that happened?" she asks softly. I nod.

"Was it... was it a house fire, or...?"

This is one thing I've never discussed with Elise. She's never asked. She's never even *mentioned* my scars, almost like she didn't even notice them. I've never discussed it with anyone, actually.

"My mom used to work for Mateo's dad." Smiling very slightly, I say, "She was a *maid*. Before Maria, before he...

insisted on *owning* his maids. He probably started that because of her, honestly. She worked there for years, before I was even born she started working there, and she became friendly with his wife, Belle. She was miserable, hated Matt, he was horrible to her. Abusive. He started cheating on her to hurt her. He was every bad part of Mateo on steroids and without any of the charm." Glancing up at her, I say, "You've met Dante, right?"

She nods, her attention rapt.

"He's more like Matt than Mateo. Anyway, after years of abuse, Belle fell in love with someone else. She wanted to leave Matt, but of course, you don't leave a Morelli. She got pregnant, and no one was sure by whom. She already had a daughter with Matt, but that was earlier on, when he was less violent. She was terrified of him, and… they weren't even sure he would let her keep the babies, because he found out about the affair so he didn't know if they were his. One night it all blew up. He attacked her and my mom was there, she saw. So she went to get his sister for help. Bianca came and they tried to help, to stop him, but I guess he hurt her pretty badly. Bianca and my mother helped her escape. My mom packed her some things, Bianca snuck her out. And she disappeared. It seemed like she was the one woman who successfully escaped them. As it turned out, my mother… knew where Belle went. They continued to exchange Christmas cards every year, to check in, since they had been such good friends. Matt moved on, started tormenting Mateo's mom until she killed herself. Played with Joey's mom for a while. But he never stopped looking for Belle until he found her. And when he did? He found the Christmas cards."

Elise's eyes are wide with horror. Even though she can probably figure out where this is going, it's like she's hoping for a different ending. "So… it was retaliation?"

I nod. "He brought a shoe box over to our house one night. Had the Christmas cards from over the years, pictures of me she'd sent to show me off." With a slight smile, I tell her, "I was a cute kid."

She rolls her eyes lightly, but her eyes wander the left side of my face, taking in every ridge, every welt. "You've always been handsome," she informs me. "I don't doubt it."

"I'm no Mateo," I joke.

"Don't do that," she says firmly, shaking her head.

Her compliment makes me more uncomfortable than anything else she's ever done, so I get back to the story. "Anyway, he dumped out the Christmas cards, tortured my father in front of her, had my mom... hurt. And then he set me on fire."

"Did he...?"

"Killed them both."

She slowly exhales, looking weighed down by this story. "I'm so sorry, Adrian."

"My mom begged for mercy. That's the part I really remember. That's the worst part. How she begged him, realizing what he was going to do, and...then the bastard made me live."

Elise moves closer all of a sudden, wrapping her arms around me and pressing her body against mine. Hugging me. I'm tempted to pull back, not wanting her pity, but the scent of her shampoo hits me, the feeling of her arms secured around me, and I decide maybe sympathy is okay. A tentative hand comes to rest on her back, but she's still full-on wrapped around me.

"I'm sorry I made you talk about it," she says, her voice muffled since her face is pressed against my shoulder.

Yearning. That's what I feel. There's no pain from the memories I just shared with her, just a deep yearning as she holds me, wanting *this*—more of this. I don't care about anything outside of this embrace.

But I don't even hug her back, so she eventually pulls away.

Worse, she looks a little embarrassed. "Sorry," she murmurs, with a slight smile. "It seemed like the time for a hug."

"You don't have to apologize," I murmur. "I'm... just not terribly affectionate."

She shrugs like it doesn't matter, but it clearly does. "I never had anyone to be affectionate with. Always thought it'd be nice."

I never really thought that before, but it's different with her. I'm not *opposed*, and I don't know why my stupid mouth won't open so I can tell her that.

I just can't shake the feeling that I'd be playing on her sympathies. She's not being affectionate because she wants me, but because she feels bad for me. Not because it's something she *wants*, but because it's something she can offer.

I don't know how I can ever not feel like I'm taking advantage of her.

For literally the first time in five years, I wonder if this is possible. In my head, before it was real, before she was here, this should've been easy. But that was assuming we were on the same page. That was assuming we got out and Elise was happy about it, happy to be free again, happy to move on with her life.

I never considered how hard this would be if she didn't feel that relief. If she'd been damaged, molded into some kind of Stepford wife.

"Well, I bet the oven's heated up by now," she says lightly, breaking away from my wall of silence to warm up the damn food.

CHAPTER SEVEN

"YOU SHOULD bring Elise by for dinner tonight."

I glance at Mateo in the back seat, messing around on his phone as he tosses out the casual invitation. "Meg coming tonight?"

He shakes his head. "Not tonight." Then, with a slight smirk, he said, "Vince and Mia will be there, though."

"It's not Sunday," I point out.

"Maria's understaffed. Someone's gotta bring me my salad." He says it lightly, like a joke, but I can already anticipate Vince sulking about it.

I shake my head. "You're such a dick."

He looks up just long enough to flash me a grin, then he goes back to his phone.

"Can I ask you something?"

"Why am I such a dick?" he asks, pulling a fake pout. "Tragic childhood."

I roll my eyes. "No, something real."

I have his attention now, and he drops his phone back into his pocket. "Of course."

"Did you kill Elise's dad?"

"Yes," he says, without even the slightest hesitation.

I nod, sighing. I kind of figured, but that's going to make meeting her desire to see them quite a lot harder. "Her mom still alive?"

He shakes his head, a wordless no.

"Great."

"Why?" he asks.

"She wanted to see them. See if they were okay."

He shakes his head, glancing out the window. "Women have an astounding capacity for forgiveness, I swear to god. Why would you want to see the assholes who literally sold you?"

I scoff, shaking my head. "I don't know, Mateo, why would you admire the man who *bought* you?"

"I've been good to Elise," he states, like that makes it all right.

"Because of me," I point out.

He smirks. "I would've still been good to her—just a different kind of good."

"Sometimes it's so hard to remember why I want to keep you alive," I tell him.

He smiles, unconcerned. "How are things going for you two? Is she everything you hoped she'd be?"

I don't immediately answer. I don't even think I'm going to, but then suddenly I say, "She's still working on deprogramming."

Mateo quirks an eyebrow at me. "Deprogramming?"

"You have her trained. She doesn't know what to do with herself now that she's not stuck cleaning your house and cooking your dinner."

Mateo sighs heavily, as if disappointed. "You're trying to fix her, aren't you?"

I look at the rearview mirror, glaring at him.

"Does she *want* to be fixed?" he asks.

"Like you care what women want," I mutter.

"Adrian, just enjoy her, for fuck's sake. Jesus Christ. You

worked five years for the girl. Have you even fucked her yet?"

"We don't need to talk about my sex life," I inform him.

"You certainly have enough opinions about mine," he shoots back, rolling his eyes.

"She thinks I bought her," I tell him. I don't know why I tell him that, it's not like he'll be similarly disgusted by the idea.

"You did," he says, simply.

I scowl at him in the rearview mirror. "I didn't buy *her*, I worked to *free* her. Why doesn't anyone realize those aren't the same thing?"

"Is she pissed about it?"

"No."

"Then who cares?" he replies.

"It's pointless to argue an ethical stance with you," I state, shaking my head.

"It's not *pointless*. I understand the ethics, they just don't matter in this situation. Get out of your own way and let yourself be happy for once."

I pull up behind the abandoned warehouse, throwing the car in park and climbing out. Mateo doesn't usually come along and get his hands dirty with this kind of stuff, but since Meg got shot, he seems to want an outlet for some pent-up aggression. I guess I can understand that.

"Why'd you wear a white shirt?" I ask, as he removes his jacket and drapes it over his arm.

"I like them to see their own blood spatter," he states.

That surprises me since he has a thing about cleanliness, but I don't remark upon in. I'm honestly surprised he doesn't wear hazmat gear to punch a guy in the face, but I guess since he's got us here, he only has to do as much as he wants to, anyway.

"Did you ever look into the daughter?" Mateo asks as we head inside.

"I'm gonna check it out a little more, depending on what we get from this guy."

"She's technically a Castellanos."

"She has nothing to do with the old man," I point out.

"Fruit of his looms," Mateo tosses back.

"I've found some pretty disturbing shit there, frankly," I tell him. "I have to dig a little more, but I'm inclined to think he's a bigger bastard than we realized."

"Still, streets running red with blood and all that," he says casually.

"Why don't we focus on the blood of the people actually involved before we branch out to innocent bystanders," I suggest.

"You're such a Boy Scout, Adrian."

I roll my eyes, rolling up my shirt sleeves to go beat some asshole half to death. "Oh yeah, I'm a real angel."

Because it's just easier and because I'm going to have to do it eventually, I go ahead and take Elise over to Mateo's for dinner. She's eager during the car ride over, and I don't know if it's to see him, to be back at the place she still thinks of as home, or maybe to see the people she used to live and work with. I don't ask.

She pops into the study with me for a few minutes, but neither of us is quite sure how to work that. Mia is sitting on Vince's lap and Meg's not down here since Mateo won't let her out of bed, but Elise and I don't behave like a couple. It becomes apparent after a few minutes of awkward lingering—I wanna take a seat like I usually do, but I don't know what to do with her. She's sure as hell not going to sit on my lap, and I don't want to make her linger by the chair. Usually she's the one getting drinks if she's in here, and I catch her casting a few longing looks toward the drink cart.

Eventually she bails and heads to the kitchen to help Maria

with dinner.

"She knows she doesn't have to do that anymore, right?" Mateo remarks, seeming slightly amused as she runs back to her old job.

Vince stands up, displacing Mia, and goes outside to take a call. Literally as soon as Vince is out of sight, she heads over to the alcohol cart and grabs Mateo's decanter, heading over to his desk to refill his glass.

"Thank you," he says, giving her a warm smile.

With an indulgent roll of her eyes, she says, "I know you hate getting it yourself."

"So much work," he agrees, lifting his glass to his lips and watching her over the rim.

Mia suddenly frowns, almost unthinkingly reaching out and running her thumb over his knuckles. "What happened to your hand?"

I glance down at my own knuckles. They're in worse shape than his, and Elise certainly didn't notice *mine*.

"Had a slight disagreement with someone's face," he remarks.

She sighs, leaning against his desk, standing beside him and looking over at him. "Don't you pay people to do stuff like that for you?"

"Why should they get to have all the fun?" he asks, glancing over at her.

"As long as it wasn't Vince this time, I guess I shouldn't complain," she remarks.

Mateo's eyebrows inch upward. "Does Vince need to be punched again?" He holds up his other hand, free of nicks or bruises. "I've still got this one. If he's acting up, just say the word."

Shaking her head disapprovingly, Mia pushes off the desk and goes back to the alcohol cart. Without looking back, she grabs a glass and pours some, then brings it over to me.

"Oh, thanks, Mia. You didn't have to do that," I tell her.

"Maybe I *don't* need a new maid," Mateo remarks as she walks back that way. His eyes are on her, dancing with amusement and mischief as he says, "Should I order you a costume, Mia? I bet you'd like costumes."

She looks back toward the door, checking for Vince, then gives him a completely insincere glare.

He winks.

I sigh. Working for him has to be taking years off my life in more ways than one.

By the time Vince comes back, Mia's ready to climb onto his lap and make believe she wasn't flirting with Mateo while he was gone. Which suits the rest of us, because Meg's on bed rest after taking a bullet for him, and we have to try to like the son of a bitch.

We're all a bunch of liars.

I shouldn't have brought Elise here. I don't want her to get swept up in Mateo's shit.

Throughout the rest of drinks I think about that, solidifying the thought in my mind. Then we head to the dining room for dinner, and Elise comes out with my salad, beaming like she's doing something she actually enjoys.

"Thank you," I say, as she puts mine down in front of me and takes a seat to my left.

Smiling, she nods. "Of course."

I glance down at the opposite side of the table where Mateo sits. Mia is just placing his salad in front of him, then putting down Vince's. Vince looks quite unimpressed, glaring at Mateo's salad plate while Mia takes her seat between them.

"This is nice, isn't it?" Elise murmurs, oblivious to any mounting tension down by Mateo.

I watch Vince stab a grape tomato, probably envisioning Mateo's head. "Yeah. Nice," I mutter.

I tell Elise her mom and dad moved.

I hate lying to her, and I shouldn't lie for Mateo, but I really don't want to tell her. Since she agreed to go with him for their safety in the first place, I can imagine how it would make her feel to know it had all been for nothing.

So, they live in Florida. I looked up her father's business, put together enough of a story about them relocating and opening up shop in Destin, and just like that, Elise's parents are doing okay. It seems to please her, the idea that they're doing all right. I hate agreeing with Mateo, but I can't figure out why she would wish them well, either. When she left her father's house that night, he had to have assumed she was heading for a life of constant rape and abuse. What kind of man would let his daughter go through a thing like that to save his own skin? You'd have to kill me *twice* to put my daughter through that kind of shit—and even then, my ghost would probably come for you.

I decide Elise's homework for the next day will be that—asking if she wants kids. What kind of life she'd like to have, whether or not she wants a family. She seems to have accepted that she's mine, and even though I'm not positive she'll end up staying (I can't even make myself kiss the girl) I guess I should consider it. It's not something I've ever thought about seriously, since kids weren't exactly in the cards, given my lifestyle. But Elise may want kids, and if I *do* end up with Elise... well, that's worth knowing.

I guess it might be kind of nice. An image of a little girl with blond pigtails rockets to the forefront of my mind, standing at a kitchen counter with Elise, learning how to make muffins.

Ouch. Goddammit. I rub my chest, feeling an actual stab of

some fucked up emotion. Don't have the time or inclination to deal with that right now.

"I'm so tired," Elise tells me, turning and pulling her hair over her shoulder. "Will you unzip me?"

"Do you want kids?"

I don't mean to ask, but I can't get that little girl out of my head.

Spinning around and meeting my gaze, she says unflinchingly, "Yes."

I nod, but I'm not even sure why I'm nodding. It feels presumptuous, and I suddenly want to tell her I didn't mean with me, but didn't I? I keep my mouth shut, because nothing good can come from opening it. I just keep nodding, like a busted bobble-head doll.

"Do you?" she finally asks, after what feels like an hour.

I stop nodding. My palms sweat. Jesus, why is this apartment always so hot?

"I don't know," I answer honestly. "I never really thought about it before."

She nods, turning back around, since I didn't unzip her. My fingers awkwardly find the zipper as she continues, "I want a little girl. Candace."

"You already have a name picked out," I murmur, tugging the zipper down, the temperature in the room climbing with every inch of exposed, perfect skin.

Glancing back at me with amusement, she says, "Don't worry, I haven't named the boy yet."

"Two kids," I murmur, suddenly wanting to rip off my clothes and jump in an ice cold shower.

"I've never seen you scared before," she says, laughing at me. "It's kind of fun." Then, grasping the damaged hands I didn't think she'd even noticed, she says, "You probably did this without flinching, but I mention procreation and you look at me like I'm the clown from *It*."

Then she drops my hands and peels the dress from her arms, tugging it off until she's only wearing a bra and panties. Right there, in front of me.

I turn to give her privacy, but that brief glimpse of her perfect, barely-covered body is now emblazoned in my mind. My eyes dart to the door, wondering if I should leave, but she's talking again, and I don't want to be rude.

"I should read some more tonight," she says casually, like it's normal to be undressing in front of me. "We haven't read in a few nights. I miss it."

"What do you want to read?" I ask, since at least *this* is something I'm comfortable with.

"*Jane Eyre.* I know how much you love Rochester," she teases.

"And listening to you butcher French," I add.

"Nope, I'm making you read those lines," she states, as my ears register the sound of fabric falling around her. "You can turn around now."

I do, and she's grabbing her literature book and climbing across the bed. The nightshirt she's wearing doesn't adequately cover her ass as she climbs across the bed, but I've already seen a split second of much more, so I don't even feel as bad as I might've.

My head is swimming with all the new information, but as Elise cracks open her book, searching toward the back for the story she wants to read me, the crushing weight begins to dissipate. I don't have to deal with all of it now. All I have to do right now is strip off this damn suit, climb into bed, and listen to Elise read me some Brontë.

CHAPTER EIGHT

I CAN'T sleep.

I toss and turn all night long. At one point I do fall asleep, but only long enough for my eyes to burn like hell when they open again and it's still dark.

Something is lodged in my brain, gnawing away at me. I can't stop thinking about it, and I don't *want* to think about it. Thinking about it makes it real, and it can't be real. I can't accept the ramifications if it is.

It's just before four when I give up on sleeping. I climb out of bed, dead tired, and drag my ass to the shower. I go back to the bedroom to get dressed and watch Elise for a minute, so peacefully curled up in bed. *Our* bed.

I shouldn't have set us up in Chicago. I could've found work somewhere else. As much as Mia grates on me sometimes, I'm no better; I can't handle being in such close proximity to Mateo without getting sucked into the path of his destruction, either.

I let myself into his house and put in the alarm code. I'm partially glad he gave me my key back, but I hate it nearly as much, because sometimes I don't want his trust. It's too heavy.

Much the same as years earlier, I make the trek in the middle of the night to his bedroom. He'll probably be getting up soon to hit the gym anyway, but when I ease open his bedroom door and slip inside, he's still asleep. Meg is snuggled up against him with her back to me, an arm thrown over his chest. Not like last time, not like Beth.

She wants him. She loves him. She's devoted to him.

And he's goddamned Mateo.

I walk to his side of the bed noiselessly, but he must sense a disturbance, because his eyes open.

"It's me," I say, so he doesn't pull a gun on me.

Sighing heavily, he turns and looks at me. "You've gotta stop watching me sleep, Adrian. It's fucking creepy."

"Are you fucking Mia?"

His features turn to stone and he spares a quick glance over at Meg, still asleep. With a decidedly less easygoing glare, he tells me, "No."

"Are you lying?"

"I have no reason to," he states.

I glance at Meg. "I can think of a couple."

"Those are reasons not to do it, not reasons to lie about it," he states, passing a hand over his face. "What the fuck is this, Adrian?"

"You can't keep doing this to Vince."

"For the *last* time, I am not doing anything to Vince. I gave him a house. I gave them space, freedom away from me. I didn't have to—if I wanted to keep Mia for myself, I wouldn't have."

"She's coming around a lot more lately."

Eyes widening, he says, "Because of *Meg*. That's Meg's doing, not mine."

"Meg trusts you, you know."

He looks at me the way I usually look at him. It would amuse me, his lack of humor, if not for all the thoughts brewing in my mind right now.

Since I'm not going to get anything else out of him, I turn to head out of his bedroom.

"You came here just for that?" he asks.

"No, I'm going to the surveillance room. Couldn't sleep. Work to do."

I don't expect to see Mateo until much later, but he comes to the surveillance room with wet hair an hour later. He comes with two cups of coffee, passing one to me.

"Thanks," I murmur, lifting the mug to take a drink.

"What's going on?" he asks, flicking a glance at the screen I'm viewing. It's everybody having drinks in his study, the night before Meg was shot.

"I don't know. Maybe nothing. Just couldn't sleep, figured I might as well do something."

"Trouble in paradise?"

I glance up at him warily, but don't answer.

"You treat her like she's your sister, you know," he remarks.

I don't respond, turning my attention to the screen so he'll see that I'm ignoring him and leave.

"She's never going to fuck you if you're treating her like a sister," he continues.

"I don't need advice on how to get laid, thank you very much."

He takes a sip of his coffee, but seems to reject my assertion. "You need to start touching her. The whole night you never touched her once. Light, easy touches—her shoulder, her wrist, her arm, her leg, her hip, her back, whatever you can touch, innocent as can be, but you need to make contact."

"I don't need your advice, Mateo," I inform him, still watching the screen.

"Just trying to help," he says, shrugging.

"Don't need your help," I reply evenly.

"You're being stubborn."

I give him a sideways glare.

His eyebrows rise and he shakes his head. "Fine, fine. Not like I have experience here or anything."

"I don't want to appeal to her on the same level you do. I'm not you. I don't want to be. I will foster something healthy with her, or I'll foster nothing and kick her out of the nest once she's recovered. I'm not taking advantage of her. I'm not *you*."

He shakes his head, sighing as he turns to leave. "Always doing things the hard way."

I roll my eyes and rewind the damn tape. I've been staring at it, trying to ignore him, but he's aggravated me and I don't want to risk missing anything.

I'm supposed to go to Saturday night dinner this week to welcome Colin into the fold as Meg's new bodyguard, but it only takes five minutes with him and Cherie to make me regret that recommendation. I want to stay and talk to Mateo about it after, but I finally get some good information about Castellanos. More specifically, where he's supposed to be this coming week.

That's a little more pressing than dealing with McGregor.

The rest of the night is gone before I know it, calling around to set up meetings, making plans to move against Castellanos.

Problem is, I haven't had a chance to verify my suspicions after reviewing the security tapes and looking into who might've been behind Meg's shooting. Bigger problem is, I just don't want to. So instead I make plans without them, and don't even tell Mateo, that way he won't accidentally share the information with the wrong people.

If I can take out Castellanos on a small scale op like this, I may be able to navigate around outright war. No one can find Salvatore at this point, but if we strike down his old man and cease fire, maybe he'll resurface. Mateo and I have talked a little bit about this, but now he's more reluctant to make any kind of peace, after Salvatore set him up to think he was banging Meg. I'd like to remind Mateo he doesn't hold grudges, but with Meg still wounded and everything so fresh, he's not listening.

My to-do list somehow grows longer with each thing I check off.

Normally I join Mateo in his study for pre-dinner drinks, but tonight I follow Elise to the kitchen with the ladies. Mia and Meg are shoulder to shoulder, chatting as they prep food, but Elise heads where I want to go—to Cherie.

After the customary greetings, Elise asks what she can help with and gets to work setting the table. Me, I linger by the stove, leaning against the counter by Cherie.

Flashing me a smile once Elise is gone, she says, "So, how are you doing? I never get to talk to you anymore."

"I'm good."

"How's freedom?" she asks lightly.

"Small," I tell her.

She grabs a salt shaker and dumps some in her pot. "Well, it would probably be bigger if you wouldn't have run right back to Mateo's rescue," she points out.

"Meg got shot."

"Not your problem," she reminds me, putting the salt shaker down and stirring.

"Someone's going to kill him," I state.

"Without a doubt," she replies, raising her eyebrows.

"I couldn't let that happen."

She shrugs, as if to say without words we'll have to agree to disagree. I know she's not Mateo's biggest fan, but I'm still surprised she's so ambivalent about his potential demise. Mateo's never been *bad* to Cherie, but he's never been good to her, either. She's the only person in his life who doesn't seem to find him charming—even as a kid, she always liked me more.

"It wouldn't make a difference anyway," I tell her, though I'm not sure if I'm trying to convince her, or myself. "The world wouldn't *really* be better off without him."

"You sure?" she asks.

"Dante wouldn't be a better head of the family, believe me."

"Vince would," she says quietly, almost under her breath.

Dread rolls over me that she would even think that, let alone say it. I ease back, glancing around the room, trying not to look at the cameras. "We shouldn't talk about this," I decide, not wanting her to get in trouble.

"You like Vince."

"Cherie." I stare at her, lowering my voice. "That's never gonna happen. And he's way too young, anyway."

"Mateo was young when he pushed Matt out."

I rub the back of my neck, moving away from the counter, pacing a couple feet away. "This isn't what I wanted to talk to you about."

She merely raises her eyebrows noncommittally and places the spoon down on a dish, turning to face me. "Then what *did* you want to talk to me about?"

Now I kind of *do* want to talk to her about this, but not where Mateo could listen in on the conversation if he felt like it. *Definitely* not mere feet from Meg and Mia, both of whom would report straight back to Mateo if they overheard us. I lean in close, so I can speak lowly. "You can't say shit like that, Cherie."

"He's a jerk," she whispers back.

"Has Vince mentioned this to you?"

"Of course not," she says, rolling her eyes. "Vince doesn't even want to *be* in the family business, let alone run it."

That eases a little of the weight on my shoulders, so I ease back, sighing. I'm already running out of juice, but I should say what I came to say. "You need to stay away from McGregor."

Nodding knowingly, she turns back to the stove. "I knew that's why you came in here."

"He's not a good guy, Cherie."

"I'm not convinced good guys exist," she states. "I've sure never met one."

"Even so, he falls too far on the bad end of the spectrum. You don't want a guy like that. Wait until you start college, you can meet someone *normal*."

"Mateo's sending me to school *in* Chicago. With *Mia*. It's going to be just like high school. As soon as people find out who I'm related to, no one's going to want to have a relationship with me unless they're a total weirdo. If he would've let me go away, maybe, but Mom didn't want him to, and he doesn't care what I want."

I'm rethinking my newfound desire to have a daughter. Sure, they might have cute pigtails and make muffins with their mom for a time, but then they'll grow up and want to date assholes. Is it really worth it?

"I could try talking to him, if you really want to go away to school."

She shakes her head, aggravated. "It won't matter. Mom has that smug look when we talk about it, so I know she's already talked to him. He's not gonna piss off Mom—she might start putting his decorative pillows out of order or something."

I bite back a smile. She's not wrong.

Meg drifts over toward me, just seeming to realize I'm in the kitchen. "Are you lost? Drinks are that way," she says, indicating the door.

I shake my head, glancing down at her abdomen. "Just trying to talk some sense into this one. How are you feeling?"

"I'm much better," she assures me.

"Where's your bodyguard?"

Meg smirks, her gaze drifting to Cherie, then back to me. "Having drinks with the boys."

"Is that what he's paid for?"

"I'm pretty safe inside these walls," she points out.

"I wouldn't say the same for him," I mutter, glancing back at Cherie before heading for the door. I'll have to warn him off, since Cherie won't listen to me.

"No murdering," Meg calls after me. "Mateo's orders!"

When I get to the study, that smug, Irish son of a bitch is sitting in my chair. Joey and Vince are across from each other, talking, and Alec is in the other one.

Even though I normally don't, I decide to go stand by Mateo at his desk.

"All well with the ladies?" he asks.

"I don't trust McGregor around Cherie," I state.

"He's just a harmless flirt," Mateo says, dismissively.

"I don't know if he is or not, but Cherie's gonna feed into it and make it all worse."

"I already talked to him about it," he assures me.

"You did?" I ask, relaxing a little. He's not always as protective of Cherie as the girls he has a vested interest in, but I know Colin won't cross Mateo, regardless of what he boasts to Cherie.

Mateo nods, taking a drink from his glass. "He's assured me that he'll keep his hands to himself until she's of age."

I stare at him, my stomach twisting up in knots. "Of *age*? You mean in a month? You talked to him and got his word that he wouldn't try anything for a *month*?"

Mateo nods, glancing at me. "She's going to grow up sometime."

"Not with *him*! Are you insane? He's a *murderer*."

"We're *all* murderers," Mateo points out, as if amused. "Literally everyone in this room."

"And I wouldn't want any of us with Cherie," I point out.

"Come on. You're not going to tell me you're okay with that? He's too old for her."

"Okay, again… you're saying all these things that could be said about any one of us and our respective female counterparts. Do Meg and Mia deserve less than Cherie? Does Elise?"

I shake my head, irritated with him for not looking at Cherie and seeing a little girl who needs protecting from a lecherous ass like Colin McGregor. It feels almost identical to how I felt all those years ago when he wouldn't protect Elise against that Rick asshole, except I actually care more about Cherie than I cared about Elise then.

"Why don't you let Cherie go away to school? If you're going to pay her tuition, you can pay it just as easily in another state. Somewhere warm and calm without us around to keep her in a box. If she wants to grow up, let it be with some douchebag in college who wears polo shirts and plays beer pong."

Mateo is already shaking his head. "Maria wants to keep her close."

"He'll hurt her, you know he will," I state. "He's not you, he's not looking for a nice girl to settle down with him and keep his bed warm; he's just looking for another conquest."

"I think Cherie is smart enough to make her own decisions regarding who she sleeps with," Mateo states, pushing away from the desk to go refill his glass.

"How?" I ask, following. "She has *no* experience with guys, let alone dogs like him."

"Hey now," Colin puts in, from my chair. "I have two ears, y'know."

"I haven't said anything you don't already know, McGregor," I inform him.

He nods in acknowledgement and goes back to bullshitting with Alec.

I roll my eyes, liking him even less.

"You worry too much, Adrian," Mateo tells me, replacing

his decanter on the cart and retrieving his glass. "It'll be okay."

I narrow my eyes, settling back against his desk, and look at Colin. Maybe I'll just kill the bastard. He's a mercenary, so it's not like I'd be robbing the world of some precious jewel.

As if reading my mind, or perhaps just recalling history, Mateo says, "And don't you dare kill him. I'm in the middle of a gang war; I can't be worried about this stupid shit right now."

"If he puts a single finger on her, I make no promises."

"Well, you should tell him that, not me," Mateo reasons. Then, patting me on the shoulder, he says, "Better yet, get to solving my Castellanos problem so you can move on with your life—then you won't have to think about any of this anymore."

As soon as he says it, he tips his hand. I can see him realize that he took it a little too far, but now that he's caught, he just smiles. "Unless of course you want to stick around, make sure everything remains... pure."

"You son of a bitch," I mutter.

"Colin's not going anywhere anytime soon, so if you're that worried about it..."

"Yeah, I get it," I say, rolling my eyes. "You'd really sacrifice Cherie's well-being to trap me into working for you again."

"You say that like it's unimaginable," he says dryly. "Come on, Adrian. It's straight from my playbook. I'll move her ass in with him, if I have to."

I shake my head, surprised it's even possible to be disappointed in him at this point. "Wow."

"I'll make sure Cherie makes it past 18 without being defiled by the Irishman—all you have to do is stay."

"I could make sure of the same thing for a lot cheaper," I inform him.

"Except I just said you couldn't," he points out.

"Didn't stop me last time," I mutter.

A faint hint of steel creeps into his tone, though his smile remains. "And look what happened then."

My gaze snaps to his, narrowing. "You don't have anything to trade me this time, Mateo. If I wanted to play by your rules, I could win this in a minute."

"If you play by my rules, you'll lose," he informs me, the smile waning. "You're my friend, Adrian, but don't forget your place." Leaning in just slightly, he says, "I gave you Elise, and I could take her away just as easily."

"You don't own her," I grind out, my jaw locked so tight it's painful.

"I don't have to," he answers silkily.

Slamming the glass down on the edge of his desk, I push away and head for the exit.

I almost walk right out the front door, but then I remember Elise. Storming back to the kitchen, I tap her on the shoulder, grabbing her arm and hauling her toward the door.

"What are you doing?" she asks, confused, glancing back at the bread she was just arranging on the plate. "I wasn't finished with that."

"We're leaving."

"Why?" she demands, looking more than a little disappointed.

I don't have an explanation to give her, so I don't say anything; I just haul her out of Mateo's house reluctantly one more goddamn time.

CHAPTER NINE

I'M QUIET the whole way home, stewing in a mix of anxious, self-conscious and murderous thoughts. Mateo's cocksure attitude doesn't usually get to me, but it does this time because he means it. For someone so goddamn paranoid, he would push me, even knowing what I'm capable of, because he doesn't believe he can lose. He doesn't believe he can be toppled.

I've never been so goddamn tempted in my life to help topple him.

He thinks he has all the power. He only *has* what he has because of me.

I glance over at Elise, beautiful, gentle Elise, watching out the window since I won't talk to her. She's all dressed up in a navy blue dress Mateo bought for her before we left, her hair pulled back into a neat up-do, little blond tendrils escaping. God, she's so beautiful. *Too* beautiful. She sits in this boring-ass car, regal as a queen, and…

And he'd take her from me, just to prove he could. He doesn't even want her, just like he didn't want Mia when he first took her from Vince, but Mateo uses sex as a weapon. He uses *everything* as a weapon, and he knows how long Elise yearned for him. He's kept it in his back pocket, never acting on it, rarely even encouraging it, but always making sure I knew.

Mere days ago I wanted to believe that was over, that now he has Meg and he'll stop that shit, but I gave him too much credit.

Vince is right. Once you cross him, Mateo has no loyalty to you. I survived crossing him once, but he doesn't want to fuck me; *I* won't survive a second time.

Or he won't.

Either way, it ends badly. Either way it's not the life I want to make for Elise.

Never has regicide sounded so appealing. Maybe I should take over his goddamn family myself. Put in Vince, like Cherie suggested. If I got rid of Dante, I could probably do it. Joey's older, but Joey loves Vince, he'd pass the torch without a struggle. He doesn't want that kind of responsibility anyway.

Of course, Vince reminds me a little too much of Matt, and I'm worried what would happen to him if he had Mateo's power. He'd probably end up being mean to Mia. I might not be able to control him. Our whole operation would be vulnerable, especially with all this shit we have going on with Castellanos right now. We won't survive a change in management right on the heels of this, not without a major loss of people, at the very least. And he's so young.

"I wish you'd tell me what happened."

I glance over at Elise, emerging from the helpless rage that's threatening to consume me. She looks so sincere, like she really wants to know why I'm upset, but I don't feel like having another Mateo fight. I don't feel like tiring her out that way. I don't feel like adding to my already mounting fears that he could do what he threatened. As hard as she fell for him with no encouragement, I can't imagine the agony of seeing him exert even a soupçon of effort to turn her head.

I haven't even done a damn thing to claim her as mine. Aside from their claims that I *bought* her, anyway. I haven't kissed her. I never touch her.

It's like the goddamn car's closing in on me.

"I don't know if I want to help Mateo finish this," I finally say, stealing a glance in her direction.

Her brow furrows with displeasure. "Why?"

"Because it's not my problem."

"Someone tried to kill him," she points out, like I've forgotten. "They almost killed Meg."

"But they didn't."

"But won't they try again, if you don't take care of it?" she asks.

"Probably. But that's the life he chose."

She doesn't say anything else, but she turns her head back toward the window, watching the scenery fly by as we approach our apartment, instead of looking at me. Her obvious disapproval only makes me feel worse.

When we get home, it's too early for bed, so Elise changes into her pajamas and goes in the bedroom, cracking open her literature book to read some *Jane Eyre*.

I don't think I'm invited until she starts reading aloud, even though I'm still in the living room.

I duck my head in and she pauses, glancing up at me. "Want me to start over?"

I shake my head, since I already know what I missed. "Go ahead."

She nods and picks up where she left off, reading as I peel off this goddamn suit and pull on a more comfortable T-shirt instead. It's still hot as hell in this apartment for some reason, but I pull on sleep pants and climb in beside her.

When she gets to the end of the chapter, she puts her hand between the pages and closes the book, looking over at me. "Don't you own shorts?"

I smile slightly. "I have a pair, but I don't wear them."

"It's really warm in here tonight; you're going to burn up."

The burn scars creep down my hip, down my leg, but she's never seen me out of pants, so she doesn't know that. I just shrug, nodding toward the book. "Come on, don't keep me in suspense."

She cracks a smile, opening the book up. The sound of her voice relaxes me, melting away my troubles, making me forget about the stress of the day.

I don't do a damn thing for Mateo on Monday.

I planned to, after Elise finished reading last night and curled up in our bed, her long blonde hair spread out across the pillow. Because I don't want to fight him. I don't know if I can win, and I have a hell of a lot more to lose now than I used to.

But then I dreamed about them all night. When I closed my eyes, Mateo's hands were roaming every inch of her perfect body, his mouth on her neck, her eyes closed in rapturous pleasure. Him, with his goddamn Disney prince face, with his pretty gifts and his unmarred body, with his power and his wealth and his disregard for what's right—he had no problem pouncing on Elise's attraction to authority, I'll tell you that.

When I woke up, I couldn't stomach helping him. Sure, maybe another day where I don't ferret out the rats in his own circle could bring him another day closer to his own demise, but you know what, the bastard dug his own grave. If someone else puts him in it while I take a personal day, that's just too damn bad.

I'm calm by the time I head home. I've prowled the city all day, doing not a damn thing, and it was nice. My aggression has largely melted away. At a certain point I even thought about answering some of the calls I'm ignoring, because this isn't a great time for it. With the Castellanos thing coming up Thursday, I should be focused, not scattered, not rebelling.

I walk through the door, expecting Elise to probably be making dinner. I put on a suit today even though I didn't need to, and that reminds me I need to go to the dry cleaner.

As soon as I walk in, Elise lights up like a Christmas tree. She comes over and throws her arms around me, so close to my face I think she might kiss me, and my heart nearly gives out. She doesn't, she just grins at me, but like I'm a goddamn prince.

"Well, hello to you, too."

"Thank you," she says, a huge grin lighting up her beautiful face. "Thank you, thank you, thank you."

I don't know why I'm being thanked. I try to remember if I did anything worth any measure of gratitude before I left this morning, let alone *this* level, but I come up blank.

She lets go of me and steps back, all but skipping to the counter. My heart stutters then sinks when she leans down and smells a huge bouquet of pink and lavender roses. They're in a cube vase, tinted purple, and I can see the card sticking out of it.

The white card, with the gold edges.

Mateo's cards.

I go to it like a magnet to a refrigerator door, plucking it from the flower arrangement and reading it.

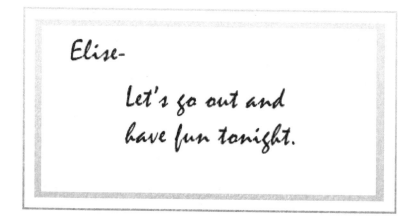

Elise—

Let's go out and
have fun tonight.

"That dress. Oh, my god. I've never seen a prettier dress in my whole life."

She keeps talking, but the sound of her voice is drowned out by the tidal wave of rage crashing through my veins.

"I didn't even know Aladdin was playing," she gushes, clutching an envelope, still grinning at me, still not catching on that I have no idea what the hell any of this is.

Well, I do.

Of course I do.

But she doesn't. She apparently thinks all of this is from me. Because she doesn't recognize his card.

I'm going to meet him at the gym tomorrow. Take him up on that open invitation. Because I'm going to beat the living fuck out of him.

"I'm so excited!"

I force myself to emerge from the rage fog and look at Elise, beaming, happy. This is what I wanted, right? Sure, I wanted to be the one to make it happen, but she thinks I was. In all likelihood, she'll never know I didn't as long as I fall in line.

I feel like Vince right now, and I fucking hate it. Only I'm not, because he doesn't actually *want* to steal my girl—he just wants to show me how incredibly easy it would be if he decided to.

Elise might as well have a lit sign above her head with an arrow pointing at her, announcing, "So easy!"

Placing a hand on mine, she says, "Now that you're here, I'm going to get dressed. If we want to make dinner before the show, we have to get going."

She disappears into the bedroom and I lean against the counter, trying to get my bearings. The roses seem so guilty, like they're complicit in this scheme. I want to dump them down the garbage disposal and watch the blades rip them apart.

I want to tell Meg what he did to Mia.

I've covered his ass so many times, and this is how much loyalty he has to me.

Elise emerges, and I forget all my feelings of vengeance. She looks incredible in the long dress he had sent over for her. It's so sexy, with a split clear up the left side. Her entire smooth, perfect leg is visible every time she moves, and then she strikes a playful pose at the end of the hall, and it's not just for a second. I have to shift, hoping there's no visible evidence of the arousal that's just hit me like a truck.

He must like her in blue. He bought her blue again. To match her eyes. I'm never buying her anything blue again.

"Wow." I don't even mean to say it, it's hardly more than a breath, but Elise shines even brighter, basking in the compliment.

She flexes her ankle, showing off the nude pumps on her feet. "These aren't even as uncomfortable as I thought they'd be," she tells me, looking down to admire them.

I recognize the red soles. He always bought Mia that brand.

I've never felt sorrier for Vince than I do right now.

She comes over and drapes herself on me again, hugging me, lingering close. I think she's gonna kiss me again, but she doesn't. Maybe she's giving me a chance to. I don't.

"This is gonna be fun," she tells me.

I nod my agreement, forcing a smile.

When we get to the restaurant, I'm relieved to find the reservation's in my name, not his.

I'm not psyched this is where he sent us, since the bill's going to be astronomical, but Elise is enchanted. The setting is romantic—we're seated near the bar at a small table for two, but there's candlelight and soft music that she keeps absently swaying to in her seat. Whatever fruity drink she ordered seems to be doing good things for her. She looks so happy. So vibrant. I want to be able to do stuff like this with her all the time.

Goddamn Mateo.

I hold my breath when the waiter brings over our bill, but when I open it up, it's already been paid.

Hell, if I would've known he was paying, I would've ordered a bunch of shit I didn't even want, just to be petty.

Elise had two drinks, so she's loose and having fun as we leave the restaurant. On the way to the car, she reaches down and grabs my hand. It's only for a minute, since she has to release it for me to open the door for her, but the way her blue eyes twinkle as she slides in almost stops my heart.

God, this girl.

Next is the show. Since dinner and the tickets were paid for by Mateo, I go ahead and buy us drinks for while we watch. I probably shouldn't let Elise have another, since she's still pretty happy from her drinks at the restaurant, but I do anyway, because she's having so much fun. Every new scene change, she grabs my arm, touches my thigh, pats my hand with excitement. She's never so touchy. Her face is lit with pleasure from the time the lights dim until the last curtain falls, and then she's standing and clapping her hands, throwing her long blonde hair back over her bare shoulder and clapping some more. A little reluctantly, I stand beside her, and she rewards me with another beaming smile.

As we all file out of the theater, she grabs my hand again. It's a nice summer night, not too hot, no wind. Instead of following everyone to the parking area, Elise dawdles, sighing and swinging my hand.

"Let's just go for a walk. It's so beautiful out tonight."

I'm inclined to agree, and seeing her like this makes it even more beautiful. I'm not much of a hand-holder, but I wouldn't let go of her hand right now for anything.

"We should go out more often," she tells me, leaning into my left side.

"We can go out whenever you like," I tell her.

"I wasn't sure. Also I didn't know how much fun this would

be. I went to a show when I was 14, my first one. My mom took me and my friend, and it was magical. I loved it. But I've never gone with a guy before." She gives me another mysterious little look. "Actually, this was kind of my first date, I guess."

"Well, I hope it was a good one," I say honestly.

"It was a great one," she tells me. "I always used to..." She trails off, laughing a little. "This is going to sound so boring and lame compared to this, but back when you used to tutor me, I always used to imagine us going out one day—not like this, just, like, to a bookstore, because I knew you loved books. And if we're being honest here, sometimes I *hated* the books you picked, but I didn't want you to think I was stupid, so I tried to like them."

This surprises a little laugh out of me. "You should've told me. I would've never thought that."

"I always had these daydreams that we could go on an outing—like, I'd imagine you suggesting it one day while we were studying, and us grabbing coffee and a pastry, and picking out books. The bookstore first, so we could do the coffee and pastries after and discuss the books we bought, of course."

"That sounds... perfect."

She nods vehemently, glancing over at me. "Not that this wasn't. Because it was. *Good job*, A plus, gold star. This was awesome. But I think our next date should be my books and coffee date."

"Our next date, huh?"

She swings my hand, nodding, not looking at me. "Assuming you ever ask me on another one," she says lightly. "You're obviously in no rush."

I don't know what to say to that. She's right, I'm not, but she makes it sound like a bad thing. "I didn't think you'd want me to be," I finally say.

"Why?" she asks, glancing over at me.

I shrug, brushing my thumb across hers. "You didn't really get much of a choice in all this. I didn't want you to feel pressured."

"You could never make me feel pressured," she says, like that's an absurd thing to say. "You've waited for me for *five* years. You waited for me to *grow up*. How much time do you think I need?"

"But you didn't even *know* I was waiting for you all that time. You didn't know you were going to get passed off to me. You've said time and again that you feel like I *bought* you, and I don't want that. I don't want you to feel obligated to me. I don't want you to feel like I own you."

"What if I wanna be owned?" she asks lightly, flirtatiously. "Maybe you should try taking what you want and see what happens."

I smile, shaking my head. "I think I should've stopped you after the first two drinks."

"Yes, because I couldn't *possibly* mean that," she says, rolling her eyes dramatically.

There are a lot of reasons I don't think she means it, but I start small. "I'm older than you."

"That's sexy," she states.

It's a little disarming to hear that, but I hold onto my objections like they're gospel. "And two weeks ago you wanted someone else."

Her smile drops at that one. "I didn't *want* him two weeks ago," she mutters, watching the sidewalk as we walk. To my immense regret, she also drops my hand. "I didn't want him after the Mia thing. I told you that. I get that it's weird that I liked your best friend, but to be fair, you never *once* indicated any actual interest in me. Never. I waited; I searched for it, and nothing. We spent so much time together for *years*, and you never once tried to kiss me or touch me or spend time together outside of our studying. And I enjoyed that, obviously, but... it made me think you weren't interested in pursuing me. I had *no* idea you were doing all that for me."

"But when you found out, you said no," I point out. "When he first told you that you could go with me, that he'd let you leave... you said no."

"I did," she acknowledges. "I was a little nervous, and like I said, I wasn't unhappy working for Mateo. I got lonely sometimes, sure, but I liked living with Cherie and Maria—they're closer than my mom and I ever were, and they always included me. Maria loves board games, and she's such a generally grumpy person, but you should see her beat someone at a board game. She's such a sore winner," she says, grinning. "She just gloats, and she doesn't even say anything, but she has this smug little look on her face."

I crack a smile. "That sounds nice."

"On Sundays we have our own family dinners in the servants' quarters. And for Christmas she makes these amazing cookies. And Mateo was never stingy, so we always got to order presents for one another and decorate the house. I never got much for presents as a kid. My mom would buy these really cheap, generic things that would break before winter break was even over. Not that it's about the gifts, but..." She looks up at me and shrugs. "It was home. If you wanted to be a part of it, I would've been fine with that, I would've offered you an invitation, but I didn't want to leave it. Especially for just... nothing. I had no idea why I was leaving, I was so confused, and Mateo just expected me to understand, he didn't explain it. And I know you hate that I liked Mateo, but it wasn't really *sexual*, I just... I like the way he runs his family. I like the way he ran our home. He was like my boss, and yeah, I was fine with that. And yes, sure, I had a crush on him for a time, but who *doesn't*? I didn't have a lot of other options. *You* never expressed an interest in me, so I didn't even put you in the same category once you stopped tutoring me."

"You could've liked Alec, or Vince, or Joey."

"Vince is too young," she says, shaking her head. "Alec's boring. Joey..." She rocks her head back and forth. "Joey was okay. I never really got to talk to him. I think Mateo warned him off."

That surprises me. "Really? Why would he do that?"

Giving me a pointed look, she says, "Well, now I assume it's because he knew *you* liked me. Joey's a charmer. Not Mateo level, but…"

Yeah, I wouldn't have enjoyed watching Joey flirt with Elise, that's for damn sure.

"That Irish guy, now if *he* would've come around…"

My jaw falls open, and she gives me a devious little grin.

"I'm gonna kill that asshole one of these days," I swear, shaking my head.

Elise laughs, taking a left as we come to a crosswalk. "I'm just teasing you."

I feel a prickling on the back of my neck. The road I followed Elise down is quieter than the one we were just walking, but the man who's been walking behind us turned, too. I assume it's a man, anyway. I haven't looked back, but judging by the footfall, it's not a woman.

Probably nothing, but I eye up the next turn anyway. If he follows us again, there might be a problem.

Elise is still talking, but I'm no longer paying attention. I reclaim her hand, clasping it a little tighter. This would be no problem if she wasn't with me, but the thought of something happening to her terrifies me. I care too much. There's a certain level of emotional distance when I'm doing my job—there's never terror. I'm never afraid. Lack of fear is why I'm good at it.

But right now, as I pick up the pace and he does, too, my heartbeat pounds in my throat. I don't want Elise to see me kill someone, and I don't want her to get hurt if this is an actual threat.

And then Elise steps out of her goddamn shoe.

"Oh," she says on a laugh, stopping in the middle of the road, backing up a step to slide it back on.

And there it is. I can turn to look at the guy now, but when I do, he's pointing a gun in my face.

CHAPTER TEN

THE MAN'S large, rough hand closes around Elise's tiny bicep. She gasps, looking back to see who's touching her, and I go for my gun.

"Oh, my god," she says, her voice shaking as he pulls her back against him, putting the gun to her head, then swinging it to point at me. This little fuck. He doesn't even know where he wants to point the gun.

I relax a little. My fingers brush the butt of my gun, but I don't pull it out. This guy's gonna panic if I do.

Not one of Antonio's guys. They'd know where they want to point the gun.

"Please don't hurt me," Elise says, her voice somehow smaller. I frown at her, but she's not looking at me, she has those big blue eyes trained on her assailant. Does she really think I'd let him hurt her? Granted, she's never seen me in action beyond launching Rick through a wall of shelves, but she knows what I do, what I'm capable of.

"Relax," I say, keeping my tone calm. "I'm gonna grab my wallet."

"No," he says, the gun wobbling. This poor fucker's *shaking*.

"You don't want my wallet?"

"Yeah, no, I do. But nothing—nothing funny. Put your hands up, where I can see them. Both of them," he says more adamantly, putting the shaky gun to Elise's temple.

"Okay," I say, immediately letting go of the gun and raising my hands. His damn nervousness is the real threat here. I spook this asshole, he might accidentally hurt Elise. "I can't give you my wallet if my hands are up. Let's just bring it down a notch. Everything's fine. We're all cool here. Let's just... relax."

"Why are you so fucking calm?" he demands, clearly not calm. Maybe a little high? Man, he should've picked a better mark.

"You can take whatever you want, man. It's just stuff," I tell him. "I just don't want anyone to get hurt. If you let me get my wallet, I can give it to you, and this can all be over."

Elise turns her head to look back at him again, and he slowly lets her ease away from his body. He maintains his hold on her arm, and I contemplate what I want to do next. I really wanna shoot him. Like, really, really bad. And I could—but we're technically in public, and Elise will see. Do I want to commit a murder right in front of her? Not especially.

Once she turns to face him, the guy finally gets a good look at her, and then I kind of do want to kill him, even if she has to watch. His gaze darts around her body, at the cleavage spilling out of her low-cut dress, the thigh she is inexplicably exposing instead of hiding under his perusal. If I didn't know any better, I'd think she's trying to hold his attention.

Oh.

I slowly lower my right hand, bringing it toward my gun. My heart pounds as I keep my gaze trained on him, knowing if he catches me, he'll get scared and fire his weapon.

Elise bites down on that damn plump lower lip of hers, and inexplicably takes a small step closer to the man. "Please don't hurt us. I'll do anything." Her voice all sweet and scared and innocent. Goddamn.

Dude's Adam's apple bobs, but before he can respond to her offer, Elise grabs his arm, yanks him toward the ground, plants her elbow in his spine, shoves him back, and kicks him right in the face.

My jaw drops as the guy does, and then she skitters forward, kicking the gun away from him and into the street.

"You picked the wrong fucking people to rob, asshole," she states, no trace of sweetness left in her tone.

The man shoves up off the ground and I pull my gun, but he's not pursuing—he runs, awkwardly and as quickly as he can away from us.

Elise spins back to face me, grinning. "Wow! Can you believe that just happened?"

"What. The. Fuck?" I can really only stare at her, and she's so weirdly *excited*.

"That guy—" She snorts, shaking her head. "Man, what a schmuck. Can you imagine, someone trying to rob *you*?"

"Me?" My eyebrows rise, my eyes widening. "I didn't do anything. You just beat that guy's ass."

"Oh." She shrugs, like it was nothing. "Not really. I mean, he ran, and I'm not exactly dressed for it, but…"

"How did you know how to do that?"

"Ju taught me."

I blink at her, shaking my head. "Mateo's nanny?"

She nods. "After all that happened with that Rick guy a long time ago, I realized I wanted to be able to defend myself if it ever came up again. You might not always be there, and it's not always the best guys who come around, you know. When I told Maria what happened, she sent me to Ju."

I knew Mateo's nanny had background in self-defense—that was a requirement for him, in the event anything ever happened, he wanted one last line of defense for Isabella. But I *didn't* know she was teaching the other ladies self-defense.

I mean, on reflection, that's a really good idea, particularly if you live with Mateo, but suddenly Elise doesn't look so fragile to me anymore. Suddenly I realize, if Elise didn't want my attentions, she could simply knock my ass out.

And damn, that's sexy.

I move toward her without realizing my own intention, fisting a hand in her long blonde hair and pulling her against my body. A little breath of surprise whooshes out of her, but she braces her hands on my shoulders and doesn't pull back as I lean in and crush my lips against hers. Her body molds to mine and she kisses me back with matched fierceness, as if she's been waiting for this, too. I rotate our positions, walking her back against the building until she's planted against it. Her peek-a-boo thigh comes up and hooks around my hip, luring me closer, and arousal surges through me, almost incapacitating in its force.

She pulls back and looks up at me, the moonlight on her beautiful face, her blue eyes sparkling with warmth... desire?

"Let's go home," I murmur, hearing the hoarseness in my own voice.

Elise nods, biting down on that bottom lip as she drops her leg.

She grabs my hand again, but then on second thought she releases it, darting out into the road and grabbing the gun our assailant was too afraid to retrieve. She jogs up ahead to the trash can on the sidewalk and drops it in.

Finally she comes back to reclaim my hand, explaining, "Don't want another bad guy to find that."

I barely get the door locked.

For five long years, I have awaited this moment. Elise watches me with interest, backing up toward the bedroom. She might have it in her to be aggressive, but she doesn't want to—she wants me to do it.

So I do.

I chase her down the hall and she grins, throwing herself inside the bedroom, letting me back her up against the wall. As I move in, the distance between us vanishing, her playfulness gives way to something a little heavier. Her fingers go to the lapels of my jacket, tugging it off me. I shake it off the rest of the way, tossing it to the side, and she starts on the buttons of my white dress shirt. Once it's open, I'm hit by a minor case of nerves. I don't like people seeing my scars, and her skin is the exact opposite of mine—smooth, creamy perfection.

Before she can finish peeling it off, I shrug it back on. Elise pauses, frowning.

"You don't wanna...?"

I don't know if I'm more afraid to see disgust or compassion on her face. I don't want her feeling bad for me.

"I'm fine," I say, pausing. "I just—why don't we wait a minute to take that off?"

She understands why, but she doesn't drop it. Her gaze drops to my chest and her hands brush my sides as she touches me all over, her left hand brushing taut, normal skin, the skin of a man she should be touching, and the right touching the mottled flesh I don't want her to see, even in the dark.

"I already saw this the night you came home drunk, and if it bothered me, I wouldn't deserve to be here with you anyway."

"I don't want your... sympathy."

"I wasn't offering any," she says, almost lightly. "It's just, while I'm not at all opposed to the sight of you in an open dress shirt, this is my first time, and I'd like for us both to be naked."

Even though I assumed that's where this was heading, hearing her address the reality that we're approaching sex knocks some of the resistance out of me. Apparently counting on that, she takes advantage and peels the shirt off, her gaze never leaving mine.

There's a certain measure of calculation in Elise that I didn't expect, but I kind of like it. This girl knows how to get what she wants. I may not always understand why she wants it, but the more time I spend with her, the more facets I see. The more I realize… maybe she *doesn't* need as much fixing as I thought.

Erasing all thoughts of literally anything else, Elise bends her head and her soft lips brush my chest, just below my collar bone. She leaves a trail of fire behind her—every single time her lips brush my skin, I think I'm going to combust. Then she gets to my nipple and her tongue darts out, circling it, then suckling.

I need support. I need to move this to the bed.

Reaching down to grab her hand, I tug her back that way. I'm already so hard it hurts, and she's still fully dressed.

Well, as fully dressed as she can be with that evil thigh split.

This is her first time. I need to slow down.

My eyes are glued to her, watching as she reaches around and unties her dress. I expected to have to unzip this one, but apparently it wraps around, because a moment later, she drops it in a pool at her feet. I swallow, my eyes wandering over her body. She's not wearing a bra, only a lacy scrap of nude underwear, and as my gaze hits her bare body, her perfect, smooth, beautiful skin, feelings I've shoved down for literally years come rising to the surface. I don't just want to touch her, I want to *consume* her.

I move toward her, skimming my hands down her bare shoulders, watching her face for any sign she's not feeling it as my hands move in, catching the weight of her full, beautiful breasts in my palms.

She's too perfect. It's too corny to say, so I keep it in, but she is. Countless nights, more than I'd ever admit to, I've lain awake thinking about this moment, what she would look like, how she would respond to my touch, how she would taste. I lean in now, finally free to find out.

Her arms find their way around my neck again and she leans

in to meet me, a little smile on her lips as she presses her forehead against mine.

"Like what you see?" she teases.

I press my erection against her thigh. "What do you think?"

She nods. "So do I."

She turns around, dislodging my hands and climbs across the bed. I wince a little, seeing her ass up in the air like that, nothing but a lacy thong covering it.

Jesus, I wish I'd have known we were having sex tonight. I needed to prepare for this.

I climb on the bed with her. Prepared or not, we're doing this. I guess if it doesn't last too long this time, that's not the worst thing in the world; she's a virgin, so it's not going to be the greatest for her.

Looking at her like this, waiting for me in bed, mostly naked... well, I need to do something about that mostly part. I hook my fingers around the flimsy fabric still covering her and tug it down. She lifts her hips to help me and a moment later, I fling them off the bed behind us.

Now she gets a little shy, positioning her hands to cover herself. I shake my head, tugging them away.

"No hiding," I tell her.

"Then I think you should..." She flicks her finger toward the lower part of my body, still dressed in slacks. "It's only fair," she adds.

In a way it's more uncomfortable undressing in front of her than anyone before her. I've never cared what anyone else thought, not really. I care a lot about what she thinks.

I shove the rest of my clothes off, kicking them onto the floor, but I don't look at her. She doesn't wait; she sits back on her heels and reaches a hand out, her fingertips moving slowly down my hip, her long hair falling over her shoulder as she inspects the damage. Perhaps because I told her I didn't want any, her face betrays no sympathy as she explores me, but when she finishes, she says simply, "I hope he dies."

Smiling slightly, I reply, "Yeah, me too."

CHAPTER ELEVEN

ELISE SMILES at me, then without further mention of my scars, she leans in to give me a gentle kiss. Her hand comes up to touch my face and she sends shivers all down my spine at the brief contact. I love this, just kissing her, her touching me. I want her on top of me, so I grab her by the hips and position her so she's straddling me. Judging by her little smile, she approves of this position.

"Should we... Do you have a condom?" she asks.

"Oh, not yet," I tell her, leaning in to catch the rosy tip of her left breast in my mouth. Her breath catches, her hands fisting in my hair—or they would've, if I wouldn't have cut it all off. Never again.

I push my hand through the long locks of her hair, cupping my hand behind her neck and drawing her close. I release her breast, capturing her mouth again, arousal growing as she opens for me, not quite sure what to do, but waiting for me to take charge. I do, dominating, my tongue sweeping in to tangle with hers. My free hand drops, splaying across her breast, brushing my thumb across her nipple. She moans into my mouth and I nearly lose my shit. As much as I regret pulling back when she's getting into it, I want to make sure she experiences pleasure before we get to the sex, and if she moans like that again, I'm not going to be able to wait.

"We're gonna do this more next time," I promise.

"What are we gonna do now?" she asks eagerly, following my lead and crawling off my lap. It's funny, the way she sits there looking at me, like I'm her tutor again, about to give her an assignment instead of an orgasm.

I smile, shaking my head at her, then I catch her legs and flip her onto her back. "Right now I'm going to kiss you."

"Oh, good," she says, her arms heading for my neck again.

"Nope," I say, dropping to place a little kiss on her flat tummy, then a little lower. Then a little lower.

Her face flushes as she realizes where I meant.

"Oh, you don't have to do that," she tells me.

"Trust me," I say, tugging her knees apart. "I want to."

She covers her face with her hands, as if she can't watch, but then she peeks down at me between her fingers. "Really, honestly, you *don't* have to—" Her words cut off as I drop a kiss to the inside of her left thigh. She tries again, "We can just—" I drop a kiss just a little bit higher, and she sighs.

"Does that feel good?" I ask, moving my attention to her other thigh.

"Yes," she says, but reluctantly, like she hates to admit it.

"Good. Don't be embarrassed," I tell her, since she obviously is.

"That's easy for you to say," she mutters. "I don't have my head between your legs."

Unable to stifle a smirk, I tell her, "I promise if you did, embarrassment is not what I would be feeling."

"Why don't you just kiss my face?" she suggests. "I'm perfectly comfortable with that. Or my boobs—they miss you. They told me."

"Oh, did they?"

Nodding vehemently, she says, "They're very sad that you

went away. They're starting to take it personally. If you don't come up here *right now* and pay attention to them, they may never want anything to do with you ever again."

"Why don't you give me about two minutes to change your mind? I promise to make amends with those two as soon as I'm done," I assure her, indicating her breasts.

"It might be too late," she informs me.

"I *promise* you're going to like this," I tell her, shaking my head at her extravagant attempts to delay her own pleasure.

She covers her face again as I ignore all her attempts and move my face between her thighs. There's nothing like the sounds of her gasping as my tongue pushes inside to taste her, her breathless sigh, the helpless moan that escapes her as it hits her clit and sends a jolt of pleasure through her body.

"Adrian," she utters, half moan, half gasp. And I'm wrong, because *that's* the greatest sound that's ever hit my ears. Her gasping my name in pleasure. I want that replaying on a loop in my head for the rest of my life. With that goal in mind, I unleash years of pent up desire and devour her like I'm a starving man and her pussy is a king's feast.

"Oh, my god, Adrian."

I love how vocal she is. I love every gasp, every moan, every second that she grasps the sheets in ecstasy. I love when she can't take it anymore, and she cries out in pleasure, her body arching up off the bed, my mouth still attached to her.

"Adrian," she says, on a sigh, reaching down to touch me.

I finally let up, kissing my way back up her abdomen, then her chest, paying the attention I promised to each perfect inch of her breasts.

"That was… I'm a big fan," she tells me, her hands coming to rest on my back, just touching me as I continue to kiss her.

"I told you," I say, lightly biting down on a nipple.

Elise sighs, closing her eyes. "I'm kind of peeved we haven't been doing this all along now."

I grin, rolling over to grab a condom out of the night stand. "This next part might be a little less fun, since it's your first time. I want to let you be on top this time, that way you can control the pace."

"I'm game," she tells me, watching as I rip open the condom.

Once I get it on, I lie back on the bed and let her climb on top of me, straddling me. The view of her from this angle might kill me—Elise basked in moonlight, her long blond hair draped over her shoulders, her perky tits playing peek-a-boo. The mental image I'm already getting of her riding me is brutal, and the reality's bound to be better.

I assume I'm going to have to walk her through it, but Elise leans down, apparently wanting to kiss me again before she gets started. The sensation of her naked body against mine while we kiss might be manageable on most days, but it's been too long and I can't let her do it too much. I almost wish she *wasn't* a virgin, so we could do this again later tonight.

Nah, who'm I kidding? It's worth a brief first time. There will be plenty of times after, and I'd want to kill any man who dared touch her.

Actually I *have* killed every man who dared touch her—it's just there was only one.

Thinking about murder isn't even helping me last longer, so I finally have to pull back. I don't want to explain it to her, and I figure she likes a little dominance anyway, so as her lips linger close to mine, as she tries to kiss me again, I grab her hair and tug her back—not too hard, but with enough force to make my point.

"Ride me."

Excitement sparkles in her eyes at the command—sensuous, purely sexual excitement. It makes me even harder, and I did *not* think that was possible.

Elise smiles, scooting back and grasping my dick in her soft hand. Lifting up, she guides me between her legs, and as she slowly lowers herself onto my cock, I watch her face. She's going so slowly, and this is the most exquisite torture I've ever experienced in the duration of my life.

When she gets about halfway, she has to stop. Grimacing apologetically, she says, "Sorry."

"You're fine," I assure her, slowly exhaling as she lifts herself off me again.

I can see her starting to get a bit anxious as she tries again, but again, she must encounter pain so she stops.

To get her attention, I reach out and touch her shoulder. Her gaze jumps to me, like she's worried she's messing it up, and I offer a little smile.

"Relax," I tell her. "It's worse if you tense up. Also, unless you break my dick off, there's no way this isn't going to be awesome."

That makes her laugh, and I feel a little better to see the tension melt away.

With a bit more confidence, she shimmies her hips, grasping me again. "Okay, let's do this," she says.

"Ready when you are," I assure her.

"I promise to be better at this next time," she tells me. "I'm gonna read some books."

"Trust me, you're doing great."

Elise guides me to her entrance again, holding my gaze this time as she slowly lowers herself, this time taking all of my cock inside her body.

"Oh, fuck, Elise," I murmur, throwing my head back against the pillow.

"You like that?" she teases, her soft hand trailing down my chest as she slowly lifts herself again, then lowers herself again, less slowly that time.

"I like that a *lot*," I assure her.

"Good," she says, grinning as she does it again. And again. And again. It must have stopped hurting, because she picks up the pace, riding me like an old pro. She really starts getting into it, running her hands through her hair, caressing her breasts. When she's not playing with her own breasts, I get to. She's driving me wild. I finally grasp her hips, urging her to fuck me faster, and though I really *want* to hold on, to watch Elise ride me all night long, pleasure erupts like a volcano inside me and my fingers dig into her hips as I groan through my release.

"Fuck," I say on a sigh, lying there motionless in the bed.

Elise lifts herself off me and curls up by my side, leaning in to give me a kiss. "Good?" she asks, like she needs a performance review.

"Very good," I tell her. "I'm sorry about that."

Her eyebrows rise. "About what?"

"That should've lasted longer. It's been a while."

"Oh," she says, actually flushing. I would laugh, but I can't right now—too much energy. She can ride me like a fucking cowgirl, but I *mention* sex and suddenly she's an angel again.

"You don't have to be shy about sex, Elise," I inform her.

"It's not that," she says, but with the distinct tone of a vaguely annoyed woman. "I don't like to think of you with anyone else."

That sort of surprises me. I mean, *I* certainly wouldn't like to think of her anyone else either—her infatuation with Mateo, when I knew there was no sex, was at least part of why he and I had such a strained relationship. But that it bothers *her*... well, that makes me feel pretty damn good.

"Trust me, it's been a long time," I assure her, curling my arm around her and bringing her close to me. "I didn't feel right about it. I know that's kind of dumb, since you and I weren't together, but—"

"Not dumb," she interrupts, letting her hand drift across my chest. "If you've been with anyone else since you met me, I don't even want to know."

I raise my eyebrows, but don't volunteer anything further. "Okay."

"And if any other chick tries anything again, tell her what I did to the guy who tried to mug us, then tell her she's next," she adds, causing me to actually laugh.

"Trust me, I'm all yours," I assure her.

"Damn straight," she says.

"I had no idea you were so possessive," I tease, placing a little kiss on top of her head.

With an amused smile, she says, "Yet another reason I could've never made it with Mateo."

I groan, even though she's completely right. "You used the M-word in bed. Why would you do that?"

"Hey, you were just talking about having had actual sex with other women; I'm only referring to someone I had a crush on."

"You're so mean," I tell her.

"You want mean? How's this? You know what the sexiest thing about Mateo is?"

I grimace. "God no, and I don't want to."

Ignoring me, she goes on, her tone titillating, "It's his *big*, sexy... library. And I spent most of my time in there with you anyway."

She laughs as I squeeze her in retaliation for those two seconds of torture. "You and your damn *Beauty and the Beast* parallels."

She grins, nodding her head. "Yeah, you're right. I hadn't even thought of that though, now *you're* the one who brought it up." Snuggling against me, she says, "We need to add that movie to our collection. All this talk about it is making me wanna watch it."

"Never."

"Oh, come on," she says, jabbing me in the side.

"Every time that big hairy bastard's on the screen, I'm going to think of Mateo."

Elise props herself up on an elbow, rolling her eyes. "That's silly. Let's be honest, if we're casting *Beauty and the Beast* with the people in our lives, Mateo isn't Beast. He's Gaston."

I think about it for a second, but I haven't seen that movie in a lot of years. It comes back to me now that she says it, and it surprises a smile out of me. "Yeah, he kind of is, isn't he?"

"Definitely," she says.

"Doesn't that make me his chubby little sycophant friend?" I ask, amused.

"No way." She shakes her head, letting her hand drift across my chest. "You're my Beast."

Her touch is relaxing, and I feel better about this interpretation of one of her favorite cartoons. If we ever have kids, maybe I'll let them watch it, after all. "Didn't he end up killing Gaston in the end?"

"Nope," she says evenly, still running her hand tenderly across my chest. "Beast is the hero. Gaston died because he's Gaston, and he can't stop until he wins or he dies." Tilting her head back to look up at me, she adds, "Beast even tried to save Gaston, but he couldn't. At the end of the day, Gaston gets just enough rope to hang himself with, and so he does."

"That sounds like a Gaston thing to do," I remark, solemnly. I don't actually remember if that's true of the movie, but it sure is of Mateo.

She nods, resting her head on my chest again.

"You think I should keep working for him." It's not a question, but she answers me anyway.

"I think you will. You're the hero. You have to try to save him, no matter how many times he tries to hang himself."

I shake my head, amused that she can think of *me* as any kind of hero.

A little less amused because I know she's right.

Mateo could storm the gates of Hell, and my dumb ass would be right behind him, trying to keep the demons off his back.

CHAPTER TWELVE

SINCE I took the day off yesterday, there's a lot to get done today. A *lot*.

I start early, heading to Mateo's in time to grab breakfast. He's at the table, reading his paper and drinking his coffee. He flicks a glance in my direction as I enter, but since I'm not in his bedroom in the middle of the night, he must not be too worried about the possibility of me killing him.

I don't greet him right off. I head into the kitchen to grab some food and coffee. Then I take Meg's seat at the table, right next to him.

Finally he speaks. "Have a good night?"

I meet his gaze, unamused. His lips curve up ever so slightly, but he goes back to reading his paper, not even expecting a response.

I've considered it from all angles. I'm Mateo's chief enabler, so once the rage subsided, of course I dug a little deeper, tried to find his real intention. It crossed my mind, of course, that he's been on me about pushing my relationship with Elise forward anyway. He knows me—he probably thought it'd take me another five years to ever get this thing off the ground at the pace I'd set. Maybe he just wanted to give me a shove. Maybe it wasn't really a threat, maybe it was only meant to kick my ass in gear. Something nice, to make up for the scene in his study Sunday night.

Mateo's kiss, after he's done fucking you.

But the reason I know it wasn't is the card. His card, in his handwriting. He ordered the flowers and specifically left his card for the florist to put in the bouquet. They could've used any old generic flower card at the shop, but he wanted Elise to get *his* card. After the night we had, the night she gave me full credit for, he wants to remind me that it was all founded on his lie. That Elise could end up finding out who all that was from, to maybe consider that it could have been him in my place, and where would that leave me?

He left a breadcrumb for her to trace back, if she ever felt so inclined.

Of course I ripped up the card and threw it in the garbage before I came over here this morning, but his cards are distinctive. If she saw one on his desk when we're having drinks, or on a gift he gives to Meg or Mia, she would remember she'd received one, too.

I should've told her the truth, taken away his power, but I couldn't.

And he counted on that.

"If I work for you again—and this is *if*, I have not decided yet—I want a lot of money."

Mateo looks up, a flicker of victory flashing across his face before he can stop it. "Done."

"A *lot*. Like... even for you, a lot."

Mateo nods once more.

"And don't ever buy Elise panties again," I add, picking up my cup of coffee.

"What, you didn't like them?" he asks innocently.

"Or flowers. None of that bullshit. You know I don't have your pride issues, but don't disrespect me."

His amusement fades and he puts down his paper, giving me

his full attention. "You know how much I respect you, Adrian."

"I don't like being the target of your games," I inform him. "I realize no one does—except maybe Mia," I add, rolling my eyes.

He smirks at this.

"But *I* don't, and it's hard enough to be on your side watching what you do to everyone else. Don't start doing it to me, too. Our friendship has limits, and Elise is over the line. I'm not Vince; I won't put up with what he has and continue to serve you."

"I understand that. I don't want Elise, you know that. She's always been for you."

I nod, accepting that. Logically I knew it was just a threat—but I also know he doesn't make threats he won't follow through with. Doesn't mean he wants to, but if he makes a threat and you force him to deliver, he'll do it, no matter the cost. Beth had the poor judgment to test him on that one.

Taking a breath and pushing it out, he steeples his hands on the table. "If you sign on to work for me, I want a commitment this time," he finally says. "No freelancing. No contract."

He wants forever. He wants to know I'm not going anywhere. Not so he can abuse me however he wants, like Vince, but so he knows he'll never have to again.

I don't ever want us to be enemies, so I agree with that. I'm still hesitant as hell about it, but after last night with Elise, the stakes are higher. She's mine now, and that's scary and exhilarating and a hell of a lot more responsibility. If I'm going to be working for Mateo again and going after Castellanos, I'm going to need better security on her than the apartment can provide.

I have to wrestle my own tongue to get my next words out. "It might be easiest if we stayed here until everything's settled with Castellanos."

Mateo nods in agreement. "Yes, I would've already suggested that, but I didn't think you'd be of the same mind."

"Someone tried to mug us last night." His eyes briefly flash with alarm, but I shake my head. "Not one of his guys, just some unlucky asshole. But it could've been, and it's different now, with Elise. I've never been real worried about it before, but..."

He nods his understanding, glancing off at nothing, probably recalling Meg's shooting. "Yeah. I've considered bringing Vince and Mia back, just until it's all over. I don't think he's important enough for them to go after, but once we start striking at their people—"

I interrupt, shaking my head. "Don't do that."

"It'd be for their safety."

"It'd be for *her* safety," I correct, holding his gaze.

Mateo rolls his eyes. "So I don't want her to die—sue me," he says, mockingly raising his hands in surrender.

"She's Vince's girlfriend, no one's likely to go after her right now. It's more dangerous for Mia if you give anybody the impression she's important to you," I point out.

"Not if she's in my house," he states. "I won't let her leave."

My eyes widen, hearing those words, even if he didn't mean them that way. "Yeah, that's what I'm afraid of."

He frowns in consternation, but seems to be considering my words. "Maybe I'll split Colin between them. Meg can't leave the house right now anyway."

"Mateo..." I shake my head. "You said you were letting her go."

"I did."

"Then stop worrying about her. She's Vince's partner, not yours. If he's worried about her safety, he'll take care of it. You'll only stomp all over his pride if you swoop in *again* and start overshadowing him."

"I think Mia's safety is slightly more important than Vince's ego," Mateo says, rolling his eyes.

"What would Meg think about this?" I ask, more because I want to see if it makes him look guilty than anything.

It doesn't.

"Meg is equal parts ice and love—she loves Mia, so she'd be equally as concerned."

I shake my head, pushing the oatmeal around my bowl. I'm filling up with Mateo's problems again, and it's not leaving much room for an appetite. "Tell me the truth, Mateo. Are you planning on taking her from him again?"

"No," Mateo says, lifting his coffee cup and taking a sip. "Not planning on it."

I'm uncomfortable with that second part. "No bullshit. Is this a problem I'm going to have to deal with again? Forget about me judging you; for practicality's sake, I need to know."

"You'll judge me regardless," he says, smirking. "It's what you do."

"Mateo."

"I already said no," he states.

I still don't believe him. I want to, I really want to, but he doesn't sound sure enough, and he's not an uncertain person. With last night so fresh in my mind, the feeling, however brief, however watered down, of what Vince must have gone through, it's hard to let go.

"You'll make him an enemy if you do," I tell him.

"Because we're so close now," he says, rolling his eyes.

No, they're certainly not that. "If this is happening... You can't keep me in the dark about it, Mateo. I can't protect you if you do."

He meets my gaze, probing a little more than I'm comfortable with. "You think Vince has the balls to take me on?"

"I don't know," I say, tiredly passing a hand over my mouth. "But I know he loves that girl, and I know you have a tendency to drive people past the bounds of sanity with your bullshit."

Seeming to consider this, he nods, almost like he agrees. He probably does. He's not an idiot; he knows what he does to people. "Well, like I said. I have no plans to take Mia from Vince."

I don't know if he's wording his refusals that way on

purpose, to drive me batshit crazy, or if he's lying to himself, but he just made my predestined bad day a whole lot worse.

As the last strains of *Life on Mars?* drift off into the brief silence before the next track plays, I turn the radio off. The only thing worse than listening to music in the car is having to get out before a song finishes. Vince and Joey should be here any minute, and it wouldn't be the first time I've made someone wait for me to finish a song before I get out, but I'm not in the mood for it today.

My mood today is *black*. Even the sight of Elise's bare body curled up in bed beside me this morning failed to make me feel lighter. Breakfast with Mateo made it all worse, and now I just want to get this shit over with.

I decide to head inside. They know where I'll be. It's not unusual to gather here, to talk in the back room Mateo likes. He makes us sweep the damn building for bugs weekly. I don't know how he stays so concerned about that shit. I've been in this life so long, I hardly even think about the police anymore. They're nothing. Not for us. Mateo invests enough money in them—frankly, they should send him a Christmas card every year for how much he gives, not just to the individual cops on his payroll, but to the department itself. Mateo knows how to make the right friends, I'll give him that.

Me, I'm not much for making friends. I could never do what Mateo does. I don't like people enough, and he has more inherent charisma in his thumb than I have overall.

That's what makes us a good team though. He keeps things running smoothly with his god-given talents; I keep things under control with mine.

Speaking of things I need to keep under control, Vince and

Joey finally come strolling in.

I turn to look at my chair.

Not my chair, like the one I'm going to sit in, but *my chair*.

See, there's a lot to be said about mixing things up. It's good to have the edge of unpredictability, it's good when people don't know what to expect from you. But there's also something to be said for having something dependable, some unbending part of your routine—something that strikes fear into the hearts of hardened, grown fucking men.

For me, it's my chair.

Nothing fancy, nothing special, just a rusty, once-gray fold-up chair that sits along the cement wall in this old abandoned building. A light hangs over it for dramatic effect, blood stains on the legs, since I don't see the point in cleaning it every time, and I like the dread it stirs in the people who notice.

No one's worried about cleanliness when they take a seat in this chair. After all, no one ever leaves my chair alive.

Joey's eyebrows knit together as he glances around the empty room, expecting to see more than just me.

Vince shifts uneasily, his gaze moving to the chair like he knows.

They both should've known.

I could've moved a second chair over there in anticipation of their arrival, but I didn't, because I want them to experience every second of this. They both watch now as I drag a second chair across the cold, dirty floor and set it up to the left of my chair.

"Have a seat."

CHAPTER THIRTEEN

VINCE'S EYES bounce from the chair to me, while Joey's go wide. I watch him dart a glance over his shoulder, like he's prepared to run, but to do so would be to admit guilt. To do so would mean he dies like a bitch, face down on a cement floor.

I watch him decide against this. I see the desperate fear morph to a pitiful kind of hope, thinking of the years we've known each other—I literally knew Joey when he was a little kid, bringing me his Hot Wheels, trying to steal my attention away when I was busy playing with Mateo. I was there when Luciana told him with a sick sort of pleasure about how their father used to keep his mother locked in the basement, tied to a cot while she was pregnant with him. Luciana had a psychopathic streak in her that typically skips the Morelli women and only lands with the males, but she went through a lot shit in her life, too. Probably fucked her up.

Yeah, Joey and I go way back. I understand why he hopes that will matter. Logically he has to know it won't, since there's some shit you just don't do, and betraying Mateo Morelli tops that list.

Nearly getting his unborn child killed? That doesn't even require a list; it's just common fucking sense.

But these guys are young, and Joey seems to have even less of that than Vince.

Vince doesn't come across as hopeful. He doesn't look behind him at the exit, doesn't consider running. Without argument, he walks over and drops into my chair, folding his arms across his chest and glaring.

Joey's still by the door, and I'm starting to lose my patience. "Move your ass," I tell him.

Joey plays dumb. "Adrian, what is this about? What's going on?"

"You know what it's about. Sit your ass down so we can talk. Unless you're not interested in a trial, and you want to skip right to the sentencing?"

His breathing already labored, Joey hauls himself across the room and takes a seat next to Vince.

Now that they're both seated and I'm standing before them, I take out my gun. I didn't bother before now—could've grabbed it fast enough if one of them tried to run. I didn't expect they would. I *did* expect Vince to look more scared than he does though, given he's the younger of the two, the newest to all this shit, the most reluctant.

Joey's gaze darts to my gun, then to my face, then to Vince. "Either of you two want to start?" I ask.

Of course they don't. Even once caught, people want to believe you might not know. They want to believe a reprieve is coming.

Well, most people. Some people just spill their guts, hoping that will earn them mercy, but no one in the Morelli family expects that, so I'm not surprised when neither man speaks.

"Okay," I say, turning and beginning a slow, purposeful pace in front of their chairs. "I'll start. Which one of you stupid motherfuckers told Castellanos where to find Mateo the night Meg was shot?"

Joey's head falls back, a dread-filled, "Oh, fuck," falling

right out of him.

"No volunteers?" I ask after a few seconds. "All right, we'll come back to that. I don't recommend you stay silent on this one." I stop pacing, staring Joey straight in the eye, then Vince. "Who else in this family knew?"

"No one," Vince mutters.

"No one?" I question, my eyebrows shooting up. "Not Mia?"

A bitter little smile tugs at his mouth and he shakes his head. "Definitely not Mia."

"Why should I believe you?"

Vince meets my gaze. "Because you know as well as I do that she would've fucking told him."

I close my eyes for a split second, uttering a string of internal curses that would make a sailor blush. "Are you stupid, Vince, or just fucking suicidal?"

"Not everyone worships at the altar of Mateo, Adrian," he says, loathing permeating each syllable. "I would've been loyal to him all my life, but where's his loyalty to me?"

"He let you keep her!" I remind him, wanting to punch him in the face instead of shoot it.

"Oh, what a fucking nice guy," he shoots back. "He let me keep my own girlfriend? What a goddamn saint, I'm sorry, my fucking bad."

"And Meg? You feel good knowing you almost got her *killed?* What do you think Mateo does if Meg dies, Vince?"

For the first time, I see a shred of remorse. "I never wanted Meg to get hurt. I thought..." He trails off, shaking his head.

"No, finish your fucking thought."

"I thought Castellanos would send someone good enough to get the fucking job done; I didn't think Meg would get hurt."

I shake my head, honestly flabbergasted. Even having figured it out, even *knowing* what he did, I can't believe he's admitting it like this. I can't believe he's standing by it.

Joey isn't.

"We fucked up," Joey finally says, shaking his head. "We fucked up bad. We wanted to call it off, man, but it was too late."

"No, we didn't," Vince disagrees. "I didn't want to call it off."

Joey stares at Vince, his eyes wide. Finally he looks back at me, though he looks as baffled by Vince's suddenly steel spine as I am. "Well, *I* did."

"Vince, what the fuck is wrong with you?" I ask, because I'm genuinely confused. He knows what I'm capable of. He knows what happens to men who sit in this chair, and he damn sure knows what happens to people who do the shit he's admitting to right now.

Meeting my gaze unflinchingly, he asks, "You want me to lie?"

"No, I want you to not be an asshole," I state.

Pointing at his chest, he demands, "*I'm* the asshole? See, I don't think I am. I think *he* is. *He's* the fucking villain, Adrian, and everyone *loves* him. What the fuck is that?"

"She doesn't love him," I state, since it's clearly only Mia he cares about.

"Yes she fucking does," he says, shaking his head. "Don't do that. Don't try to lie. You know she does."

"*If* she does, it's not like she loves you. It's…" I trail off, shaking my head. "He's the boss, Vince. Would you rather she hated him? If you want her to be a part of the family, she has no *choice* but to kneel to him."

"Yeah, well, maybe I don't want her *kneeling* to him," he states, folding his arms again.

This kid's a ball of fucking rage. How have I missed this? I knew he was pissed before they moved out of the house, but I thought their own space helped ease the burden.

"I thought you were over this," I state.

He meets my gaze, just a hint of sadness breaking through his resentment. "You know, the last time we had a fight, a really bad one, I thought she wanted to leave me. But she wouldn't. Not because she can't—Mateo gave her back her freedom, and I'm not one of those assholes, I'd never force her to stay with me; but I wasn't afraid she'd leave. Not because she loves me too much. Mia loves me, but not as much as I love her. I fucking adore her. I love her heart, I love her mind, I love the fact that even knowing the life I have to live, she can still look at me and see something good, but none of that is why she won't leave me. She won't leave because she wants to stay in his family. Because if she fucking left me, Adrian, she wouldn't see him on Sundays."

Sympathy suddenly hits me in the gut, because I completely understand how he feels. For years I've had to watch Elise's infatuation with Mateo, watch her look at him the way I look at her. I feel bad for the kid, and I completely understand why this happened.

It just doesn't matter *why*, because it shouldn't have happened, regardless. Loyalty to Mateo is how you survive this family—a lesson Mia picked up quick, and Vince seems to have forgotten.

I hate the next question I have to ask. "Was this Joey's idea or yours?"

"Mine."

There's a challenge in his eyes. No remorse, again.

Joey's gaze is darting from me to Vince, but that relaxes him a little. I don't know why—the asshole was complicit, no matter whose idea it was.

I nod my head, easing back. I hate what I'm about to do. I hate it *so* fucking much.

"Goddamn you, Vince."

I hold his gaze, but I can feel Joey watching me as I pull back the muzzle. I raise my arm, aiming directly at Vince's forehead.

He swallows, but he doesn't look away from me. "Tell Mia I'm sorry."

I push out a breath, my finger flexing on the trigger, and then I swing my arm and fire at Joey's forehead before I can second guess myself.

Vince jumps as Joey's body slumps, toppling to the floor beside the chair, a disgusting new stain on this cold cement floor and my own soul.

"Jesus fucking Christ, Adrian!" Vince screams, launching out of his chair and over to Joey. The kid covers his mouth, staring at the motionless body of his closest friend.

He doubles over, breathing deeply and letting it out.

I think he might throw up, but he doesn't.

"Sit back down," I say, like I'm heartless.

His gaze jumps to mine, and for the first time in his life, he looks at me like he's seeing a monster. "You just... you just..."

"You did that," I tell him, calmly.

His chest is pumping, his face pale. I know how close he was to Joey, I know what he must be feeling right now. Right now he probably wishes *I* was dead, but he falls back the few steps and drops his ass back into my chair like I commanded.

I take a step closer. "If Mia wanted Mateo, she would have him. He gave her a choice, Vince. Did he borrow her? Yes. Did he steal her? No. Because she didn't *want* to be stolen. When she went to that poker game, he gave her a choice. She could have him and stay, or she could have you and leave. *She chose you.* He respected that. What else matters?"

A flicker of doubt crosses his pale features. "He gave her that choice?"

I nod once. I'm not sure this is true, but I know what he needs to hear. "He wanted her, but she wanted you more. And now he has Meg, and unless some treasonous fucking asshole gets her killed? He's not going to come sniffing around your girlfriend anymore, Vince. If Meg died, he would. If he ever finds out you were behind it, I feel fucking *sorry* for Mia, but that would be on *you*. This thirst for vengeance? You need to squash it. It's over, it's done. Think of it as your 'one night with the king' sacrifice and move the fuck on. Mia has. He did worse shit to her than he's done to you; hell, *you* did some pretty bad shit to her yourself and she still loves *you*—so learn from your girlfriend and *let it go*. Because you're going to get yourself killed if you don't."

"Going to?" he questions.

I straighten, sighing. "I've always considered you a friend, Vince. That's not why I'm considering letting you walk out of here, though. I've had to kill friends before. Like just now," I add, indicating Joey, dead and bleeding out all over the floor. "The thing is, I owe a debt to Mia. If not for Mia, unaccountably thinking of *me* during the darkest time of *her* life, Elise would still be in Mateo's house mooning after him to this day. I gave up five years of my life to buy her freedom, and she didn't even want to fucking leave—not until Mia interfered, anyway. Mia showed her that Mateo hurts people. She made her see it. She made her *clean it up*."

At that, Vince swallows, his eyes dropping. I can only imagine he's recalling how horribly he treated Mia when Mateo was abusing her—and I hope he is, because that was fucking shitty.

"And so, I'm going to pay that debt right now. I can't guarantee you're going to walk out of here alive, the rest is up to you, but I'm giving you something you don't deserve—a second chance."

Vince's gaze tries to drift back over to Joey, but he makes a visible effort to keep his eyes trained on me.

"You don't want Mateo to die, Vince. Castellanos doesn't take over if you destabilize the family like that, Dante does, and you don't want Dante running things. He won't fuck your girlfriend, but he's mean, and he's not afraid of a gang war. He wants more territory; he's not afraid to lose people. Mateo knows that more territory means more lives lost. Maybe yours. He doesn't want that. You may not like him, and I get it, but you could do a lot fucking worse."

Vince's eyes finally drop, first to my chest, then down near my feet. "We talked to his dad."

"Whose dad?"

His gaze returns to mine. "Mateo. Matt."

Even now, hearing the old man's name makes my gut burn with fury. "Why would you talk to him?"

"It was his idea to remove Mateo. He wants Dante in his place. Wasn't about Castellanos, we just... there was no one inside the family we could go to. We were just using the old man's hatred of Mateo for our own purposes. If Dante took over, he'd take down Castellanos anyway."

Now this is fucking news. It's not bad enough I have two traitors to deal with, now I might actually have a whole fucking rebellion on my hands?

Vince's gaze flickers over to Joey, then back to me. "He's not dying, you know. Mateo tells everyone he's sick, but he's not. Mateo just keeps him drugged up to keep him out of the way so he can stay in charge."

"Does Dante know about any of this?" I ask.

Vince shakes his head no. "I don't think so."

I rake a hand through my hair—or, I try, forgetting I cut it all off. "Fuck me," I mutter.

This mess just keeps getting bigger and bigger. It was one thing having to go up against the Castellanos family, needing to locate Antonio and talk Mateo out of massacring everyone with even a drop of his blood in their veins, but now I'm told my own army's infiltrated with this kind of bullshit, riddled with problems on the inside, too?

"You shouldn't have come back," Vince tells me, as if he can read my mind.

"No shit."

When I left, there was a part of me that wondered if I'd miss it. Right now I can't imagine why I would.

Sighing, I look back to Vince. "I want to let you walk out of here, Vince. But I need to *know*, really know, that you aren't going to pull anything like this again. And if Mateo finds out you were involved? We're both fucked. I am putting *my* neck on the line for you, kid, and if you make me regret it, I will bring so much fucking agony on you that you'll beg me for death. I need to know right now that you will *never* betray Mateo again."

I'm tense, waiting for his response. Given his attitude up to now, I'm not confident he'll swear to it, and I'm not looking forward to ending his life. Vince's gaze drifts over to where Joey fell—family. Mateo's own brother. The kid I used to play baseball with, even though I fucking hated the game.

Vince looks back at me, and finally he nods.

"Good," I say simply. "I really didn't want to pump bullets into the heads of two more people I fucking like."

Vince's brow furrows as he reminds me, "You already put a bullet in his head."

"I wasn't talking about Joey."

Fire jumps in his eyes again, this time directed at me instead of Mateo. "Mia had nothing to do with this."

"And it wasn't Joey's idea," I point out, holding his gaze. "You may not be afraid to die, Vince, but are you prepared to keep getting the people you love killed?"

He all but snarls at me, and I realize we probably won't be friends after this.

Finally he spits, "I won't betray him again."

I nod. "Good." Glancing over at Joey, I add, "Clean this up."

"Are you fucking kidding me?" he asks, his eyes widening.

"Nope," I say, heading for the door.

CHAPTER FOURTEEN

ELISE COOKS dinner, but I can't enjoy it.

She keeps stealing glances at me, in the floor, sitting at a damn box instead of a table, but she doesn't ask questions. I appreciate that, because there's nothing I could tell her.

When she's clearing away our dinner plates, I finally say, "I need you to pack up some things tonight, whatever you need for at least the next couple weeks."

Frowning, she drops to the floor beside me, curling her legs up to her side. "Why? Are we going somewhere?"

I nod, meeting her gaze. "We're going to stay at the mansion for a little while. There's some stuff going on that could get dangerous, and I'm going to piss a lot of people off. I need to know you're safe so I can concentrate on my own tasks."

She smiles just a little, but I can tell she's making an effort to tone it down so she doesn't aggravate me. "Okay. When do we leave?"

"I'm gonna take you over in the morning when I go for work. We'll stay in my old room while we're there. Same as before, if you need to go somewhere, you need to take an escort. Not Vince."

"Why not Vince?"

"Just… not Vince."

"Okay," she says, nodding.

"I don't think he will, but if Vince offers to take you anywhere, don't go. And don't say anything to Mateo about these instructions."

She frowns, but nods again, accepting my orders. Maybe it is good she's a little trained.

Jesus Christ, listen to me.

Shaking my head in self-disgust, I lean back until I'm flat on the floor, staring at the ceiling. Elise comes over and curls up next to me, her arm settling around my waist.

"Are you sure you're okay?" she asks.

"Just had a bad day."

"Is there anything I can do?"

"Do you have a time machine?"

"I did once; it broke."

"Damn."

Elise sighs, just a little sigh, and her finger slips through a gap in my shirt. I don't respond, but then she undoes a button, making a bigger space. Then another. And another.

"What are you doing?" I ask mildly.

"I wanna make you feel better," she tells me.

I feel dirty from the day. I shouldn't even be letting her touch me, but my body overrules my brain's judgment on this one. Especially when she unbuttons my pants and slides her hand inside, grabbing hold of my cock.

I let myself get lost in her ministrations as she strokes me, in the way her soft hand moves up and down, up and down. She pushes her hair back over her shoulder and leans down, dropping kisses down my chest, down my abdomen. She gives me a playful little look, then she releases me so she can tug my pants down.

My instinct is to tell her she doesn't have to, but the prospect of Elise's lips around my cock is too tempting to pass up.

Elise sits on her knees beside my hip, biting down on her bottom lip as she grasps my cock again, tugging it a few more times before taking the plunge. She takes just the tip in her mouth at first, then slowly works her way down my length.

"Oh, fuck," I mutter, closing my eyes. I open them again fast, because I don't want to miss this, but Jesus, that feels incredible. Her tongue slides around the tip as she pulls back up, not quite coming off, just creating suction. I clench my hands at my sides, digging into the carpet like I want to grab onto her hair. Finding a rhythm, she moves her mouth over my cock again and again, involving her teeth a few times more than I'd like, but this is likely her first one, and I'm not complaining. She could probably bite my cock off, and I'd just be grateful its last memory was that of her warm, wet lips wrapped around it.

I don't know if she's prepared for me to come, but right as I'm about to warn her, she speeds up and pleasure explodes, the evidence pouring out of me and right into her mouth.

She takes it like a champ, swallowing and then running her lips over me one more time to make sure everything's tidy.

I laugh a little, because she's still cleaning, even when she's giving me head.

Elise comes back up to lie down beside me once she's done. "What?" she asks, because of the laugh.

I shake my head, smiling faintly. "You're just adorable."

"Thank you," she says, pulling my arm around her so she can snuggle into my side.

"Thank *you*," I say, leaning over and dropping a kiss on top of her head.

"You didn't give me an assignment this morning," she tells me.

"I forgot. You still want me to?"

Nodding, she says, "I like it. Though if we're going to be

staying at Mateo's again, I can probably help out around the house while I'm there, so I'll have more to do. I mean, Meg was supposed to replace me and she went and got promoted to wife, so Maria probably has a lot to do."

"Damned inconvenient," I agree, my mind tempted to wander back into Mateo's murky bullshit. I pull back, refusing to go there. This is my time off, I will fill it with Elise, not him.

"Can I ask you something?" she asks.

"Of course."

"Who did you love before me?"

I turn my head to look over at her, and she blushes a little.

"I mean, not that you love me," she amends. "But you know what I mean."

"There really wasn't anyone. I know you wouldn't think so, given my age, but before I got trapped in Mateo's world, I really wasn't doing too much. I didn't expect to live too long given the things I did do, and any... relationships I had were short-lived and usually meaningless."

"That sounds sad," she says. "I don't think I'd ever have a relationship like that."

"No, I don't imagine you would," I agree.

"Are you ever afraid you might get killed doing what you do?"

I glance over at her again. This isn't a cheerful line of questioning. "Sure. It never really used to scare me, but I'm a lot less keen on the idea now."

"You weren't afraid to die?" she asks, propping herself up, resting her chin on my chest.

I shake my head. "Not really."

"I'd be afraid," she says, quietly. "Like, really afraid. Last night was pretty exhilarating, but I couldn't do what you do."

I smile slightly, trying to imagine Elise, even with her little kickass mugger moves, doing what I do. "No, I don't think it'd be a good fit."

"I'm gonna stick to making muffins," she tells me.

"That's probably for the best."

"I like that you're capable of it, but I don't like that you're ever in danger."

"You like that I'm capable of...?"

"Taking care of things," she says evasively.

"Violence?"

She shrugs. "You do what you have to do."

I guess living in a mob house throughout your formative years, even if sheltered from the darkness of it, can desensitize even a normal person to that sort of thing.

"It makes me feel safe," she adds. "When I first met you, when you first defended me like that, it just... right off, you seemed like someone trustworthy. Someone good. When you first came on the scene, I thought you were a Morelli I just hadn't met yet."

I scoff a little at the idea. "Really?"

She nods, smiling slightly. "It's not such a stretch."

"You can usually tell a Morelli by the look of them, if not by the behavior."

"I didn't know. It was a little harder to tell with you," she says, her eyes drifting to the scarred left side of my face.

"Yeah," I say, absently touching it. "The Morelli men are uniformly pretty."

"You're more intimidating and ruggedly handsome, but I think this has a lot to do with it," she says, reaching out and brushing my cheek herself. "It's hard to look at you without it, but if you just look at the one side, you can tell you have a certain prettiness to you, too. The scarring just gives you that 'don't mess with me' look, where Mateo is more... 'come mess with me. I'll destroy your life, but don't mind that.' And Vince, he's young, but he's like the sulky James Dean type. Alec—I really don't understand where his nose came from, he'd be pretty otherwise. And Joey, he looks the most like you. I think because he has the lighter hair, more golden chestnut than black."

The mention of Joey makes me sad. "His mom was blonde," I explain, though she didn't ask. "Normally the Morelli genes are dominant, but... it happens. Luciana had lighter hair, too."

"What happened to her?"

"She tried to kill Mateo."

"Why?"

I shrug. "She was crazy. Like, really crazy. She was technically Matt's eldest child, and even though there's no way a woman could head this family, she didn't want to accept her role. Felt she'd been born to more. It was kind of bizarre, considering he killed her whole family, but when she came back, she sucked up to Matt. Just worshipped him for some reason, like she was somehow at fault for what her mother had done and she wanted to make up for it." I roll my eyes, because I personally think Belle was completely justified, but the Morelli men don't accept infidelity. They'll dole it out, but they sure won't take it.

"And yet she tried to kill his son?"

"Matt and Mateo have had a bumpy relationship," I tell her, thinking of what Vince told me today. About Matt not really being sick, just drugged up. I can certainly see Mateo doing that, but I would think he'd let me in on the secret.

"Who killed her?" she asks.

"Mateo."

Her eyebrows rise, like she's surprised. "So he actually does get his hands dirty."

"Sometimes. He doesn't have to, but he feeds the darkness from time to time."

"Do you ever do that? Kill if you don't have to?"

I shake my head, meeting her gaze. "No. I don't have the desire in me; I just do it out of necessity."

She nods, like she was prepared for a worse answer, but pleased with that one. "Good. What do you think you would've done if you didn't have to do this?"

"I don't like to consider it," I tell her, propping my hands behind my head, so I can see her better. "I think another life would've suited me better, and it's too late to change gears now."

"Like what kind? How would I have met you if we didn't both get sucked into Mateo's world?"

"Maybe you would've been my student," I say, smirking at her.

She grins in approval. "Yeah? High school or college?"

"Oof, college," I say, grimacing. "I didn't *like* that you were 16 when I met you, for the record. Typically I don't go for younger girls; I like to stay in my own age bracket."

"How very un-Morelli of you," she jokes.

Well, sort of. It's not really a joke, I guess, since it's consistently true.

"I wonder if I would've always liked older guys," she says, still resting her chin on my chest, but gazing at the wall beyond me.

So do I, and that makes me sad, too. She may daydream up scenarios in which we would've met outside of our circumstances, but we never would've. She would've been a normal girl with a normal life and she would've cycled through relationships with normal guys her own age until she found one smart enough to keep her.

I know *I* didn't cheat her out of that, but she got cheated nonetheless, and now I'm benefitting from it.

"Are you happy with me?" I ask her. I know it hasn't been long, and she'd probably say yes regardless, but I can't really shoulder any more guilt today.

"Of course I am," she says.

"I don't feel like that warrants an 'of course,'" I tell her. "You don't have to say what you think I want to hear, you know. I only want the truth. I won't be disappointed in it."

She reconsiders, and despite what I just said, my heart stops as her generally pleasant smile melts, giving way to actual deliberation. Finally she says, "I mean, it's had its ups and downs, and it hasn't been that long, but I like where we are now. I feel less like you're trying to change me now, like you've accepted me more, and that helps. You had me kind of twisted up the first week. When Mateo told me I was coming here, I had certain expectations about what that meant, and then you didn't act on any of them. And I wasn't even sure I wanted you to at first, which is why I felt so... unsure about this whole thing, but then you gave me time to adjust. But then it was a little too much time, and I started to feel like Mateo misread what you wanted me for, and then I couldn't figure out *what* you wanted me for, and no, I guess I wasn't very happy about all that. But I'm the sort of person who always finds the bright side of any situation. That didn't start when I went with Mateo; I was always like that, even as a kid. And it just so happens, there are a lot of bright sides to this for me. I already told you I had a crush on you back when you tutored me, so the groundwork was there, I only stopped because we stopped spending time together and you weren't interested. Maybe Mateo wasn't either, but he never expressly said that, and he gave me just enough encouragement to..."

"Keep you on his hook," I say with a nod of understanding.

She nods, pursing her lips. "Yeah, I guess. Or maybe he didn't even mean to, I don't know."

"No, he did. You were his back-pocket threat to keep me in line."

"You wouldn't have let him hurt me," she says, frowning.

"Nope. But he figures you would've let him... *not* hurt you."

She flushes at that and doesn't say whether or not she would've. I'm half relieved and half consumed with dread, but I can't focus on any additional dread tonight, so I let it go.

"I kinda want to go to bed," I tell her.

"It's 7:30," she points out.

"It's been a *really* long day."

"Want me to read some Brontë?"

"I would."

"And then we could have sex," she offers.

"This pot keeps getting sweeter," I state, eyebrows rising in surprise.

Elise grins and pushes up off the floor. "Let me clean up the kitchen first and I'll be right in."

I stand, too, figuring this will be a good time to take a shower. Before I do, I approach her at the counter, lightly wrapping my arms around her and giving her a hug from behind. "Thank you."

"For what?" she asks, sounding surprised as she twists to look back at me.

I place a soft kiss on her lips. "For being happy with me."

Her whole face seems to soften with tenderness and she turns in my arms, wrapping her arms around my neck and leaning in to press her forehead against mine. "Thank you for letting me."

She's so close I can't resist giving her one more kiss, then I break away, otherwise I'm never getting to the shower. She gives me a playful little wink as she turns around to clean up the counter, and I sigh, thankful that I have her, 'cause there's no way in hell I ever did anything to deserve her.

CHAPTER FIFTEEN

AFTER I drop Elise off at the mansion, I head to the bakery to see Mia.

Well, not really to see Mia, but since she's there, that's what ends up happening.

"Did you come to check up on me?" she asks as she refills the chocolate cannoli tray.

"Nope, I'm a customer," I tell her.

"You want a cannolo? Did you know that's the singular form of cannoli? I didn't, and this old Italian lady yelled at me. A lot. It wasn't pretty."

I smirk. "I did know that."

"Well... you could've told me," she states. "She invited me over for spaghetti sometime when she realized she overreacted, but it was a pretty uncomfortable few minutes."

The shaggy haired baker heads up front, a dopey smile on his face until he sees me. His smile droops, then falls off completely, and he sets another tray down for Mia with less enthusiasm.

Then before she can even thank him, he disappears to the

back.

Mia glances after him, then shrugs to herself. "How about an apple turnover?"

"Actually I need a strawberry cassata cake," I tell her.

She lights up, all pleased with herself. "I hooked you with the piece I made you take home, huh?"

I nod, even though the cake isn't for me. "It's weird seeing you here," I remark.

She finishes the cannoli tray and places it on an empty counter behind her, then she grabs a cake box for me. "Yeah, I know. I'm so used to Francesca here. You guys still haven't heard anything about her?"

I shake my head, glancing through the doorway to the back. "He ever say anything about it?"

"Mark?" she asks, raising her eyebrows. "No."

"He's been an awful good sport about coming back both times the place closed without warning. Does he make enough money to have a nest egg when he goes a couple weeks without a paycheck?"

Mia shrugs, like she's never thought of it and can't imagine why I would.

I'm gonna have to look into him. Just to be safe.

"How's Elise like the new place?" she asks me.

"We're actually going to be staying back at the mansion for a little while," I tell her.

"Oh, cool," she says, smiling. "Then I'm sure I'll see you around a bit more."

"Are you at the mansion more than Sundays now?"

"I like to pop over and check on Meg. She's bored and all cooped up in the house. Plus she likes when I bring her treats."

"And Mateo?"

Levelly, almost like she was expecting it, she says, "Doesn't like treats."

I wonder if he talked to her about my suspicions. I realize

that's an incredibly suspicious thought to have, but I don't put it past him at this point. "In Francesca's stead, I'd usually expect Mateo's woman to run the bakery."

She smiles thinly, dropping my cake in the box and closing the lid. "Yeah, well, I'm filling in until she can."

"Right, right. Took a bullet for him and all."

Her eyes narrow and she slides the cake box across the counter, leaning in. "Something you wanna say, Adrian?"

"Nope," I say, grabbing the box. "What do I owe you?"

"On the house," she states, straightening.

I give her a mock salute, putting the cake under my arm, and head out the door.

A cute redhead is sitting on the couch, watching television when I come through the door. She appears startled, which I guess makes sense, seeing as no one ever comes to visit.

I try to remember her name. I wanna say it was something Ukrainian? Damned if I can recall, it's been years since I've actually looked at this person.

"You can take the rest of the day off," I tell her, as she pushes off the couch and warily approaches me.

"He needs more medication with his dinner," she explains, casting a glance at the old man on the daybed, his wily brown eyes dim with age. He watches me, a vague smirk on his face.

"I'll give it to him," I tell her.

Nodding uncertainly, she approaches the counter of the little kitchenette in his suite to grab a bottle of pills. "I'm not really sure what I should do," she tells me.

I look her over once more. She flushes, thinking I'm being an asshole, but I'm just trying to determine whether or not I should send her to Mateo. He's never gone for a redhead before, but I don't want to invite more trouble into my life. That said, he does need a maid, and we probably can't release this girl back into the wild right now.

"Go downstairs. I'll be down in a little bit."

She looks decidedly uncomfortable with these instructions, but she's trained well enough to listen anyway.

Once she's gone, I put the cake box down on the counter.

Matt Morelli glances at the cake, then meets my gaze. "Here to celebrate my birthday?"

"I think I missed it by a couple months," I tell him. "Better late than never."

The old man sighs, maneuvering himself into a sitting position. "Should've called first. Ilya and I had shows to watch for a couple more hours."

Ilya, that's her name.

"I'm sure she'll be heartbroken in the absence of your company," I state, turning to open the cake box.

"They always are," he agrees.

I roll my eyes at that one. There's never existed a woman whose heart was broken by losing this man, only by the heinous shit he did to them.

"You got any knives?" I ask, opening and closing drawers in search of one.

"No. Strangely enough, Mateo won't let me have any," he says, as if amused.

"Well, he knows you." I grab a spatula instead. It won't be as neat, but hell, who do I need to impress?

"I can't believe it's taken this long for you to walk through my door, Adrian. To what do I owe this pleasure?"

"I think you know," I tell him, grabbing a plate and plopping an enormous slice of cake down on it.

"Why don't you humor an old man," he says, playing at docility.

I shake my head, grabbing a fork and walking over to him. I hold out the plate and he just stares at it. His eyes move over the huge slice of cake, but then they wander to the hand holding it. My left hand. The scars end before they reach my fingers, but the marbled skin nearly reaches my knuckles.

"Your favorite," he remarks.

It takes me a second to realize he means the cake. I put a mocking hand to my heart. "You remembered."

His lips curve up again, another little smirk. I don't think he remembers how to smile. There's too much evil in him for such a harmless expression.

"Cake, huh? That's how you're gonna do it?"

"Do you still possess the strength to feed yourself, old man, or should I do it for you?"

His feigned amusement fades at that, his dark eyes flashing at the insult. Matt's never been able to handle a real insult. He snaps the plate up and settles it on his lap, but doesn't move to take a bite.

"I'm disappointed," he says, looking up at me. "I expected more from you."

"You thrive on violence. You don't deserve anything you'd enjoy. I know how much you hate sweets," I tell him. Then, because it brings *me* joy, I tell him, "It came special from Belle's bakery. I know how many good memories you have there. Why, it was probably prepared on the same counter where she let another man fuck her."

Even after all these years, the bitter old man snarls at me for the visual.

Maybe he's why Mateo doesn't hold a grudge. He's seen what holding grudges does to a man, how it breaks you down, controls you.

I nod at the plate. "Get going on that. I don't have all day." I go back to the dining area, opening the fridge and drawing out two beers. I pop the caps off on the countertop and head back to the living room, holding one out to Matt. "Something to wash it down with."

I drop onto the couch where Ilya had been seated, reclining and propping my feet up on the coffee table. Matt looks at the plate again, but still doesn't touch it. I'm probably gonna have to feed the old bastard. I thought maybe he'd accept his end with some kind of dignity, understanding it's been a long time coming, but I guess I shouldn't have expected so much.

"Your son's dead," I tell him. I take no joy in Joey's death, but I figure he should probably know.

"Which one?" He doesn't sound like he cares. He doesn't even seem excessively curious; he just knows he's expected to ask.

"Joey. Suppose he can thank you for that."

Matt shakes his head, taking a sip of the beer. "Joey was always weak. Like his mother."

Joey's mother had been the youngest of Matt's toys—to my knowledge, anyway. Only 17 when he locked her up in the basement, torturing and impregnating the poor girl. Most women lasted a few years with him, but Stacie barely made it through her pregnancy. She wanted nothing to do with Joey at birth, and she was dead before he turned four months old.

"Does Mateo know?" Matt asks.

"Nope," I say, before taking a swig of my beer. "Mateo doesn't know shit, and he's never going to. I don't think he'd give a damn at this point—he certainly doesn't give a damn about *you*—but just on the off chance, I wouldn't let you hurt him one more time."

Matt shakes his head, his lips curving up again. He always has this one smile, the kind that's meant to fuck with you, to make you think he knows more than you do. "Your mother ruined you," he states.

I chuckle, shaking my head. Of course now he wants to talk about my mom.

"She was so kind. Too kind. Protective. Such a good friend.

Just like you."

"We must have different definitions of ruination," I state. "Most people aspire to teach their kids qualities like kindness and loyalty. I wouldn't expect you to know that."

"Kindness and loyalty are for followers, not leaders. You could've been a leader. Feared. Respected."

I don't bother telling him I'm already both of those things. I have nothing to prove to this man.

"You have the look of a man who's walked through hell, thrown off every demon that dared come at him, and emerged stronger for it. People revere that."

"Okay," I say, already growing tired of whatever little game he's playing. "We both know you don't like me, so whatever you're up to, you can stop."

"I don't dislike you, Adrian. I'm just disappointed you never met your full potential."

"I'm sure you can imagine how deeply that wounds me," I tell him flatly.

"You should have embraced your darkness," he tells me, the excitement brewing in his eyes telling me we're approaching his point. His grand finale. I'll let him get it out, then I'm shoving that cake down his throat. "You've worked so hard over the years for Mateo, haven't you? Cleaning up his messes. Building his empire. Ensuring that he keeps everything I left him. Giving him more power, more wealth—building him up and up and up, and what's he done for you?"

Turning me on Mateo? Really? *That's* his play?

I have to smile. "You've lost your touch, old man."

"Do you remember what your father did for a living, Adrian? Before I killed him?"

I don't feel pain, but I still feel anger. My smile melts right off, twisting into something less pleasant. Something more like his.

"He was a banker," he tells me, nodding. "A *banker*."

"I'll make a note in my scrapbook," I reply.

"Do you *feel* like a banker's son, Adrian?"

Suddenly uncomfortable, I take another sip of my beer.

"Your mother and Belle, they became good friends, you remember? And your mother, your protective, sweet mother... sometimes she'd try to intervene when my temper got the best of me. To protect Belle. To... divert my attention."

My heart beats a little faster, but I keep my face expressionless. He's not going where I think he's going with this. I'll jam that fork down his fucking throat.

"You're not a banker's son, Adrian." The words slide off his tongue, sick pleasure dancing in his eyes. "You're mine."

He's lying. I know he's lying. He has to be lying, because there isn't a lot that bothers me, but *that*? That would gut me.

There's nothing in the whole world I want less than to be a Morelli.

But he knows that, I remind myself. He knows that. I'm not his secret son. Matt's just a liar, and maybe he's trying one last ditch effort to save his own skin, or maybe he just wants to make one last splash before he dies. His motive doesn't matter. What's important is that I don't let him get to me—because he's just a rotten liar. That's all.

His brown eyes practically glow as he awaits my response. So I grin, cocking my head at him. "That's the best you got, huh? You think we're in *Star Wars* now?" I snort, shaking my head and doing my best Darth Vader impression, "'Luke, I am your father.'"

He *hates* being made fun of. The excitement in his eyes only moments ago has turned to pure loathing, and at least that I can deal with.

I smile, shaking my head. "I'm sorry, Matt. I'm sorry. I should've just let you have that one. Let's have a do-over." I wipe my face clear, launching forward, dramatically ducking my head and staring at the coffee table like my whole life's just been undone. "You're... you're my real father? Everything I've known is a lie? I... I'm two months older than Mateo—everything that's his should be mine? *I'm* the eldest son of Matt Morelli?" I clasp my heart, falling back against the couch.

Matt's eyes narrow and he shakes his head in disgust.

"Is that better?" I ask him, regular now, kicking my feet back up and tipping back my beer.

"You didn't get your brother's gift for showmanship," he says silkily.

That's like a knife to the gut, hearing him refer to Mateo as my brother.

"Eat your goddamn cake," I snap.

"Believe me or don't," he says, finally using his fork to chop off a little piece of cake. "Makes no difference to me."

"If it made no difference, there was no reason to say it," I point out.

He raises the cake to his mouth, but speaks before taking a bite. "Sure there was. This is the last time we'll see each other. My last chance to tell the truth. Don't say you've never wondered."

"Of course I haven't," I say, watching him finally take the first bite.

It won't be long now. Matt's deathly allergic to strawberries. At Mateo's 10th birthday party, he picked a strawberry cassata cake. Matt couldn't eat it, but when someone got him a slice of cheesecake (the only cake he does like), they used the same knife.

Before he finished half of it, his throat closed up and he had to be rushed to the hospital.

That's when strawberry cassata cake became my favorite. When it nearly killed this evil bastard.

Now here it is, 23 years later, to finish the job.

"Few more bites, and I'll get out of your hair," I tell him.

"You're not staying?" he asks, looking unimpressed. "Never took you for a coward."

"Nah, it's just... if there's anyone in the world who deserves to die alone, it's you."

"A man who kills for a living shouldn't be so judgmental,"

he informs me, taking a sip of the beer. When he swallows, it looks like he struggles a bit.

I push off the couch, walking over to him. I grab his fork, getting a big bite full of strawberry. As I shove the bite into his mouth, I tell him mockingly, "Now I can add patricide to the list of my sins, huh?"

He chokes it down, and I grab his beer, taking it over to the sink to dump it out. I'm done here.

"What do you think he'll do?" Matt asks. "What do you think he'll do when he finds out, Adrian? Mateo has no loyalty, no sense of *family*. Mateo is out for himself, and no one else."

I shake my head. It shouldn't even surprise me that this old bastard is using his last remaining moments on Earth to try to get to me to kill his son, but somehow it does.

"Go to hell, old man."

He gives me that conniving smirk again. "I'll be running the place by the time you get there."

CHAPTER SIXTEEN

IT'S A little harder to sit at the dinner table, opposite Mateo at the head of the table, and not think about Matt's words.

He's full of shit, and there's no way he could be telling the truth… But what if he is?

Not that it would matter, in the great scheme of things. It wouldn't change anything. That's what I tell myself. But my mind keeps circling back to it. It sure would be a hell of a thing, wouldn't it? It would also go a long way in explaining the one thing I never could figure out.

Why did Matt take me in after he killed my parents? I knew Mateo had begged him to, in the way that kids do, but why say yes? It had always plagued me, if I really gave it enough thought.

Not like I'd even want what Mateo has. That's not the part that bothers me.

It's more the prospect of what would change if Mateo knew. Depending on how long Matt's had this up his sleeve, it's possible Mateo *will* find out. It'd be just like Matt to leave behind a bombshell like that, a final farewell, one last 'fuck you' to all of us.

Should I tell him and get ahead of it? There aren't usually secrets between us, on account of my position in his life, but if Matt *does* leave something for Mateo with this information, will he tell me? I don't like to think Mateo would turn on me, but… well, I'm a realist.

Not like he has a reason to. I couldn't care less about their bloodline bullshit. I don't *want* anything to change.

It's mulling that over that I make a decision: I'm going to give Mateo the commitment he wants. I'm going to work for him. If I start to notice him behaving strangely toward me, then maybe we can talk about Matt's last words, but until or unless that happens, I have to shrug this off as his last attempt at a mind game. He's pissed off at Mateo for rejecting him, for locking him up, taking away his freedom, and taking his place at the head of the family. He absolutely deserved it, but now he's had years to nurse that grudge, to turn on his own son.

The little redhead—Ilya, her name's Ilya—comes out of the kitchen and puts down the bread baskets. Mia watches her, confused. Meg frowns, glancing at Mateo, but he doesn't even look up.

"Um… who's that?" Meg finally asks.

"Who?" Mateo asks, straightening a crooked fork at his place setting.

"The beautiful redhead with the piercing blue eyes?" she asks, smiling cheerfully.

Mateo smirks at her description, still not looking up. "New maid."

"Oh, good," she says, nodding and reaching for her empty wine glass. Then she sighs, and grabs the water instead.

He reaches across the table for her hand, giving it a reassuring thumb-rub.

"No, it's good," Meg says, picking up steam. "We need to hook her up with Joey."

I glance at Vince—the darkening of his features comes as no surprise, but the way Mia goes pale does. She stares at the table, then steals a glance at Mateo. He's still paying attention to Meg, so he doesn't see it.

Vince looks over at Mia and she must notice out of her peripherals because she returns his look… but there's ice in her eyes when they meet his.

Vince looks away.

So does Mia.

I glance around the table, but no one else seems to have noticed.

Mateo releases Meg's hand and glances at Joey's empty seat at the table. He looks across at me, but thankfully the new maid comes back out and saves anyone from having to respond.

Meg's friendlier to the new maid this time, smiling and thanking her with that look she used to give Mia, like she has a new friend in her sights. I wonder if Meg actually likes any of these girls, or she's just cunning enough to know she needs to keep the pretty ones close so they won't want to tempt Mateo.

Although, considering Mia is sitting at the dinner table on a week night when they only have to come on Sundays, I'm not sure how foolproof that plan is. I felt confident he'd let Mia go when he let her go live with Vince, when she didn't come around as much, but something's shifted. Meg changed something between Mia and Mateo, something she didn't mean to change, and I don't know how that's going to ultimately pan out.

I resist the urge to get lost in that whole mess for the moment, bringing my attention back to the table, to Elise seated beside me.

"How was your day?" I ask her.

She smiles, but casts the maid a less fond look than Meg. "It was good. I helped Maria out a little."

"You shouldn't have to now; Maria has help again," I tell her.

She rolls her eyes, like I'm a real dolt. "Yeah, I know. Thanks," she says, dryly.

I shake my head, but can't help smiling a little. "Only you would be annoyed that you don't get to be a maid anymore."

"She's too nervous," Elise states, grabbing a piece of bread. "She's not gonna last."

"She's had a long day," I tell her. "I'm not even sure she will stay, but... I needed to put her somewhere until we figure it out."

Dinner is long tonight—I'm not sure why. Everyone at the table seems a little off, all for our own individual reasons. Vince wants to leave as soon as it's over, but Mateo invites us to the study for the drinks we didn't have beforehand.

I'm just about to tell Elise she can go with the girls, but Mateo adds, "The girls can come, too. I have something to share with everyone, anyway."

Mia and Meg exchange questioning glances and we all head for Mateo's study.

Usually Mia sits on Vince's lap when she's in the study, but tonight she sticks close to Meg. Initially Meg heads toward Mateo, but when she sees Mia's her shadow, she goes over and sits on the sofa by the wall. Mia sits beside her, and Vince sits in an arm chair facing her, sulking.

He couldn't have possibly told her, right? That would be insane. Even he pointed out that she didn't know because she would've told Mateo, so what purpose could it possibly serve to clue her in after I've already bailed his ass out?

The possibility of that makes me decidedly uncomfortable. If Mia tells Mateo, and Mateo finds out I knew, I'm going to be in deep shit.

Maybe I should talk to Vince.

Of course I can't in this damn house, because Mateo can watch the footage later.

I probably should've killed Vince. I have too much invested and too much on the line to leave a loose cannon rolling around, and I'm not completely convinced Mateo isn't going to snap Mia back up anyway. I wish he'd have just told me that when I asked him before I met Vince and Joey at the warehouse.

Too late now, I suppose. I've already assured Mateo that

Vince wasn't in on it, so I can't exactly change the story now.

Now that I have Elise and I'm making a commitment to Mateo—aligning my life with his for the duration—I really need to stop taking these kinds of risks. I need this op to go well tomorrow; I need to get Castellanos out of the way and work on settling things back down again. There are too many loose ends, too many wild cards, too many variables. We used to operate with more security—Mateo's ship has never had these kinds of holes before, and that was what made us strong.

Until fucking Mia.

It would be almost hilarious if that one damn girl was the downfall of the great Mateo Morelli.

Well, he'd still be his own downfall, I guess, she'd just be the catalyst.

Hopefully the storm is winding down. I've told Vince what he needed to hear, and he's faced consequences. Maybe he'll settle down and I can repurpose him.

Maybe he should marry Mia.

I don't know if that would solve my problems or make them all worse later, but I like the idea. Maybe then he'd accept that she's really his—hell, maybe *she* would—and I could put him to use, instead of always having to keep one wary eye on the damn kid.

Something's gotta give. I made the call to spare him and now I need to figure out a way to iron out the subsequent wrinkles, because this constant state of overbearing stress isn't something I want in my daily routine. Not to mention I don't *want* Mateo's empire to fall (most days), and strife from within is a sure way to open us up that that danger.

Not that Mia seems like she's in the mood to marry him tonight. She won't even sit with him. I'll run the idea by Mateo, see what he thinks. She'll probably marry Vince if Mateo tells her to.

Mateo perches at the edge of his desk, like he usually does, but his carriage is less casually commanding tonight, more imperial. His expression holds none of his usual lightness, and his arms are crossed in a foreboding manner as he surveys his subjects. We aren't friends right now, we aren't family—we're his subjects, and it's a deliberate deportment.

"I don't like to bring unpleasantness to the dinner table," Mateo begins. "In fact, regardless of what many of you think," he says as his gaze swings to Vince, lingering there before moving over the rest of us, "I don't enjoy having to be the bad guy at all. The problem is, when I'm a nice guy, when I ease up, when I try to enjoy peace for a while, people start fucking up." He spreads his hands in a sort of "what are you gonna do?" gesture. "You may have noticed Joey missing from dinner tonight." His gaze moves to Vince again, and I dart a glance his way, just to see what Mateo's seeing.

Vince's expression is closed off, pokerfaced.

"Joey's gone," Mateo states, impassively, as if the death of his own brother means nothing to him. "Joey betrayed me," he adds, his gaze moving over the ladies—Mia and Meg. His gaze sweeps back toward Vince, but he lands on Alec to be fair. "Now, unfortunately, there are a number of people in this room who have been less than loyal to me at one point or another, but unlike Joey, you're still here." He pauses just long enough, before concluding firmly, "That ends now. I want the most loyal group, not the largest. I won't punish anyone for past wrongs, you know that's not my style, but from here on out, if you think to betray me, you better damn well succeed. If you don't, you are *done*. I'm giving no more warnings, no more pardons, no more staying the executioner. No more mercy. I don't care if it hurts me as much as it hurts you. Everyone in this room knows what I expect. You betray me, you're gone—just like Joey. This applies to every. Last. One. Of. You." To emphasize his point, he meets each of our gazes as he makes that announcement. "I have varying levels of affection for each one of you," he states. "That doesn't matter. I've had to kill people I loved before. I'm sure I will again. Hopefully it won't be any of you," he adds, his lips finally curving up, but not with any legitimate humor. "It's in your hands now."

I glance to Mia and see Meg has taken her hand. Mia is watching Mateo, her expression pensive.

Elise, Alec, and Mia are the only people in the room who *haven't* betrayed Mateo. Meg, Vince and I should all be dead.

The mood in the room is understandably solemn. No one speaks, though I'm sweating at the possibility that Vince *did* tell Mia, because if he did, and she's on the fence about telling Mateo, this little speech might make the difference.

Clasping his hands together to signal the end of his speech, he adds, "If anyone has anything to get off their chest, do it tonight. Tomorrow is too late."

I glance at Mia, expecting her to have the most volatile response to that, but she keeps her gaze on Mateo—and she manages to keep it calm.

Huh. Maybe she *doesn't* know. She's usually more transparent than that.

Or maybe she does, and she's going to tell him.

Now that Mateo's done reminding us all of our places, it's time for drinks. Elise automatically heads to the liquor cart, and I follow to help. Mateo gets his first, naturally, but when she pours a second, I take it over and offer it to Vince.

Vince's stormy brown eyes meet mine, giving birth to dread inside me. I need him to get his shit together. I need him to let it go.

"I'm good," he says coldly.

"Never known you to turn down a drink before," I remark evenly.

He holds my gaze, cool anger in his eyes, but he doesn't touch the glass.

Suddenly it's plucked out of my hands and I glance up to see Mia, forcing a smile and taking a seat on the edge of Vince's chair.

"Don't mind him, he's a grump today."

Vince's features register surprise as she hands him the glass, and of course he takes it from her.

"We doing this now?" Vince asks placidly, looking up at her.

She tries to smile at him, but I see her eyes narrow with aggravation. I realize she doesn't want to sit with him, doesn't want to pretend everything's okay between them, but she is anyway.

So she's not going to tell Mateo.

Vince realizes the same thing, and an unpleasant, Ben-like smile graces his lips and nearly makes me cringe. Then he moves his arm around Mia and tugs her onto his lap.

Her jaw locks, but she keeps an aggressively mild smile on her lips and doesn't say a word.

CHAPTER SEVENTEEN

I TAKE Elise to bed after drinks.

I'm not ready for sleep and I still need to talk to Mateo tonight, but when Elise gets handsy, I can't really turn that down.

She falls asleep in my old bed afterward, and I lie there for a few minutes watching her, thinking about what a lucky bastard I am. Thinking about all the nights I spent alone in this bed, wondering if she'd even want me.

I haven't had a ton of lucky breaks in life, but I'm glad I got this one.

When I head back to Mateo's study, it's just in time to see Mia leaving. She's not in her dress from earlier, but in… pajamas? She doesn't see me as she heads to the kitchen.

Frowning, I step inside. His head pops up and I can tell initially he thought Mia was coming back in, because his expression dims when he sees it's only me.

"Mia spending the night?"

Mateo nods, abandoning his desk for the pair of chairs we usually sit in when it's just us and he doesn't have to command the room. "First night back in the old room, huh? How's that?"

"Better company this time," I say lightly. I'm still on Mia sleeping here, though. "Does Meg know she's here?"

Mateo nods, not even looking aggravated as he finishes his drink. "It's Meg she's spending the night with."

"In your bed?" I question, remembering all too clearly the last time I saw Mia in his bed.

Mateo smirks. "I promise to keep my hands to myself, Mom."

"I have a feeling Vince wouldn't appreciate this."

"I have the same feeling," he agrees, meeting my gaze. I don't like the probing look he gives me, but if he's wondering about Vince's involvement with Joey again, he doesn't say anything this time.

"Listen, there's some stuff around this whole Joey thing that... I'd rather not tell you. What I'd like is for you to just give me the reins on this one, let me handle it, and don't ask for all the details."

He doesn't immediately say no, but he is understandably hesitant. "Why?"

"Because it wouldn't benefit you and I'm taking care of it, so it doesn't matter. At worst, some of it might be hurtful. At best, it's just damned annoying. I want to use my own discretion, handle it as I see fit, and it'll all be over and we can move on with our lives."

"Who is it you think would hurt me?" he asks, because he's Mateo, and he has to know.

I sigh, wishing for some alcohol myself. I don't feel like getting it though. "Your father."

Judging by his expression, he didn't expect me to say that. "Oh. No one else?"

I shake my head.

I don't know if he thought I meant the girls or Vince, but he seems relieved to know I only meant Matt. "Sure. Deal with him as you see fit."

"I already did. I just meant... the information surrounding it."

"You already…?"

"Matt's dead," I say without preamble.

Mateo's eyebrows rise in mild surprise, but then he nods. There's no emotion on his face, no sadness, no grief. "I suppose that explains why you reassigned the redhead."

"Please don't fuck her," I request.

He laughs a little, looking down at the glass in his hands. "I'm not going to fuck the redhead. Why does everyone think I'm going to cheat on Meg? I never cheated on Beth, and that bitch ripped my heart out."

"Because of the way you look at Mia, probably," I say, since it's the truth.

"Mm," he murmurs, nodding, his smile falling. "I do like Mia."

I shift in my seat, not expecting him to admit that. "And Meg?"

"I love Meg," he replies, glancing from the glass to me. "But I trust Mia more than I trust Meg. It's not even close."

"Well… Mia's been loyal to you. That makes sense. I would remind you Meg took a *bullet* for you though, so…"

"No, I know. I don't mean I *distrust* Meg, it's just… I don't have to hide anything from Mia. If Meg knew everything…" He trails off, shaking his head, his gaze drifting back to his glass. "I don't know. Mia has surprised me. I never expected Mia to be what she is. She seems so breakable—so soft and malleable and *kind*, but there's something powerful in her. Not aggressive power, but power in her gentleness, in what she can withstand. That girl would stand in the center of hurricane and throw affection at it to try to tame it."

"I think her love definitely tends toward the unconditional," I agree.

"Yeah. Meg has a few conditions."

"Mia is very loving," I acknowledge. "But so is Meg, where you're concerned. With only one exception I know of, she accepts everything about you. And Mia already covered your ass on that base, so I don't think you have to worry about it."

"I'm not trying to compare them," he says. "They're not competing. I care about them both. I just... I don't know." He sighs, glancing back up at me. "Anyway, you didn't come here to talk about them."

"We can, if you want to," I offer. It's not like we haven't had messier discussions in our time.

But he shakes his head. "I'm good." Glancing down at his glass with a faint smirk, he adds, "I am a little eager to go to bed now, so if we could hurry this along."

"Well, before we completely switch topics, I had an idea to run by you. Might clear up a few problems for all of us."

"What's that?" he asks.

I wasn't sure he'd go for this when I walked the long stretch of house to this study, but I have even less confidence in it now. I'm hoping he does. I'm hoping he *wants* to behave, that he'll welcome a way to simplify his messy feelings. He has Meg, so what reason could he actually have to say no?

But that doesn't mean he won't. Mateo is usually rational, but not always where women are concerned.

"Hear me out," I begin.

Now he's amused. "Oh, that's a great start."

"What if Vince and Mia got married?"

For a moment, he stares at me. I can't read him—he really only looks like he's processing my suggestion, then he says, "No."

"Why?"

Mateo shrugs, playing off the importance of the matter. "I don't believe Mia wants to marry Vince. I'm not going to make her."

"It would force a commitment," I point out. "I think Mia would fare better if—"

Cutting me off, Mateo says, "The answer is no. Next order of business."

Well, that went about as well as I expected. Hopefully this next thing goes better.

I've gone back and forth with whether or not to tell him about Matt, but I haven't made up my mind. On a whim, because I just don't want to open myself up to any bullshit down the road, I make my decision. Sighing, I lean forward and meet Mateo's gaze. "Before he died, Matt told me I was his son."

Every trace of amusement vanishes from Mateo's face and he puts his glass down, leaning forward to mirror my stature. "He what now?"

"I'm sure it was bullshit," I tell him, rolling my eyes. "He's Matt, so I'm sure he just wanted to fuck with me one last time. I just wanted to tell you, because I wouldn't put it past him to include a letter in his will or some dramatic shit like that. Just in case, I don't want it to come as a shock to you. Again, it's bullshit, it's obviously bullshit, but there it is."

His head is cocked to the side and he's frowning, searching my face for signs of shared features. I sigh, sitting back, because I feel like I'm on display, and I hate that shit.

"What if it isn't?" he asks.

I shrug. "Wouldn't really make a difference, would it?"

"We'd be brothers," he remarks. His gaze sharpens and he smiles slowly as he realizes, "You're older than I am."

"Barely."

"That would make *you* the Morelli heir."

"No, it wouldn't," I say firmly, semi-glaring at him. "I'm not a Morelli. Whether Matt's full of shit or he isn't, I'm still me. I'm still Adrian Palmetto. I want nothing to do with your legacy. Knowing Matt, I don't even know if my mom…" I trail off, shaking my head. It fills me with dread just considering the possibility of sharing that man's DNA, but not more than knowing what a rapey bastard he was. Mateo's not above the same behavior, obviously, but Matt certainly never had any of his victims turn into admirers afterward. Thinking of Mia in Mateo's bed, considering the possibility that it could've been my mom in her place with his dad years earlier...

It turns my stomach.

Mateo watches those thoughts play out across my face, then he suddenly asks, "Did they have an affair, or...?"

He doesn't have to finish his sentence. "I don't know," I mutter. "And we never will, so I guess there's no point thinking about it."

"You should've swabbed his cheek," he offers.

"I don't want a test. Like I said, if it's true, I don't even want to know."

Shrugging, he says, "If you change your mind, we could look into it. If it is true, you and I share DNA markers, too."

"Not interested," I reiterate.

"This is an interesting prospect," Mateo says, his flair for the dramatic making him incapable of letting it go. Bastard's probably going to steal my hair brush and test it himself.

"I don't want this to be an issue between us," I state, holding his gaze. "He did, that's why he said it. If it *is* true, it doesn't matter."

"It would be sort of poetic, wouldn't it?" he asks, a ghost of a smile on his face.

"It'd be *something*."

It'd mean a lot of things. It'd mean I murdered my own brother when I killed Joey. Murdered my own father when I killed Matt. It might mean I'm another Morelli rape baby—and *related* to Cherie, come to think of it.

Thank God he brought Elise in from the outside world.

The main thing, though, is that it could change the way Mateo looks at me. Not because he's sentimental, but because he likes power and doesn't like competition.

I go for lightness when I tell him, "If it *did* turn out to be true, just know you don't have to lock me up and drug me to keep me out of your way."

He sort of smiles, but it doesn't reach his distant eyes. As soon as I utter the words, I realize Mateo never told me that. As far as anyone in this family knew, Matt was sick. Mateo never told me he just wanted his father's power.

Not that it bothers me. I've lived this life; I know the circumstances. I *know* Matt. I know how much he hurt Mateo—and literally everyone else—over the years. I know there's no love between them. Even if Mateo would've confided in me that Matt was healthy, fully capable of handling the family affairs himself, I would've supported locking the old bastard up and drugging his ass.

But Mateo never told me.

And I just told him I knew.

He doesn't call me on it, though. I wait for it, but he merely nods his understanding. I guess he figures maybe Matt told me, since I was obviously in with him today.

But Mateo still feels distant, and as much as I hate to admit it, that makes me nervous.

"I'm trying to be open with you," I tell him.

"I appreciate that."

"Don't start plotting against me," I say, not bothering to pretend he wouldn't.

Instead of assuring me he won't, he asks, "Have you made a decision about coming back to work for me long-term?"

"Yeah." I search his face for something accessible, but come up empty, so I watch for changes instead as I say, "I'm in."

His expression relaxes just slightly, but the promise of my loyalty is not enough to disarm him this time. I can imagine the thoughts going through his mind—probably running through what he would do in the same circumstances. We're not alike, but we both have a ruthless streak, an ability to hone in on what we want and go for it, regardless of what's in the way. I decided I wanted Elise and gave up five years of my life in service to someone I more or less hated just to get her—not even knowing if she'd want me once I did. In pursuit of that end, I've done heinous, unconscionable shit that even I don't think is right—but I did it. To get what I wanted.

Mateo doesn't have to work that hard for things, but that's because he was born to excessive privilege. Not just financial wealth, charisma, and good looks, but power, influence, respect. I came into the world with little, lost what I had, and had to fight for every inch of what I have now. If what Matt said is true, I shouldn't have had to.

Me, I can let that go. It doesn't matter to me. I never wanted it anyway.

But I don't know if Mateo will believe that. He knows it's consistent with who I am, but it isn't what *he* would do, and that has to color his perspective, at least a little.

He would swear his fealty, kneel to the king, and then overthrow him.

Nothing I say to him tonight's going to resolve this, so I give up trying. I'll let him stew in it for little while, consider the best and worst case scenarios. Then tomorrow I'll wake up and go kill his enemy for him, because that's what loyal soldiers do.

CHAPTER EIGHTEEN

"HARDER."

I groan as Elise rides me harder, pushing her hands through her hair, lifting her incredible hips and dropping them, sheathing my cock in her amazing fucking body. When I'm inside her, I never want to leave.

"Adrian," she says, gasping, lowering her body until she's clutching my shoulders. She grinds against me, her beautiful face tense as she rides me, seeking out her own pleasure.

"That's it, baby," I murmur, the words falling off my tongue like they belong there.

"Oh, my god," she breathes, grinding more furiously against me until her whole body shudders with release and she collapses, smashing those perfect breasts of hers against my chest. "Oh, Adrian. Oh, my god."

"My turn," I tell her, flipping her over onto her back.

With a relaxed smile, she says, "Do whatever you want to me."

My cock really likes when she says shit like that. It's not that hard to please though—anything that includes Elise naked, and especially anything that includes being inside her, it's pretty ecstatic about. I'm still not used to her. It doesn't feel like I ever will be.

As I hike up her legs and plant myself between them, easing my cock inside her tight pussy, I still can't believe I'm allowed to do this.

"I love the feeling of you inside me," she says sweetly, turning me on even more than I already am.

Being inside of Elise is the single greatest feeling I've encountered in my 33 years, so if she feels even a fraction of that, I believe her.

While she's on my cock, I grab her legs and rotate her sideways. She gasps a little as I rotate her, but when I ease out and thrust back inside of her, I get a guttural, "Oh, shit."

"Yeah?"

"Oh, yeah," she says, with more enthusiasm as I plow into her again. "Oh, fuck."

Watching her get excited for me makes it hard to hold on, but as long as what I'm doing is working for her, I'm gonna drag it out.

"Adrian," she says on a gasp, reaching for me, but giving up and clutching the pillow. "Adrian, Adrian, Adrian."

I fucking love when she does that. When she feels pleasure building, she just says my name over and over again, a little pleasure chant, falling from her perfect lips.

God, she makes me so happy.

Even today, even knowing what a grim fucking day it's going to be, I get to start off by making love to Elise, by kissing, touching, and fucking this beautiful human being.

How can I complain about that?

Elise comes a second time, and the sounds of her pleasure prove too much. I can't hold out anymore, but I don't have to.

Collapsing against the old mattress I used to sleep on alone, I pull Elise's naked body against me, trapping her breasts with one of my arms.

It's too soon, but it's hard not to tell her I love her. I won't say it until I know she'll only say it back if she *means* it, but God… I love the fuck out of this woman.

As if she knows what I'm thinking, Elise relaxes into me, her hand coming up to rest on my arm over her breasts.

"I wish you could stay home today."

"Oh, me too." I'm trying to block out today's to-do list, to hold onto this perfect morning, but reality won't wait forever.

She turns over so she can look up at me. "Is it going to be dangerous?"

"They shouldn't know we're coming. We've got more guys. It should be okay."

She stares at my chest, her hands coming to rest there. "I hate this part."

Yeah, so do I. Never bothered me much before, but now that I finally have someone worth coming home to—hell, someone who makes calling Mateo's house *home* not only palatable, but roll out of me naturally, with no objection—it raises the stakes.

"When this is all over, you should take a few days off. We'll stay in bed the whole time, and only come out for food and water."

I smile at her, leaning down to brush a kiss across her lips. "Actually when all this is over, Mateo's taking Meg on a vacation. He shouldn't need me if he's not here. Maybe we could go away, too. Somewhere tropical. You like the beach?"

"I *love* the beach," she says, grinning. "When I was younger, I always used to dream of living in a house on the beach someday. It's so peaceful. There's something about the waves lapping at the shore that just soothes me."

"Then I'll buy you a beach house someday," I tell her.

"You'll buy *us* a beach house," she amends, poking me in the chest.

I can't help smiling. "Yeah. Us."

When I finally drag myself out of bed to shower and head downstairs for the day, I can't even wipe the stupid smile off my face.

Mateo's at the table alone, sipping his coffee and reading his paper. He looks up as I come in, and even once I've thrown some food on a plate and returned to the table, a ghost of a smile still hangs on my lips.

"What's got you in such a good mood?" he asks, quirking an eyebrow.

I don't even try to play it cool as I drop into the seat next to him. "Elise."

"Yeah?"

"Elise is awesome."

He grins, putting his paper down. "Good. It's nice to see you happy."

I shake my head, reaching for my cup of coffee. "I can't believe she likes me."

He laughs a little, probably surprised by my candor, but I don't even care. "I'm glad she does," he says earnestly. I know *he* doesn't especially care if Elise was pleased with wherever he decided to send her, but he knows *I* do.

"You won't need me when you and Meg go on vacation, right?"

"I shouldn't," he says, shaking his head. "Unless you want to come. Have a couples getaway."

"Oh yeah, that's what I want to do with my time off," I say, rolling my eyes.

"I figured," he says lightly.

"You going to Paris?"

Rolling his eyes, he says, "Fuck Paris."

"Elise wants to go to the beach," I tell him. "I can think of worse ways to spend my time."

"Actually, that's where I want to go," he says, cracking a smile. "Maybe we should reconsider the couples getaway."

I shake my head. "You tell me which ocean you're visiting, I'll pick a different one."

"That's not very brotherly," he tells me.

I give him the deadest expression I can possibly muster, but he just grins and takes a sip of his coffee.

"We're going to have to have a funeral, you know."

"*You're* going to have to have a funeral," I state, turning my attention back to my plate. "That has nothing to do with me."

"He left a will, too," Mateo points out.

I sigh, not wanting to even think about it. The old man probably left emotional landmines there, too. "I hope that's not you someday," I tell him, flicking a glance at him.

"I like to think I'm an improvement over the last Mateo, thank you very much."

"Hopefully Meg's baby will be an improvement over the current one," I say. "Who knows, maybe three or four generations down the road, someone normal will carry your name."

Mateo smirks. "I wouldn't count on it."

"It'll be nice for him to have a mom." His smile falls, not dramatically, not with any kind of excessive sadness, but he looks a little pensive as he nods his agreement. Since we're talking about it, I decide to go ahead and tell him, "Elise wants kids."

His gaze returns to me. "Do you?"

I shrug. "It's not something I ever thought was in the cards for me, but… sounds nice."

Mateo nods. "It's pretty nice."

"More people to keep safe," I mutter. "Sort of stresses me out."

"Well, put a baby in her now and my new one will have a friend. They'll be just like us," he adds, smiling faintly.

"The next generation," I say, rolling my eyes. Then I add, "Hopefully not *just* like us. If you turn on me and end up raising my kid, I'm going to be *so* pissed."

He knows that's only partially a joke, because he responds, "I maintain we should do a DNA test, just so we know."

"And I maintain that I don't want to know and it doesn't matter. Finding out would only make you paranoid if I am."

"But it would set my mind at ease if you weren't," he points out.

My eyebrows rise, since he didn't even make a half-ass attempt to deny it. "You're too smart to be this stupid, Mateo," I tell him, shaking my head.

"Don't pretend you have no ambition, Adrian," he says, rolling his eyes.

"Not nearly as much as you. You know what I *do* have?" I ask, meeting his gaze, because I'm so fucking serious right now, and I want him to see that. "Loyalty. To you. You want to be able to count on me, we've gotta stay on the same side. You have nothing I want; I have no *interest* in usurping you. Don't be a dick."

"You know how I struggle with that." He says it like a joke as he picks up his coffee cup, but I roll my eyes, because it's not a joke at all.

Turns out Castellanos was *not* there. Not Antonio, not Salvatore.

Didn't stop us from taking down eight of their guys, but despite emerging the victors, all we won was a goddamn street fight. Worthless in the great scheme of things. At *best,* worthless— at worst, inflammatory.

My good mood subsides.

So does Mateo's, when I have to report back to him.

Up until now, the Castellanos family didn't *want* war with us—Antonio did. Now his family is likely to get on board, and Antonio is still out there somewhere, alive and calling the big-picture shots. And considering the level of his obsession with taking out Mateo up to this point, it seems likely he'll take advantage of the turning tides and redouble his efforts.

Mateo stares pensively out the window. I'm not driving this time since I need to focus and strategize with him.

"We have to strike again," he says. "Now, fast, as soon as we can. Don't give them time to respond. Don't give them time to regroup. We fired first; we have to keep at it. We have to finish this."

I sigh, leaning back in the seat. I was already prepared for this—had our guys prepared for this—but it wasn't how I wanted things to go. "Yeah, I know."

"I need you to start preparing to fight dirty, too. I know you don't want to, but you need to start putting the pieces in place. Maybe we get lucky, maybe we catch one of them skittering out from the woodwork, but just in case... I like the daughter."

"I don't like it," I tell him, even though he already knows. "She's not even important to him and it sets a bad precedent. Adds fuel to their fire. Give me a little more time."

"I want to make a statement. They're both hiding like cowards; I want it to be clear I'm not."

"I understand that, but there *is* a target on your back right now. We can't get to Antonio or Salvatore. My next move is the take out Rizzo, since he's next in line. He's not hiding; he's calling the immediate shots right now. Let's not take any unnecessary risks with you to prove a point."

Mateo shakes his head, looking as tired of all this as I feel. "I just want it to be over. I don't care what we have to do now; I just want it to end."

I nod. "I'm working on it."

CHAPTER NINETEEN

THE SECOND strike is more successful than the first, in that we actually get the target we're gunning for.

It's less successful in that they had already prepared for us enough that they hurt a couple of our guys and killed one. Soldiers, no one crucial, but I don't feel good about it. We're fighting outside of our element here—this isn't Mateo's style. Mateo's a thinker, a planner, a manipulator before he's a fighter. He wins by outsmarting people more often than he wins by using muscle. Wars are won through that kind of thinking—not brute force. He knows in a lot of cases you don't have to resort to this level of violence to get what you want—you fight smarter, not harder.

And I have a bad feeling that Salvatore Castellanos is fighting smarter.

Sure, he's hiding right now, but even that's not his style. Look at what it's doing though—getting to Mateo, making him want to show himself, make a statement. He's overreacting. We're overreacting. Meanwhile Salvatore's the one knowing his enemy, knowing how to *play* his enemy, and… well, winning.

It doesn't look like he's winning if you just look at the body count, but he's fighting the way Mateo would usually fight—and he usually wins.

He's pushed too many of Mateo's buttons.

Now Mateo isn't thinking straight, and that's dangerous. We might be able to win with brute force, but we're not doing things the smartest way, and that bothers me.

I need Mateo to dial it back. I need him to focus on being cunning and manipulative—they're not the greatest traits within the family, but they make him a damn good opponent on the outside.

There's too much on the line right now, though. And with this bullshit Matt just dropped in our laps, his trust in me is shaken.

I feel a little shaken myself when I realize we are poised to *lose* this war.

"You're not even watching the movie."

I anchor myself back in the moment and look over at Elise, curled up beside me in the sitting area in my room, watching me instead of the television.

"Sorry," I murmur. My arm's already around her, so I give her a little squeeze and focus on the screen.

"What's going on up there?" she asks me.

"Just work stuff. Sorry."

"Hey, if the Dread Pirate Roberts isn't holding your attention, it must be big," she says lightly. "Share your woes. That's what I'm here for."

"I just feel like we're being outplayed."

Her eyebrows rise in astonishment. "You and Mateo, outplayed? By who, The Riddler?"

I can't bite back a grin. "Solid Batman reference."

Smiling, she says, "You told me you liked him a long time ago. I may have studied up on the subject."

"Such a good student," I say lightly.

"How are you being outplayed?" she asks.

I shake my head. "It just seems like they're tapping into *every single one* of Mateo's weaknesses. The first couple of times could've been incidental, but it's starting to feel strategic."

"Is he the one who wants to kill Mateo, or the one who wanted to keep peace?"

"He was the one who wanted peace. Probably not anymore."

Elise pats my hand, nestling into my side. "Well, I'm sure you'll figure it all out."

"Your unwavering faith in us is appreciated," I tell her, lightly.

"Just trust your instincts," she advises. "If they've got Mateo off his game, and he's throwing you off yours... just stop. Regroup. Do your thing *your* way, because you're good at it. He knows you're good at it, so just cut him out if you need to."

The shit of it is, I *would* do that, if not for this shit Matt kicked up. "It's complicated right now. Mateo is having a bout of suspicion. If I do that, he could take it the wrong way." I roll my eyes, thinking we really couldn't be in *less* ideal circumstances than these.

Elise sits up, turning her attention back to me and scowling. "He's doubting *you*?"

I haven't told her about what Matt said to me yet. I guess I haven't really wanted to, for a lot of reasons. I know Mateo's cameras are around. I also don't know how Elise would react to that prospect—part of me thinks she *would* like if it turned out I had Morelli blood.

I don't want to keep secrets between us either, though. Especially secrets that *could* potentially become an issue, like this one.

"Mateo's dad... you know he's a shit-starter," I say, to review.

"I know he's a demon who should die and burn in hell for the rest of eternity," she responds with a nod.

"Okay. Well... yeah. And also a shit-starter. He said something to me before he died, and—"

"Wait, he died?" she asks, lighting up. Then she smacks me on the arm, eyes wide. "Why wouldn't you tell me that? That makes me so happy."

I blink at her, despite smiling a little. "That's slightly disturbing."

Elise rolls her eyes in disgust. "He hurt you. He deserved to die."

"Well, yeah. Turns out he might also—No, that's wrong…" I sigh, closing my eyes for a minute, trying to clear my head. "He told me I was his son. But it's not true. I'm sure it's not true. But he said it, and I told Mateo, because I didn't want there to be issues, but that *created* an issue, so maybe I shouldn't have."

She frowns, looking a bit surprised. "Matt Morelli said he was your dad?"

"It's not true. But yeah."

"How do you know it isn't true?" she asks.

I hesitate. "Well, I mean, I don't *know* it's untrue. But I assume it is. And even if it isn't, it doesn't matter to me. But it matters to Mateo."

"Why?" she asks, still frowning. "Mateo loves you. Wouldn't he *like* if you were brothers?"

There was a time both of us probably would've liked that— before we would've understood the ramifications. "I'm older than he is."

At first, she doesn't get it. Why would that matter? Then it hits her, and I watch her face transform with understanding, my stomach twisting anxiously in response. It's hitting her that this could all be mine… and that would also make all of it hers.

"The eldest son heads the Morelli family," she finally says.

"Yep."

"Oh." Something like fear flits across her face then, and she glances over at me. "But he wouldn't hurt *you*…"

"I wouldn't want it, even if it turned out that scumbag *was* my father, but… you know Mateo." As soon as it's out, I remember who I'm talking to and I roll my eyes. "No, you don't. Never mind. Anyway, because he's an ambitious asshole, he's having a hard time accepting that I'm not. So this isn't the best time to start making my own calls without permission."

"That's annoying," she says, a bit off-handedly. I can tell she's still processing this new information, and I'm wishing I would've taken her to a bathroom to have this conversation. The last thing I need is her saying the wrong thing. Even if Mateo could accept that I'm not ambitious enough to try to take his seat at the table, if Elise said anything even remotely encouraging, he would double down. I gave up five years of my life for this girl after knowing her for a week; it's not a stretch to imagine I might try to take down someone I openly dislike (most of the time) if I thought it would make her happy to reign over his kingdom.

"Anyway," I say, so she doesn't remark further, "I guess we should turn our attention back to Cary Elwes."

This effectively aggravates her and she rolls her eyes at me. "He's not Cary Elwes. He's Dread Pirate Roberts—or at the very least, Westley. Don't ruin it."

"I just don't love this movie as much as you do. It's never going to happen. Just accept it."

"I will never accept that," she swears, as if declaring her fealty. "Never *ever*. In fact, just for that, I think we should name our son Westley."

My heart slides out of my chest cavity, right through my stomach. "Oh, good, we're talking about kids again."

Elise grins at me, her hand drifting over to caress my thigh. "Relax, I didn't mean tonight. But I want Westley on the record as my boy pick."

"I... won't fight you on that, actually. I like that name." It makes me feel a little ill that we're already naming our unborn kids, particularly given the climate of everything else in my life right now. My sort-of best friend might try to kill me. We might lose a gang war, anyway, and he won't even have to. I still haven't found Francesca. Everything related to the business-side of my life right now sucks. And as much as I think about Elise on a daily basis, I don't think there's even room in my heart for someone else—let alone two someones. It's not a very big space. She should understand that.

"Candace and Westley Palmetto," she says happily, tilting her head back to look up at me. "I love them already."

"Do you ever wish you would've been able to choose for yourself?"

"Choose what?"

"Your... me. Your partner. The person you'd start a family with. You've obviously burrowed in and made lemonade like a pro, but isn't there any part of you that wishes you could've picked someone out for yourself?"

She frowns at me a little, like she disapproves of my question. "No."

"Why?"

"What good would that do me?" she asks, her scowl deepening. "Why would I look for reasons to be unhappy? We're a good match. You're wonderful to me. We're happy together. Who *cares* if it was arranged?"

I shake my head, still mildly in wonder about the way her brain works. "We have very different ways of approaching life."

Elise rolls her eyes indulgently, like she knows more about it than I do. "That's why I'm happier than you are."

On a whim, I ask, "What would you do, if you were me?"

"In regards to which crisis?" she asks, sitting up a little straighter and turning to face me.

"My Mateo situation. My way isn't working. How would you handle it?"

Elise pauses for a moment to consider, her eyes drifting upward as she files through the information she has. "I think I'd just let him know I'm happy with what I have. I'd let him see it."

Shaking my head slightly, I tell her, "I am doing that. But Mateo isn't... He doesn't stop once he gets what he wants. He always has to have more. I don't know how to make him look at me and not think about what he would do. He could be happy with his circumstances and have everything he's always wanted—he *does,* right now, as we speak—and do you think he stops and accepts that he's content? No. He has to keep reaching for more."

"That's sad," she says, her lips turned down. "Why keep reaching if there's nothing missing?"

"There's always something missing. No one has everything."

"What could you have that you don't? You already have status. You already have respect. You've gained everything you would have as a Morelli anyway, by working for him these last five years. What more could you want?"

"Money."

"Well, he's got lots of that," she says, rolling her eyes. "He can't possibly be worried about that. Presumably now that he's done paying you in Elise, he has to start paying you in money, right?"

A short laugh escapes me at her phrasing, and she smiles, pleased with herself. "Yeah, he'll start paying me actual money."

She shrugs. "Then the only thing you have left to gain, you'll gain without hurting him." Sudden awareness transforms her face and she says, "That's it. He needs to know you love him."

I grimace.

She stands her ground. "No, listen. Mateo is not afraid you'll overthrow him because you covet what he has—he knows you're not like that. He's afraid you'll overthrow him because he thinks you don't really like him. If you only owe him your loyalty because of his position… you just found out maybe he shouldn't have his position. If you serve him because you *care,* because you love him and want to keep him safe, and want to keep him in power… then he has nothing to fear. He wouldn't care if you were brothers if you acted like one, but you openly disdain him."

"He's a horrible human being," I state.

"We all know that. But look at the people who manage to accept it—they get his trust."

"I can't condone everything he does, Elise."

She shrugs. "I can't, either, but the people he does it *to* seem to find a way. Look at Mia. She sort of baffles me, but despite his desire to literally kill her when he met her, she's like one of his favorite people now."

Elise is absolutely right—and she doesn't even know how true that is.

Expressing any kind of affection makes me uncomfortable enough, but the thought of accepting *Mateo* causes everything within me to recoil. I've spent most of my life doing exactly the opposite. It's been easy to keep that wall up for five years, despite working to keep him safe and successful every damn day, because I nursed it in my heart. Each night when I went to bed, each morning when I rose to serve him, I knew why I was doing it—to free Elise. Not for him.

But at the end of the day, I've also done plenty of things I didn't *have* to do. Things that were not my job at all, weren't even my business, but I saw a way I could help him, so I did. Sometimes I just do things because, yeah, I want the bastard to be happy.

"I'm not going to *tell* him that. Men don't say shit like that to each other."

"Then show him," she advises.

"I don't know how," I say honestly. "You may not have noticed, but this is my weakest area. I don't know how to do this shit."

Leaning in to nudge me in the shoulder, she says, "Something *you* don't know how to do. Go figure."

"I guess it's your turn to tutor me," I say lightly.

Elise nods, turning her attention back to the television. "Okay, lesson one is going to be incredibly simple and also probably really hard. Leave your judgments at the door. When he's doing something you don't approve of, just respond with love. Just let it go and love him. Don't roll your eyes. Don't get surly. Don't respond the way you do. Think, 'what would Elise do?' If I can be kind to people who buy and sell me like a pair of shoes, *you* can keep your disapproval over Mateo's life choices to yourself."

I raise my eyebrows. "See, *I'm* one of those shoe shoppers you're referring to. You say things like that and it makes me wonder—"

Apparently not in the mood for my nonsense, Elise launches herself across the couch and straddles me.

"Oh," I murmur, losing my train of thought as she yanks her shirt over her head, tossing it on the floor behind her. Suddenly Elise's boobs in a tight black bra are just about at eye-level. "That's a very effective way to change the subject."

Grinning, she swoops in and kisses me. "You think that's effective?" she asks, between kisses. Then her hand drifts between my legs, and like my cock, Elise's level of effectiveness rises.

CHAPTER TWENTY

CLEARLY BECAUSE my assignment for today is not to judge Mateo and the universe wants me to fail, Mateo and Mia both show up at breakfast this morning without Meg, and with wet hair.

Wet hair.

Mia never came to the table with wet hair when she lived here, and now despite the obscene number of showers in this house where they could've showered separately, I'm convinced they took one together.

Elise's assignment is too hard.

"Where's Meg?" I ask, watching Mia instead of Mateo. That bastard never looks guilty, but he hasn't completely disintegrated Mia's conscience—not yet, at least.

Mia keeps her eyes on her oatmeal as she scoops up a spoonful.

Mateo answers, "Sleeping."

I nod, still watching Mia. "Right. Pregnancy does tend to make women more tired, doesn't it?"

Mia isn't giving me anything so I finally look at Mateo. He's smirking, because he knows what I'm doing. Once I meet his gaze, he shakes his head, eyes twinkling with amusement, and takes a sip of his coffee.

"I wouldn't know," Mia murmurs, sipping from a glass of orange juice.

"When are you and Vince going to start popping out little Morellis?" I ask, to remind her she has a boyfriend.

Mia rolls her eyes. "Literally never."

I'm not sure why that surprises me. Maybe I *have* spent too much time with the Morelli men. "You don't want kids?"

"I do; he doesn't."

That just stresses me out more. Now my head is filling up with the colossal disaster of Mateo impregnating Mia—Meg and Vince losing their collective shit. Meg didn't leave a husband who sucked, so she could probably be managed, but Vince... Jesus Christ.

I don't even know how much I'm making yet, but I already feel sure I need a raise.

One mess at a time. I need to focus on the outside problems before I start thinking about the ones inside this family. Of course, I can't talk about work shit with Mateo right now because Mia's here.

"How about you?" Mateo challenges.

I've gotten so lost in my own disaster-scenarios, I don't know what he's asking and I raise my eyebrows questioningly.

"When is Elise going to start popping out little..." Mateo pauses, holding my gaze just long enough before slowly finishing, "Palmettos?"

I don't know if the dread washing over me is from the Morelli bullshit or my anxieties over the two kids Elise has already named—though there's certainly crossover anxiety there.

Mia sighs, not waiting for my answer, and gets up from her seat at the table. Mateo's attention turns to her for a moment, but she doesn't look at him, she just heads to the kitchen to rinse her dishes.

"Why can't anything in this family ever be easy?" I inquire aloud, though more to myself than Mateo.

"Making babies isn't so hard."

"I'm obviously not referring to that."

Mia comes back in, flashing each of us a mild smile. "Well, I'm off to work."

Mateo asks, "You have Colin's number?"

Nodding once, she says, "If I see anything funny, I'll call him straight away."

He nods, satisfied, and Mia gives me a little wave before leaving us alone in the dining room.

"I still think I should send him to keep an eye on her," Mateo says.

"I take it from the lack of Vince at this table, you had another sleepover. How was that?" I ask, somewhat stiffly.

He grins at me. "Satisfying."

"Oh, for fuck's sake, Mateo."

Mateo laughs, lifting his coffee cup and taking a drink. "How many times are you going to need reassurance that I'm not fucking her?"

"At least as many times as she sleeps in your bed. At least that many."

"She wouldn't be so glum if I'd have fucked her," he informs me.

Rolling my eyes, I shoot back, "That's not how I remember it."

This does not amuse him. He doesn't have the decency to look ashamed, but he does lose his smile.

I give up on Elise's assignment completely. "Look, I was going to try not to judge you today, but… that's not panning out. Elise thought…" I trail off, shaking my head. "Anyway, that's not going to work. Even if I could manage it today, I wouldn't be able to keep it up."

He shrugs, unconcerned. "I'm used to it."

"But I didn't sign on to work for you this time because of Cherie and Colin. Before you started your manipulative shit, I was already planning to talk to you about staying on; I just hadn't brought it up yet. I'm not loyal to you because I *have* to be, Mateo. I'm loyal to you because—for some demented reason—I *want* to be."

His gaze lingers on me, considering. Words are often flimsy, but not mine, and he knows that. I certainly don't run scared, and in personal matters, I never lie to get my way. I am, in nearly every way, the opposite of the man sitting across the table from me. I do have my own moral code, and he doesn't fit it—but neither would I, if I moved against him to benefit myself. Loyalty matters to me, and he knows that. I would need far more incentive than his position offers to betray not only him, but myself.

Finally, Mateo nods. He still holds my gaze, and this time there's no wall up. This time he feels more sincere.

"Good," he finally says.

"Are we?" I ask, raising an eyebrow.

Mateo gives me one more nod. "We are."

I'm not much for the idea of martyrdom, but I get to thinking about it when I come up with a risky idea that might work. Lying in bed with Elise's soft, warm body nestled against me, I think I must be a fool for even considering it.

It's high-risk, high-reward. If it succeeds, I save us all a lot of pain and suffering. If it fails, I probably die. I've taken on jobs with exactly those odds before, but I've never had something so worth sticking around for.

Now I have Elise.

Now I have the potential existence of Westley and Candace to consider, apparently.

It's not just me anymore, and as hesitant as I've been at

times to accept it, it doesn't feel like it ever will be again. For the first time in my life, I have *so* much to lose.

So how do I take the kind of risk I'm thinking about, putting my *life* on the line, for Mateo?

But it isn't just for him. As much as I've denied it when it came up, as much as I dislike the Morellis most days, this *is* my family. Whether or not the same blood runs through our veins, Mateo *is* the closest thing I've ever had to a brother.

I'd never admit that to him, of course. I never even wanted to admit it to myself.

But I don't want any more deaths in the family. I don't want to have more funerals. And if I didn't have all that I have now, if Elise wasn't mine, if an actual family and future didn't dangle within my reach… I would make the high-risk move. Maybe I would succeed and save Mateo's family from a war; maybe I would fail, and die.

But I'd do it. Without batting an eye. And that's what made me good.

The temptation to not be good anymore scares me. The resistance to take risks that I need to take for the good of everyone.

Well, nearly everyone.

This would've been such an easy decision before, and it isn't now, and that's a problem. Sure, I've had my first taste of happiness, but what happens if Mateo figures that out? What happens if I'm not useful anymore? Bad enough Matt had to go and make me a potential threat—what if happiness makes me less effective?

I'm going to have to take the risk. The certainty moves through me, heavy and cold, settling in my gut. I don't like the taste of fear. I'm not accustomed to it, and looking over at Elise's face, so peaceful in sleep, I wonder if it's always going to be like this. Is this a new burden I'm going to have to carry? Since she became mine, it's been there niggling at me every damn day—is it just because it's new, or is this my new normal? If I'm already feeling this way, what happens if we *do* have those kids? What happens if there *is* room in my heart for them, and they get lodged there, and I start feeling again? What if I feel the fear again? What if I feel it every damn day of my life?

My life isn't cut out for them. I don't know what Mateo was thinking, letting me have all this. Of course he couldn't have been sure I'd respond to it this way—he doesn't know yet, as far as I can tell—but he has it already; doesn't *he* feel it? Every time he steps outside this house there's a target on his back. I guess there's always been one on mine, too, but I never noticed. It never mattered.

It matters now.

But I can't let it stop me from doing what needs to be done, so I guess I just have to live with the fear. Shove it down. Hide it. Pretend it isn't there, and let it gnaw away at me every day.

I've already offered him my loyalty. The Morellis offer no take-backs.

I watch Elise's face as I move my arm out from under her, trying to move her enough to wake her up.

She just rolls over.

Dammit.

Deciding to be a little less subtle, I lean in and drop a soft kiss against the ball of her shoulder. Then I proceed in toward her collar bone, pulling her over so she's on her back, continuing the trail along her chest.

Her eyes open and she gives me a sleepy smile. "Can I help you?"

"Oh, you're awake," I say, feigning surprise.

Her sleepy smile turns into a grin and she brings her arms around my neck, pulling me down to kiss her. "Can't sleep?" she asks, when I pull back.

I shake my head, watching her beautiful face as I bring my hand up to tuck her hair behind her ears. "Can't sleep," I verify.

"What's on your mind?"

"Lots."

She smiles. "That's incredibly specific."

"When do you want to have kids?"

Her eyebrows rise, apparently not counting on that question. "I don't know. I'm pretty much ready when you are, but you don't seem like you're in a hurry."

"But when do *you* want them?" I ask her, dropping a kiss to her cleavage, then looking at her again.

Narrowing her eyes slightly, like she's trying to figure me out, she asks, "Why?"

I can't seem to stop touching her. I think it alarms her, as I trail my hand down her arm to her elbow and back, catching her wrist and bringing it to my lips, dropping a little kiss there.

Suddenly she frowns and tries to sit up. I don't let her; I want to stay here, anchoring her beneath me. "What's wrong, Adrian? Is this about the stuff with Mateo? Has something else happened?"

I shake my head, greeting her alarm with calm. "No. It's just... you know, there's some dodgy shit going on right now, and I'm in charge of some of the more dangerous operations."

"But you've always been in charge of that stuff, and you've always been fine," she points out.

"I never worried about whether I was or not. You were more a fantasy than a real goal. I knew you were the light at the end of the tunnel, but... I don't know. I don't think I ever expected to reach it."

Her brow furrows. "You didn't really want me?"

I almost chuckle at that one. "No, I wanted you more than anything. Sometimes you just chase something for so long, you can't imagine actually getting it. And maybe you do, but you don't know what to do with it."

"I think you've figured out what to do with me just fine," she assures me, wryly.

I pause, trying to find the right words to explain. "I don't know how to be the man I was before, and the man I am with you."

Elise considers my words, her pouty lips pursing. I'm just about to give up on talking, because those lips, but then she says, "Maybe you don't. Maybe it's time to move into a new phase of life, become… a blend of both. Or something entirely new. Whatever makes you happy."

"That was never a part of who I was before," I tell her.

"Well, maybe that's the problem. Maybe it should've been. No point dwelling on it now, but just be glad you found your way out of that and appreciate what you have. Which you do," she adds, reaching out and caressing the damaged side of my face.

I swore I wasn't going to say it, but nothing she's said to me has talked me out of my stupid plan, so I do.

"I love you, Elise."

Smiling back at me, without even a beat of hesitation, she says, "I love you too, Adrian."

I don't believe that, not yet. Maybe it's true and I'm overly skeptical, or maybe she's just saying it because she's Elise, and she's kind, and she *does* care about me, and she *plans* to love me, someday…

I just needed to hear it now, in case I don't get to hear it later.

"Don't be sad," she whispers. "That's not supposed to make you sad."

I try to smile, to reassure her, but it doesn't really happen.

"I mean it," she says, misunderstanding my response. She knows I'm always doubting her sincerity, blaming things on her 'programming.' Meeting my gaze, holding my face in place with both hands now so I can't look away, she tells me, "You are the best man I've ever met in my whole life. I'd be *crazy* not to love you."

I don't know if it's her words or the fierce look in her eyes, but something makes it through. It feels good and terrible at the same time, like a heavy weight is slowly crushing me, but it's the weight of feelings I've never been able to access. I'm somehow yearning for something I already have, and even as my fingertips skim Elise's torso, it feels like I'll never be able to reach her.

I don't have the capability to express what I'm feeling with words, so I do it the only way I know how.

And I don't use a condom.

CHAPTER TWENTY ONE

I'M GETTING damn tired of making the trek to Mateo's wing of the house.

I feel so damn depressed the whole way there, too. Elise is asleep again, and all I want in the world is to lie there beside her, holding her in my arms, but there's too much to take care of. Just in case I get myself killed, I need to know the lives I'm responsible for are going to be in good shape.

The door's cracked open, not latched shut, and I can see a light's still on inside. I sort of expected them to be asleep, for this visit to be just like my last, but Mateo never sleeps with the light on.

This time, I knock on Mateo's door.

"Come on in," Meg calls.

Easing open the door, I'm half-worried about what I'm going to see.

There's Mateo on the bed with Mia and Meg... and a Scrabble board.

The first part doesn't surprise me as much as the second part, and I scowl at the scene. Meg and Mia are both in pajamas, but

Mateo hasn't undressed for bed yet. His jacket's off, shirt sleeves rolled up, but he looks right at home in the center, the girls on either side of him, like at dinner.

Meg lights up when she sees me. "Adrian! Join us."

"What the hell are you guys doing?" I ask.

Mia glances over her shoulder at me. "Meg can't sleep."

"And when Meg can't sleep, ain't nobody sleeping," Meg says, about herself.

"You might think some of us should get to, since some of us have to get up early in the morning for work," Mia adds.

Meg concludes, "But you would be wrong."

Mia nods, rearranging her Scrabble tiles.

Meg grabs the bag and starts counting out tiles for me. "Come on, Adrian. Have a seat."

"I really don't want to play Scrabble."

"Please?" she asks, flashing me puppy dog eyes and a pout.

"That's not going to work on me," I tell her.

"Vince told me you're the best. He told me you even beat Mateo. I can't express to you how much I've wanted this moment to happen. I've literally fantasized about it."

"Us with Mia and Adrian?" Mateo asks, quirking an eyebrow.

"Playing Scrabble," she says, rolling her eyes.

Warily glancing between all three of them, I decide this isn't my problem and shake my head. "I need Mateo for a minute."

"Nope," Meg says, shaking her head. "Sorry, bud. It's after midnight; he's all mine until morning."

"It can't wait until morning."

"Is it about Castellanos?" Meg asks, this time seriously.

"No."

"Is it life or death?"

"Well... no."

Nodding once, she says, "Okay, then you can't have him." Now she smiles. "Of course, if you *really* need an audience tonight, you could *play me* for him."

Looking to Mateo, I ask, "Is she drunk?"

He shakes his head no. "Just crazy."

Narrowing her eyes at him, she says, "You love it, Morelli."

"I never denied that," he replies.

Mia looks as exasperated with me as I usually am with her. "Just agree to one round or we're gonna be here all night."

Sighing heavily, I approach the bed with no small amount of trepidation. "This is hands-down the weirdest thing I've ever done in this house."

Clapping victoriously, Meg says, "Yay! This is going to be awesome."

"This is going to be epigrammatic," I inform her, sitting at the edge of the bed, and uncomfortable even there.

Meg grimaces. "I don't know what that means."

Mateo smirks at her. "It means you're going to lose."

It takes me less than a half hour to soundly beat them.

"Did you cheat somehow?" Meg asks, lifting my letter tray to search under it.

"I'll take my audience with the king now," I say, dryly.

"You have to promise to come back and do this again. Mateo was crushing us before you came in." Now she waves him off, like he's insignificant. "Next time we play teams, and I want you."

"Hey," Mateo says, as if offended.

"Sorry, baby. I wanna win."

Mateo shakes his head in mock-disappointment, but Mia comes to his rescue. "That's okay, I'll take Mateo."

"Yeah," Mateo says, unaccountably sliding his arm around Mia's shoulder and tugging her against him. "Mia'll take me."

Mia turns several shades of red, losing her humor but making no move to pull away.

Meg just rolls her eyes at Mateo's attempt to annoy her, somehow less concerned about this than me *or* Mia. "She can have you; I've got an ace in the hole over here."

"You're so cold," Mateo tells Meg.

"That's why you love me," she states.

Releasing Mia, Mateo climbs off the bed. I got up as soon as I possibly could, so I'm already halfway to the door. We don't go far—just out in the hall, but he closes his bedroom door behind him so we have a little privacy.

"What's so important?" he asks, crossing his arms over his chest.

This is not what I came to ask, but I'm feeling very confused right now. "Does Mia live here now? Is she still with Vince? What the hell is going on?"

"No," he says casually. "She's just staying until the Castellanos threat has been lifted. I invited Vince, too," he adds, rolling his eyes. "He was not interested."

"In Scrabble parties and sleepovers in your bedroom? Go figure."

"I assume he doesn't know about those things," Mateo replies, clearly not caring either way.

I feel ten times heavier now than I did when I walked up here. If I die, who in the hell is going to keep this man alive? "That poor fucking kid."

"It's perfectly harmless," he assures me.

"Nothing you do is ever harmless," I state.

Mateo rolls his eyes at me, sighing. "Did you really come up here at this time of night to talk about Mia again? I'm starting to think you're the one with a thing for her."

I glare at him for that one. "Not hardly."

"Then what's on your mind?"

I shake my head, still hung up on his shit. Not even this,

specifically, just the ballpark figure of how many of this man's messes I've cleaned up over the years, that I *continue* to clean up, and he had the gall to doubt me.

Even now, when I think it's over, I don't really know what to expect from him. I always get to a point where I *think* I know what to expect from him, where he stands, and then I blink and it changes.

"You're the most unstable person in the world," I inform him.

"That's what's on your mind?"

I force myself to stop pacing and meet his gaze. "I need to know what happens to Elise if something happens to me."

Mateo scowls, suddenly serious. "If something happens to *you*?"

"Yes."

Frowning, Mateo says, "Adrian, I already told you we're good. We're fine. Nothing's going to happen to you."

"I didn't mean at your hands," I tell him. "We both know I do dangerous shit. We both know the risks of this Castellanos situation, and I'm not on the sidelines, I'm right in the thick of it, calling the shots. I want to be there to give Elise the life she deserves, but I need to know you're going to make sure she's taken care of if I'm not."

He watches me, gauging my seriousness, and finally he nods. "Of course I would, Adrian."

"None of your bullshit," I specify.

Mateo rolls his eyes. "Trust me, that's the last thing I need."

"Promise?"

Nodding, he assures me, "You have nothing to worry about. In the event anything ever happens to you, I will make sure Elise has the life you would've given her."

It makes me feel a little better, but I'm still damn aggravated that I even have to make these arrangements.

Still watching me, frowning at my obvious turmoil, Mateo

asks, "What's going on, Adrian?"

I've already decided not to tell him about this play—he won't okay it if I do. He'll know how dangerous it is, borderline reckless, all things considered. Because he does care about me in his way, he wouldn't let me do this, not even if it meant cutting the risk in half and saving a multitude of his own men.

"Thank you," I say, visibly surprising him.

"For what?" he asks.

"For Elise."

"Adrian, what the fuck?" he asks, frowning. His gaze darts beyond me, down the hall for a second, then back to me with a frown. "Are you planning something I should know about? Do you have new information?"

I shake my head. It's not new information, just a new idea, and I don't want to talk about it or he'll figure it out. Even broaching the subject would let him know where my mind is, and then he'd hone in on it, and before I could get a cup of coffee in the morning he'd be there forbidding me to take matters into my own hands.

In a sense, that would be nice. Take the burden off me.

But in a larger sense, in the practical sense, it would just mean we keep fighting a war we're going to lose against an opponent who's somehow playing better. One of Mateo's many flaws is that he thinks he's infallible. Why wouldn't he? I guess if I lived his life, getting away with everything over and over again, always winning even when I should lose, maybe then I, too, would feel infallible.

I know better.

He will someday—when it's too late.

Hopefully I'll be around after tomorrow to keep throwing demons off his back, because I don't know who else will if I'm not.

"You should be nicer to Vince," I tell him. "He's got a lot of loyalty in him and you're not using it to your advantage."

Shaking his head as if that ship has sailed, he tells me, "The damage has been done. There's nothing I can do to repair it."

"You say that like you've tried."

He shrugs. "It would be a waste of energy. The source of our strife isn't going anywhere. I'm not going to stop pissing him off, and he's never going to get past what's already happened anyway. There's nothing to be done there. We'll tolerate each other until we can't anymore."

I raise my eyes pointedly. "And then what?"

He shrugs evasively, not offering anything beyond that.

We both know where that ends up though, I know we do. If he doesn't back off, it will come down to him or Vince—it already has, he just doesn't know it yet.

Mateo usually wins, but Vince has the element of surprise now because I covered his ass. Cherie's comments from dinner float back to my mind, suggesting Vince in power. It seems ridiculous to me with Mateo at the helm, but for how long? They'll both age, assuming they don't kill each other. Vince won't always be too young, and if he's nursed resentment for years, he just might be capable of doing it. If Vince goes the way Matt went, he's going to get cold. Dark. Cruel. I saw a glimpse of it already in Mateo's study when he realized Mia was going to play nice, despite her true feelings. He took sadistic pleasure in the way she endured his affection for the sake of appearances. Having a girlfriend who fawns over Mateo is going to break him down the same way Belle's disdain wore on Matt; it's not going to be pretty.

I shouldn't have spared Vince. That was a mistake. I should tell Mateo now, consequences be damned, just in case I don't come back tomorrow. Give him a heads up. But how could he *not* already know? If another man did to him what he's done to Vince, he would do the same goddamn thing.

Mateo just doesn't think rules apply to him. He doesn't think anyone will ever make him suffer the consequences of his own actions—and Mia can't bail him out every time.

"You should let Vince out," I tell him.

"Out…?"

I meet his gaze. "*Out.* Give him some money and let him start a life of his own, removed from all this. If you're going to do whatever it is you're doing with Mia, you should give the kid what he's always wanted and just let him out. Keep Mia around, let Vince go. If you're gonna steal his girl, let him get out of your way."

"I already have a girl," Mateo reminds me, but not like he normally does, not dismissively, not amused by my judgments. He hasn't thought of what I've just suggested, I can tell. There's a spark in his eye, the spark of a new possibility.

I don't know if I did Vince a favor or fucked him over, but at least I tried.

"All right, I'm going back to bed," I tell him, turning to head back down the hall. I've done all I can for him, and all I want now is to spend every last second with the woman who makes me forget about all this shit.

"Adrian."

I pause, turning to glance back at him.

"Be careful," Mateo says.

Nodding once in response, I assure him, "I will."

CHAPTER TWENTY TWO

WHEN MORNING comes, I make love to Elise again. No condom, again. It's stupid and sentimental, but supposing I don't come home today, I kind of like the idea of her having something to remember me by.

I know the chances of getting her pregnant in two tries are low, which makes me sort of regret my practicality before. I felt like we had time, and now that I'm afraid we don't... well, now I realize what I want.

I want what Mateo has.

Not the empire, but the stuff that actually matters.

I want the woman who loves me, the cute little kids to tuck in at night after a dangerous day's work. I want to be able to wine and dine the woman I'd do literally anything for, and if she likes stupid fancy dinners and dressing up, I want to be able to give her every bit of that.

It should be a bitter pill to swallow, as much time as I've spent raging against just that, but it's not. I just feel sad that I don't have time, and the time I did have was squandered resisting.

If I do manage to pull this off today, I'm bringing my ass straight home and making up for lost time. I'm gonna put a baby in my beautiful, bewildering woman who wants togetherness and domesticity. I'll let her cook and clean, if that's what makes her happy. I'm gonna find a way to give her friends, too. Mia and Meg are both friendly enough, surely she'll fit right in if I nudge them in that direction. Maybe we won't go back to the apartment. Maybe we'll stay at Mateo's until I can get us a place that doesn't suck. It's easier for me to work from here, anyway. Plus, Maria and Cherie would be back in her life that way, and she could have back whatever bond I took from her when I dragged her out of here, thinking I was rescuing her.

If I get to come home tonight, I swear I'm going to get out of my own way. I'm gonna let us be happy.

Tonight feels like a long time from now, though.

Instead of grabbing coffee and breakfast downstairs, I head out. I'll pick something up on the road. Don't want to risk running into Mateo again. I don't want to lie to him, and I can't tell the truth until after it's already done or it won't *get* done.

The first couple of hours is spent stalking, anyway. This is the safe part. This is where I could still change my mind, if I wanted to. If I let fear rule me.

Instead I wait for an opportunity to get Antonio's daughter alone. She lives with her boyfriend, apparently, and while he's far from someone I'm worried will shoot my face off on sight, he's familiar enough with my lifestyle that he probably would if he had to.

I'm not afraid of him, obviously. He's just inconvenient, and I don't want to kill him, since I'm gonna need something from him later. Extracting information from corpses is beyond even my abilities, in most cases.

The girl works today, so eventually she has to leave. And when she bounds downstairs, her long wavy hair pulled back in a pony tail, dressed in black from head to toe, that's when I get out of my car.

I feel kind of bad about this. I've seen the video that was made featuring this poor girl, and I can't imagine she's fond of being grabbed, but I can't wait until she gets in her car. I don't know her or her habits well enough. Maybe she would be easily intimidated into getting back out; maybe she would throw the car in reverse and peel out of here. The latter can't happen, because then she might call her dad.

Which I want, just not under *those* circumstances.

She's messing with her phone (and I'm pretty stealthy when I want to be, anyway) so she doesn't notice me approaching until I'm right there. Fear leaps in her eyes and a short cry of surprise bursts out of her.

"Don't scream," I say, pressing my gun to her side.

"Oh, God," she says, shakily.

"I don't want to hurt you," I tell her. "We're gonna go back up to your apartment. Anyone up there?"

She hesitates, determining whether or not to lie to me. Finally she settles on, "No."

The lie. Okay, that's understandable. "Give me the phone," I say, since it's still in her hand.

She hesitates even longer, so I grab it from her.

I smile a little when I see she managed to get into contacts, but failed to reach any. "Were you trying to call your boyfriend or your dad?" I ask, out of curiosity.

Her big gray eyes flash with anger and she strangely reminds me of Elise for a moment. Not every day Elise, but the little badass version of her who took down the mugger.

I don't realize I'm smiling until she glares at me and demands scathingly, "You enjoy accosting women outside their homes? Does it make you feel like a big man?"

I laugh a little, shaking my head. "No, actually. I find it pretty distasteful."

At that she frowns, losing her glare, clearly confused.

"Come on," I say, taking her arm and leading her back inside. "Let's go have a little chat."

She doesn't fight me on the way back to her apartment.

Probably because she's thinking she has the element of surprise, thinking I'm taking her into an empty apartment, when her boyfriend is actually inside. He's unlikely to have a gun nearby, but he does have one, so if he happened to be out of sight and saw me first, it stands to reason he might be able to retrieve it and defend her.

I mean, he wouldn't. But she doesn't know who I am.

"Why are you doing this?" she asks me, outside the apartment door.

I don't respond. Instead I lock my arm around her waist, pulling her back against me. A shuddering breath escapes her—fear—but I'm onto the next thing in my head. I don't have time to reassure her.

"Open the door," I murmur quietly.

"Please…" She's having doubts now, since I'm holding her and I have my gun at the ready. "Are you here to hurt Ethan?"

"No."

"Are you here to hurt me?"

"I don't *want* to hurt either one of you," I inform her lowly, near her ear. "But if you don't open the goddamn door, that might change."

Swallowing, she slowly reaches for the door knob. The door drifts open and I go to move inside, but before I can, she screams, "Ethan!"

"Jesus Christ," I mutter. This girl is pissing me off. She's in a relationship with her rapist; how can she possibly be this annoying? I was expecting pliant like Mia, not this bullshit.

Fortunately her attempt doesn't amount to much, because while Ethan *does* come bounding to the door to see what's wrong, he does *not* bring a weapon.

Then he sees me, and *he* clearly recognizes me, because his face loses several shades of pigment.

What reassures me a little is that while he does look horrified, he *doesn't* look entirely surprised to see me.

His Adam's apple bobs and his gaze drops to my hold on Willow, to the gun, already outfitted with a silencer.

"Please let her go."

He keeps his tone calm, not wanting this to escalate. Not like his screamy girlfriend. I appreciate that.

I don't respond, because I want to see what he says on his own.

"Please," he repeats, holding both hands in front of him, showing me he's unarmed. "Leave her out of this."

"You know why I'm here?" I finally ask.

Swallowing again, Ethan nods.

This makes me happy. This makes me really fucking happy.

He *doesn't* know why I'm here, but that he thinks he does means if I *do* survive the first mission, my second one is going to be easy. I like easy.

"Okay, this is good. As long as your girlfriend here doesn't do anything dumb, I think we're gonna be okay. Don't try to pull any hero shit on me."

"I'm not that stupid," Ethan states.

"And *I'm* his fiancée, not his girlfriend," Willow informs me, like it matters to me in the least.

"Well, you're a pain in the ass, whatever you are," I shoot back.

Ethan really wants my hands off his lady-friend, so he says once again, "Can we just—let's step outside, we can talk, just the two of us."

"I want to talk to Willow first," I inform him.

"Willow knows nothing," he states, firmly.

"What's going on?" the girl asks, obviously out of the loop, and not appreciating it.

"Well, she does," I say, ignoring her. "She knows Antonio Castellanos—and that's what I need from her. What I need from you, we can get to later."

Ethan scowls at me, not understanding.

So I explain—not so much for him, but for Antonio's daughter. "I'm probably not surprising you with the news that Antonio tried to have Mateo Morelli killed—a few times. Most recently, he had Mateo's *pregnant* fiancée shot in the stomach.

Willow suddenly gasps, horrified.

Ethan's features tense, his jaw locking.

"Is she okay?" Willow asks, her meanness drained right out of her.

"She's recovering," I say. Since I'm still holding her against me, I feel her sag a little with relief. Now *I'm* starting to feel weird about this position, so I do finally let the girl go.

She bolts away from me, moving to Ethan's side, but she looks a little more distressed now, less angry. "My father and I don't really have much of a relationship," she tells me. "He's not a great person, obviously."

"He's scum, is what he is," I inform her, meeting her gaze.

Dropping mine, as if embarrassed by her own connection to him, she nods.

"She already knows that," Ethan states, wrapping a protective arm around Willow. She wraps an arm around him, leaning into his side for comfort.

"Just making sure we're all on the same page," I tell him.

"We are," he assures me, nodding.

"I want Willow to call him," I state, glancing from him to her. "I want you to ask him to meet you, tell him it's important, you have big news, something to lure him out."

"Why?" she asks, quietly.

I'm sure she already knows why. "He won't bring a heavy entourage to meet you," I state. "He's come completely unguarded in the past. I doubt he will now, but... he'll probably bring a body guard, nothing more."

"I can't do that," she says, shaking her head. "He's a bad man, I know that, but I can't... You want me to help you kill him, and I can't do that."

I glance to Ethan. He looks a little less sure—like he agrees with her, but only because he loves her, not because he'd be even a little sad about Antonio's passing.

Sighing, I drop my gun hand, letting it point at the ground. It's time for the *big* guns, not the little metal one.

"I've met your brother a few times over the years, but most recently when he came to me with this crazy idea that my boss was behind *your* abduction and subsequent... abuse."

Willow's eyes widen and her cheeks flush. I feel bad bringing it up, letting her know I know, but I need to tap into any negative emotions that whole experience stirred in her.

Ethan's grip on her tightens, another protective impulse. None of her negative emotions seem to be wrapped up in him somehow, even when I mention that—even when he was the perpetrator. This doesn't surprise me as much as it should. Obviously I've been working for Mateo for too long.

There's no shielding her from the truth, though. Not now.

"Because my boss doesn't like being blamed for shit he didn't do, and because *I* don't like men who abuse women, I decided to use some of my free time to do a little digging. As far as I could tell, nobody ever figured out who was behind what happened to you." I watch Ethan now, to see if he *does* know. I'm sure he looked into it, but I don't know what he found. Judging by his expression, I don't think he knows.

Then he can't help asking, "Did you find anything?"

"I did," I say, nodding. "I didn't care so much back then, and once your brother realized where I was going with it, he didn't want my help anymore—probably easier to just ignore things. So, I left it alone. Wasn't my problem, and I have enough of my own." I pause, pressing my lips firmly together for a moment. "But now it is my problem. People are dying because of your father—a lot of people. And they're going to *keep* dying if something isn't done. And so, while I really hate having to tell you this, Willow... your abduction was funded by your father."

Her head starts shaking slowly, but it doesn't stop. She just shakes and shakes and shakes her head, rejecting what I've just said.

"Yes," I say, with a single nod.

"Are you fucking kidding me?" Ethan demands, stunned.

I shake my head. "It was his first attempt to turn his family on Mateo. Tito used to work for us—for Delmonico, he had him on his crew. Fired him, because Tito's a liability and we don't really keep on liabilities. Antonio picked him up, had him assemble a crew under the guise of still working for Delmonico. None of you assholes needed much proof, I guess. When the job was done, Castellanos killed off everyone who could talk—everyone but you, because Willow wouldn't let him, from what I understand."

"Why?" Willow asks, her voice small. "How could you...?"

"He knew that coming after his children would be enough to ignite a war. He thought he could kill everyone off, make it look like Mateo just covered his tracks, and then no one would've been the wiser. Problem is, Salvatore was smart enough to bring it to us. To get all the facts before engaging a war. The facts weren't on Antonio's side."

"But why me?" she asks, shaking her head again. "Why *me*?"

Shrugging apologetically, I tell her, "I can't say with absolute certainty, but if I had to guess, he wanted one of his kids hit, just... not one he was close to, in case it all went bad."

With a little guffaw of disbelief, she says, "So, I was just the most expendable option."

"Do you have proof?" Ethan asks, features set in a thunderous scowl. "Do you have evidence that this is true?"

"I do. I have a whole folder. I'll show it to you, if you need it. I wouldn't make up something this heinous, believe me."

"That son of a bitch," Ethan says, shaking his head. He still looks surprised, but he's clearly putting it together in his mind. Then, to Willow, he says, "*This* is why he came to my house. It wasn't to defend you at all, it was to cover his own fucking ass."

Ethan is angry, but Willow looks a little traumatized. I guess I understand. Hearing that your own father cares so little for you that he used you as a pawn in the name of business, that he had you kidnapped, terrified, abused—that he ruined your life to further his own agenda? That can't be easy to swallow.

"I need to be alone," Willow says.

She turns to leave, and I want to let her, I really do, but I remind her, "Willow... I really need you to call him."

"No, you don't," Ethan says, shaking his head. Turning to Willow, he touches her shoulder and tells her, "Go ahead."

"Ethan," I say, meeting his gaze with an unspoken warning.

He meets mine, his blue eyes burning with vengeance. "You don't need her to call him. You need *me*."

CHAPTER TWENTY THREE

"HE'LL SHOW up if you call?" I ask, a bit skeptically.

Willow glances between us, then decides this isn't worth an argument and heads down the hall, closing herself inside what I assume is their bedroom.

Ethan nods, patting the pocket of his jeans, feeling for his phone. "Yeah, he'll show up for me." Turning on his heel, he heads back to the living room.

I glance down the hall where Willow went—I don't suspect she was faking her reaction, but it crosses my mind anyway. In her position, she could've retreated to the bedroom to retrieve a weapon of her own, or to call ahead and warn her piece of shit father that I'm coming for him.

Since I don't think I have to worry about the former, I ask about the latter. "Would she call to warn him?"

Ethan shakes his head, grabbing his cell phone off the coffee table. "No. Not now. That asshole put us both through hell. I'd be thoroughly pissed off at her if she did something like that now, and she knows that."

"You sure?"

"Yep."

"I still think Willow's the better bet. I know he won't bring a heavy guard to meet her, I don't know what he'll bring to meet you."

"I meet him unguarded all the time," Ethan grumbles.

This is news. Eyebrows rising, I ask, "Why?"

Glancing back toward the bedroom, he says, "Let's go outside."

I figure he means the hall, but Ethan doesn't stop until we make it to his car. He nods to the passenger side for me to get in, and though I'm not at all used to being a passenger, I do.

"Why hasn't he killed me?" Ethan suddenly asks, staring out his windshield.

I shrug. "Salvatore said it was because you're with Willow. You weren't looking into it anymore and enough time's passed now, he probably figured it wasn't a major threat. If she ever left you, he probably would've, just to tie up the loose end."

"That's fucking awesome," he remarks.

"Isn't it?"

Ethan nods. "So, how do we do this? Do you have more people coming, or what?"

I shake my head. "No. I'm gonna take him out myself."

"I don't think that's a good idea," Ethan says. "What if he *doesn't* show up alone? I mean, I do meet him unguarded all the time, but that's when he's calling the meeting. If I'm calling it, even for a good reason, he might bring a couple people." Before I can say anything, he says, "And if Willow called, he wouldn't have come. Not right now, not with everything that's going on. He's in hiding right now. He's not coming out unless there's something on the line—and no, he obviously wouldn't care if Willow was on the line."

"So what's on the line?"

Ethan sighs, glancing back at the entrance to his apartment. "Leave that to me. I know what to tell him to get him to show up. I've been doing work for Salvatore for a while now. It started out legit, but... he started asking me to do more, and I needed the money." Glancing back at me, he adds, "Willow doesn't know."

"She wouldn't approve?"

He shakes his head. "She wouldn't want me putting myself at risk."

That's understandable. Kind of hard for me to relate to, since all the women I'm around on a daily basis accept our lifestyle as normal, but I can see why outsiders would object.

"Well, what happens next isn't your responsibility. You make the call, I'll take care of the rest," I tell him.

"The hell it isn't. If I set this up and you fail, he's gonna know what I did. Then he *will* kill me. You've got Mateo Morelli's army at your disposal—why do this alone?"

"Because I don't know who I can fucking trust anymore, Ethan. We've had some bumps in the road lately and I'd rather show up to this showdown not having to worry that my own fucking people are going to turn on me."

"Oh."

"I also don't want him to see me coming. I bring an army, that's not exactly subtle, now, is it?"

"Well… he usually brings Little John with him wherever he goes, but Little John went down with the Morelli attempt." Glancing at me, as if this is news, he says, "You don't shoot at a boss and live to tell the story."

I meet his gaze dryly. "Thank you for that lesson in my own lifestyle, Ethan; I had no idea."

"You're gonna get yourself killed."

"Not if he shows up without a guard."

Ethan pulls his phone out, sighing, and stares at it for a moment. He's full of reluctance, but oddly it seems less like he's worried about crossing his father-in-law and more about me. Which, considering I've never met this man in my life, surprises me. Clearly I'm not accustomed to being around people who are still in touch with their humanity.

"What if we switch?"

Uncomprehending, I frown. "Switch what?"

"Assuming he brings a guard, and assuming *you* could take care of them quietly... what if *I* meet with Antonio? What if you take out the guards... and I shoot him?"

"You ever killed a man before?"

He shakes his head. "Nope."

"This isn't a good try-out."

"I know what's on the line," he states, looking at me. "I won't change my mind."

"It's not as easy as you might think," I tell him. "Especially not the first time. Evil bastard or not, it's not a fucking video game. You're not prepared."

"Well, maybe there's no guard, then I won't have to. Then you can take care of it. All I know is, we both have better chances if mine is the face Antonio sees."

I go over his plan in my head, and I kinda like it. I don't know if I can depend on him to pull the trigger when it comes down to it, but depending on the layout, this might be doable. Too many variables to be sure. I don't know where we're meeting, I don't know if his guard will be directly near him or just keeping watch—there are a lot of fucking variables. It's got better odds than mine though, assuming he has soldiers with him.

"All right," I agree with a nod. "Let's do it."

Ethan gets out of the car to make the call, which I'm not terribly comfortable with. Could be he's setting *me* up, but I don't get that feeling from his vibe or his language. He specifically said he works for Salvatore, not Antonio—and Salvatore doesn't have his own crew. He's an underboss, same as Mateo technically should've been before Matt died, but we aren't bound by the same rules of leadership as Salvatore's family. If Ethan did work for Salvatore, he was technically doing work for Antonio, but he didn't want to claim that because he doesn't like the old man. You don't naturally put that kind of distance between yourself and someone unless there's a whole lot of dislike there.

I also just don't think Ethan's very deceptive. I had different expectations of the guy coming in—he doesn't look so good on paper. But having met him, he's actually pretty okay.

Opening the car door, he drops back into his seat, actually looking a little excited. "All right, he's gonna meet me."

"You're sure?" I ask, catching his gaze.

"Yep."

I feel like I've been trying to kill this bastard half my life. It hasn't been that long, but it *feels* like forever. It feels a little surreal to consider it might actually be coming to a close.

"Well, what did he say? Where are we meeting him? Does he expect just you?"

"Not just me. Me and two others, but all harmless. He won't be on guard. I even made up a diversion so he'd send some guys elsewhere."

"An obvious diversion?" I ask sharply.

Shaking his head, he turns the key in the ignition. "It went with my story." Then, meeting my gaze, he says, "Relax, Adrian; this isn't my first rodeo, either."

We're halfway to Castellanos when Mateo calls me.

I think about not answering, but Mateo hates being ignored.

"Yeah?" I answer, determined to at least keep it short.

"Adrian." His tone is terse, and I instantly go on alert. "How far are you from the bakery?"

"The bakery?" I ask, eyebrows rising. "I'm nowhere near it. Why?"

"Fuck," he mutters. "All right. Where are you? I need you to meet me somewhere."

"I can't meet you anywhere right now," I tell him. "I've got my hands full with something else. Can you call Alec instead?"

"No, I don't want Alec," he says, more to himself than me. "All right, fine. I'll take care of it myself."

"You sure? I can probably call around and get you someone."

"Nah, I got it." Then, without so much as a goodbye, he's gone.

I stare at my phone for a minute, thinking that probably requires my attention… but it can't be more important than this. I consider calling him back to get more information, but I need to focus on my own thing. I'll call him back as soon as we're done.

Ethan glances over at me briefly before returning his gaze to the road. "Everything okay?"

"Hope so," I reply, shaking my head. "I'll be glad when all this shit is over, I'll tell you that."

"Yeah, I bet," he says, nodding in understanding. "There's gotta be a lot of excitement, doing what you do."

"I don't know if excitement's the word I'd use," I return, dryly.

"Thankfully I don't typically do this kind of shit. I deal in information, not violence."

"I much prefer to deal in information. If Salvatore doesn't make the right decision and we have to wipe out his whole family, you should come work for Mateo."

Laughing shortly, Ethan says, "Oh yeah, I'll get right on that."

I shrug. "He pays well."

"He's a paranoid sociopath."

"You get used to it."

Finally, we arrive. I'm a little puzzled to find the meeting place is a house—just a regular house in a suburban neighborhood.

Scowling over at Ethan, I ask, "You're not dumb enough to set me up, are you?"

"Nope," he says easily. "Just slightly smarter than that."

"Because I can't begin to explain to you the wrath Mateo would rain down upon you if you are. And you have a pretty girlfriend, so I'd think about that."

Sliding me a distinct look of displeasure, he says, "Fiancée."

"I'm never going to care."

"This is…" He pauses, looking at the garage door and sighing. "This is my old house, and this is where he's meeting us. I'm not setting you up, Adrian. Antonio Castellanos tied my 8-year-old daughter to a chair in this house—threatened to kill her. Had an asshole with a gun to her head. I can murder this piece of shit and sleep like a baby tonight, I promise you that."

Well, shit.

"I guess he wasn't invited to the wedding, huh?" I murmur.

Ethan rolls his eyes and pushes open his car door.

Once we're inside, Ethan glances around the entryway and sighs. I don't know if he's thinking about the shit we're about to do, or some sentimental shit, but after a minute he finally says, "I'll be right back."

"Where are you going?"

"Upstairs. I need to get a gun." He shows me his hands, indicating they're empty. "Didn't bring one. And I don't have a silencer."

"I have an extra in my car, but we brought yours."

He shakes his head, heading for the stairs. "Don't need it. I can get one upstairs."

"Nothing stupid, Ethan."

"I fucking get it, Adrian."

I smile a little as he heads upstairs. I do want to keep an eye on him, since this is all unfamiliar to me and I'm not exactly on comfortable ground, but first I take a walk around the house, scoping out potential spots to hide, checking vulnerabilities, windows—all the usual bullshit. I'm a little confused when I get to the kitchen and see a pink vase of white hydrangeas on the table. Ethan bringing me here to meet Castellanos gave me the impression that this house is unoccupied, and the fact that he knows we're about to dirty it up with blood and bullet holes doesn't jive with anything else.

Ethan comes back down a couple minutes later, to my relief. I actually like the guy, but I'm still not inclined to trust him—not until Antonio's dead.

"Does someone live here?" I ask, as soon as I see him.

"My ex-wife used to, but she and the kids moved in with her boyfriend," he says, rolling his eyes.

"There are flowers on the table. You trying to sell the place?"

Instead of answering me, Ethan frowns, peering out the window. "Fuck, he's here. All right, if he's alone, we're good. If not, at least one of his people will probably do a walk-through. I'd go to the kitchen, since they'll probably walk in there first."

I'm not used to being directed and I don't really like it, but there's not time to argue. I head to the kitchen, but I wish I would've had more time to prepare. I can't look out the window and watch him come in, 'cause chances are they'll be looking.

It feels like the sound of the door slamming shut resonates through the whole damn house. My pulse kicks up, and being in the kitchen when everything's going down in the living room is *not* my style. I don't even know how long to wait. If no one sweeps the kitchen in the next minute or so, I'm going to creep back toward the entryway and scope out the scene.

Waiting is hard. It's the longest two minute wait ever. And no one comes in.

I give up waiting.

He's either alone, with an idiot, or Ethan's double-crossing me and I'm in deep shit anyway. Whatever the case may be, it's time to find out.

When I approach the entryway, I see Ethan and Antonio in the living room, standing in front of a couch. I creep along the wall so I can move closer, to the area beside the stairs. I won't be able to see from there, but I need to wait another minute to make sure he didn't bring someone who may have gone upstairs first.

But then I hear the *pop* and the heavy thud. My heartbeat kicks up and I move forward, hoping that wasn't Ethan who just dropped.

It wasn't.

Ethan is doubled over, hands braced on his thighs, and Antonio Castellanos is on the floor, bleeding. Not dead though— he moves.

I don't waste another second. Hustling over to the old man's side, I meet his gaze, point my gun at his head, and fire.

"Sorry," Ethan mutters.

I step away from the old man's corpse to give Ethan a jovial pat on the back. "Don't be. You're basically my second best friend right now."

He laughs a little at that. "I'm not sure that's company I want to be in."

"You okay?" I ask, seriously.

"I feel a little… vomity."

Nodding, I assure him, "You always do the first time. Hey, look, you didn't even have to kill him. I did that."

"I really wanted to give him an awesome monologue first, let him know I was onto his bullshit, but I was too afraid he'd shoot first," Ethan says, smiling as he rights himself.

"Monologues are overrated," I tell him. "He's dead, that's what matters."

"I know, but throwing your own daughter into sex slavery to try to take down a nemesis? He should've died knowing she knew that."

"Now it's over and she can move on," I tell him.

Ethan sighs, pulling his cell phone out of his pocket and sending a text. "I'm gonna have to take her to the French Riviera to get her mind off things."

Are we *all* going on victory vacations?

Actually, the French Riviera sounds really good. And Elise loves when I speak French.

"Hey, good call," I tell him.

He looks at me questioningly, but I don't explain. "Well, I'll get someone in here to clean this up. But now that we've taken care of this, there's one other matter to attend to. You need to take me to Salvatore. I don't want to hurt him, I just want to talk."

Ethan nods. "I figured that was next on the list. And being the swell second best friend that I am, I already thought of it."

I frown and follow him to the entryway. He's just going to take me to Salvatore like that? Damn, I should've brought all this shit to Ethan a long time ago.

Only, he doesn't head for the door.

He stops at the bottom of the stair case and looks up.

There at the top, in all his cocky, smirking, pain in the ass glory, is Salvatore Castellanos.

And the icing on top of the cake? At his side, her arm wrapped possessively around his waist, stands Francesca Morelli.

The End...

Not really. I need to stop lying before I turn into a Morelli.
FAMILY TIES IS NEXT!
But for now, check out the **ALTERNATE ENDING**!

ALTERNATE ENDING

This deleted chapter is actually an alternate ending! Adrian had to end the book since it's *his* book, but what did Mateo need him for? Let's find out!

Mia

THE FRANK FAMILY should have been here to pick up their cake an hour ago.

I grab my phone and shoot a message to Meg—she's bored, and we're having a GIF-off. While I peruse for just the right Will Ferrell GIF, the doorbells chime.

I drop my phone on the counter and glance up at the man walking through the door. He looks grumpy—middle-aged, kinda puffy, a look on his face like he just wanted to stay home and watch the game, but his wife sent him here instead.

Are there any games to watch in the summer? Maybe baseball? I don't know. Sports are boring.

"Hi, what can I do for you today?" I ask him.

Mark flies in from the back—and I do mean *flies*. He has to grab onto me to steady himself so his momentum doesn't fling him into the counter.

At least, that's what I assume. But then he doesn't let me go. He pulls me into him, securing me with one arm, the other… He has a gun.

My blood turns to ice in my veins.

"I got her," he tells the guy on the other side of the display.

"Mark, what the fuck?" I manage, through the feeling of immense betrayal sinking through me.

Sweatpants says, "This ain't your assignment."

"Sal wanted me on it. He wants her alive."

"What the *fuck*?" I repeat, my eyes widening. I turn my head back to look at Mark, but his face tells me literally nothing. Where is the expressive friend who beat me at a pesto cook-off? What the hell is this bullshit?

"Well, Antonio doesn't," Sweatpants replies, eyebrows lifting like he's one-upped him.

I think there's a stand-off of some sort. Sweatpants stares down Mark, Mark stares down Sweatpants. I sweat my ass off. I can't process what's happening. Just a minute ago I was worried about a cake, and now there's Mark with a gun, and some Castellanos flunky, apparently? And also, Mark is in league with them?

"I'll take her. I'll take her right now."

"That's not what I was sent to do," Sweatpants states. "They moved on our guys. It's war, and Antonio wants blood."

"Oh, all right," Mark says, more easily than I appreciate. "Well, let me call Sal first, clear it with him. Then I'll hand her off to you. Bruce with you?"

Sweatpants shakes his head, sniffling and looking back over his shoulder. "Nah, didn't expect this to be too hard. Bruce is setting up something else."

Mark nods, his grip on me tightening. "I'll call you after I talk to him."

"Why don't you just call him right now?"

Mark jerks his head toward the ceiling. "Morelli's got this

whole place under surveillance. They're probably already on their way."

Sweatpants mutters a really filthy curse—honestly, even after listening to Mateo's mouth it makes me grimace. Then he nods in acquiescence. "All right. You need help with the girl?"

"No, she won't give me any trouble," he says, glancing down at me. Then he smirks a little, not a nice smile, and it makes my stomach hurt. He's supposed to be my friend, and I'm an idiot for believing that. "Actually, I think she likes me, don't you, honey?"

"No," I mutter, looking away from him.

Sweatpants seems vaguely amused by this.

Mark's smile turns self-deprecating. "Maybe not. You wanna escort me to the car, make sure she doesn't try to run?"

"Sure," Sweatpants says, flipping the sign on the door to closed and following Mark as he drags me out the back.

"You're going to regret this," I inform him, looking around for something, anything I could grab onto. Maybe I could hit Mark—but then there's Sweatpants, and he wants me dead, apparently?

My phone. I left my phone on the counter. How will they even know I was taken? Yes, Mateo has this place under surveillance, but he doesn't monitor it. No one will even know to look for me until I don't come home from work, and that's hours from now. I could be dead by then.

That terrifying realization settles on me and I miss a step. Mark scowls at me and tugs me closer. "I've had my eye on this one for a while," Mark goes on, conversationally. "Boyfriend's a real asshole. I've had to listen to all the girl talk. Kind of glad this is finally happening."

Sweatpants snorts. "Yeah, she looks like a real princess."

I realize it's absurd to be offended by the observations of those who plan to kill you, but I still am.

We approach Mark's car, an old, beige rust-box. I recall Adrian coming in to buy a cake, asking me about Mark. It's the only sliver of hope I have. If Adrian looked into him after he left, maybe he found something.

It's only a sliver though, because if he had? Mark wouldn't be here. I don't know how quickly they're able to find information on people, but I'm kind of banking on Adrian crashing in to save the day any minute now.

"You are so dead," I inform Mark, since all I can do at this point is lash out. "You're basically a ghost already, that's how dead you are."

"Yeah?" he asks, almost congenially. "Which one of your boyfriends is gonna kill me?"

I glare at him for that one, and he actually looks genuinely amused.

"Sorry, it was too easy," he states.

I raise my eyebrows haughtily. "It's okay. Get your laughs in while you can, Casper."

"You're so cocky for someone whose life is in my hands," he informs me. "I feel like Mateo got a much better response than this under those circumstances."

I give an outright guffaw. "You're no Mateo."

He frowns, then pulls a slight pout. "Hey now, you don't have to be mean." We're at the passenger side of his car now, and he glances from Sweatpants to me. "I don't suppose you want to be obedient and just get in the car?"

I just glare. I haven't decided how to play this. Mark wants me dead less than Sweatpants, so I probably don't want to be enough trouble that Sweatpants tags along. But I also don't want to get in the car, because as soon as I leave the bakery, I don't know how anyone will find me to rescue me.

Once I'm handed off to Sweatpants, my chances of saving *myself* significantly decrease.

So I decide, "I'll get in the car."

"Oh, good," Mark says. "That makes my life slightly easier."

I'm not happy about it, but I slide into the passenger seat of his car, crossing my arms over my chest, wanting to make sure he understands how huffy I am.

Mark shuts my door, then follows Sweatpants around the back of the car. I take advantage of the moment alone to search for something to defend myself, rifling through his glove compartment for a gun. Apparently he hasn't seen enough movies, because there's not one in there.

An explosive pop scares the shit out of me and I jump, a small scream slipping out of me.

I twist to look behind me, but then I see Mark opening the door, a grim expression on his face. He slides into the driver's seat, and I crane my head, looking for Sweatpants, but I don't see him.

"What just happened?" I ask, confused.

"I just fucked myself," he states, reaching into the center console, pulling out a false bottom, and retrieving a phone. "I need you to call Mateo."

"No," I say, frowning.

"You want him to come get you? I'm not going to hurt you. Tell him to come alone."

"No," I say again. If he wants Mateo alone, it's because he wants to hurt him. "You've been lying to me all along. You work for the bad guys."

Mark snorts, looking at me as if to see if I'm joking. "We both work for the bad guys, Mia."

I refuse to call Mateo.

Mostly because I don't want him to get hurt, and also because I don't know his phone number.

Mark doesn't know that last part, he just thinks I'm excessively stubborn.

We're at a hotel now. A cheap little one floor hotel that makes me nervous. He goes outside and makes a call, presumably to Salvatore Castellanos, and when he comes back in, he sits on the bed and stares at me.

"Call Mateo."

I shake my head again.

His head droops and he pinches the bridge of his nose. "Mia, I'm trying really hard to keep you alive. Like, really hard. But you're starting to piss me off."

"You don't need Mateo. If all you want is to keep me alive, to hand me off to my side, you could give me to anyone. Vince, Adrian—even a nobody. It wouldn't matter. If only Mateo will do, then I call bullshit. You're lying to me, like you've *been* lying to me, and I won't help you hurt him."

"I need Mateo because I need to give him *information*. I can't give it to Adrian because he'll kill me, and Vince…" He shakes his head, rolling his eyes. "I don't trust Vince. I don't want anybody else. I want Mateo."

"He won't come," I tell him, shaking my head. "Even if I called, he wouldn't come. He's not an idiot. If it looks like a trap and smells like a trap…"

"But it's *not* a trap. Look, I can leave you here in this hotel and let you find your own way, but that won't solve this thing. They're going to notice Arturo missing and it won't be too hard to figure out what happened. *I* need to get the fuck out of here, and every minute I waste arguing with you is a minute I can't afford."

"Why?" I ask, scowling. "You were clearly on their side."

"I'm not a baker, but I wasn't a spy. I mean…" He looks off to the side, sighing. "I spied, sure, but I was there to protect Francesca. I didn't technically have to come back after she disappeared, but… I wanted to keep you safe."

That gives me pause. He seems sincere, but I'm still reeling from the knowledge that he's duped me for the entire time I've known him. How do I know if I can trust anything he's saying?

"Please, Mia. Just call him."

I sigh, looking down at my hands in my lap. "I can't. I don't actually know his number, and I left my phone at the bakery."

Mark just stares at me. "You're kidding."

I shake my head. "Not at all."

"Well, can't you get it? Call Vince."

I scoff. He's *heard* my girl talk; he has to know that isn't happening.

"Meg?"

Okay, I could call Meg. Her number's really easy to remember, so I actually do have that one stored in my brain.

"You promise you're not going to hurt him?"

He shakes his head. "I'm on the anti-war side. I don't want a Morelli beef."

"Understand that if you're lying to me, I'll figure out how to work a gun and shoot you myself."

He snorts, rolling his eyes. "Okay."

"I'm not kidding," I inform him.

Mark sighs. "I'm not going to shoot your stupid mob boss boyfriend."

I give him another glare for good measure, then I finally take the phone and push in Meg's phone number.

"Hello?" she answers, a bit uncertainly.

I wasn't sure she'd answer at all, since it's an unknown number. I eye up Mark again, searching his face for any signs of inappropriate emotions. Excitement, because I'm going along with his trick? I see nothing. He looks stressed, but in no way eager.

"It's Mia," I tell her.

"Oh," she says, sounding surprised. "Did your phone die?"

"No, I don't have it on me," I say, wondering just how much to reveal. I don't want to stress her out, what with the pregnancy and everything, so I decide to keep it brief. "Listen, can you do me a favor? I don't have Mateo's phone number, but I need to talk to him. Could you give him this number and have him call me right away?"

"Sure. Is everything okay?"

"I'm not sure," I say honestly.

"I'll get it to him right now."

"Thank you."

I hang up that call and dread courses through me. I cradle the phone in my hands, staring at it, my heart starting to race with the adrenaline suddenly moving through me. I want him to call and I don't. I don't want to ask him to come here. I don't want to hear doubt in his voice, knowing he's wondering if he can trust me. I don't want to know if I'm right and he won't even come for me.

"What am I supposed to say?" I ask Mark.

"I just need you to get him on the phone and let him know you're really here. I'll do the rest."

"This is a terrible idea," I inform him. "If you're not a bad guy, I don't want you to get killed, and this seems like a really good way to get murdered."

"I'm going to use you as a human shield," he informs me.

My phone rings.

I nearly jump out of my skin, and my heart slams around my chest, anticipating his voice on the other line. I don't even think I'm in any real danger—from Mark, at least—but this feels incredibly daunting. I desperately want to answer and very much *don't* at the same time.

Swallowing, I accept the call and put the phone to my ear. "Hey."

"What's wrong?" he asks, immediately.

My heart jumps again. Anxiety pours through me, partially because of his no-nonsense, alert tone, and partially because I'm afraid of this conversation on so many levels. "I'm okay," I begin, because that seems important. "But... I've sort of been taken?"

"Taken?" he asks sharply.

"Um, some guy came to the bakery—a Castellanos guy, I think. He mentioned Antonio. I'm not with him," I add, looking to

Mark, who finally stands and comes over, but doesn't take the phone yet. "Mark from the bakery…"

Now Mark takes the phone. "Mark here," he says, with not nearly enough fear. This asshat should be shaking in his boots! "I work for Salvatore, not Antonio. I don't want to hurt Mia, but I need you to come alone to get her." He pauses, listening to Mateo's response, I guess. "Like I said, I don't want to hurt her; I just can't have you bringing your goon squad along. I didn't even intend to do this, but you guys hit our guys, and weirdly enough, nobody's very happy about it. I have *no* back-up, I sort of went rogue to save Mia, so I'd really like to leave this hotel room alive." He grimaces, falling silent. "Jesus. I wasn't—it was just the first place—" He stops again, raising his eyebrows and looking at me.

I shrug, because how am I supposed to know?

Holding up a finger at me, he heads for the door, opening it, and heading outside.

I hear mumbling, but I can't make out what he's saying. A few minutes later he comes back inside, no longer on the phone.

"I thought he wasn't supposed to have a temper," Mark states, looking at me like I've lied to him.

I shake my head. "He doesn't."

"Oh, yeah he does. I expected even-keeled sociopath. I'm very disappointed in the reliability of reputations right now."

I can't bite back a little grin. "He was really mad at you, huh?"

"I thought I was joking about him being your boyfriend," he states, raising an eyebrow.

"You know Vince is," I say.

"Does he?"

I attempt to bite back a little smile, but I fail horribly.

Mark keeps watch out the front window. There are only windows along the front of the unit, none along the sides or the back, so according to Mark, we do not have a great position. He says this as if we're on the same side, and I'm still not positive we are, but I'm being optimistic.

I point out he should've considered that when he was picking a place. He reminds me that this wasn't something he had time to plan. I guess I can't argue with that.

This not being a plan is also why I think he probably really *isn't* trying to kill Mateo. If this was a plot, it would be going more smoothly, right?

"He's here." Mark swallows, backing away from the window and coming over to grab me. I wasn't sure he was telling the truth about the human shield thing, but apparently he was. "If he tries to kill me, can you please speak up on my behalf?" he requests. "I could've left you here and got the hell out of dodge, but I'm trying to make peace and I really don't want to die for my efforts."

"I'll try," I offer.

Mark takes a breath and pushes it out, like he'd dreading this as much as I am.

"Get the door," he tells me. "Ask him if he's alone."

Mateo hasn't pounded on it to alert us to his presence, but I don't wait for that. I ease it open just in time to see him storming my way, expression stony. At the sight of me, his expression wavers, his eyes sweeping over me, taking inventory of how I look, if I've been harmed.

"Move," he says.

"Wait," I say, holding my arms out, barring the door. He scowls, but my gaze goes to the gun he already has at the ready. I glance back at Mark, making sure he isn't doing anything stupid, but he's not. He does have his gun out, but more like he wants to be able to defend himself than because he wants to use it.

"Let's all take a second here," I say. "Let's leave the guns out of this. I'm not hurt. No one needs to get hurt."

"He kidnapped you," Mateo states.

"He was protecting me," I point out.

"He hasn't touched you?"

"Of course not," I say, frowning.

He doesn't put his gun away, but he comes at me in a way that lets me know if I don't move, he'll run right over me.

So I move.

Mark grabs my arm, pulling me in front of him—his human shield.

Mateo's eyes narrow, like Mark's an especially annoying bug that he can't wait to smash against the wall. "Vince never liked you. I should've paid more attention to that."

"I'm a friend, not a foe," Mark assures him.

"Then let go of Mia," Mateo responds, reasonably.

"I know it's not much, but I'm sort of attached to my face the way it is, without a gaping bullet hole anywhere in this general vicinity," Mark says, indicating his own head.

"The longer your hands are on Mia, the less chance it stays that way," Mateo states.

Mark drops his hand from my arm, but I don't move right away. I watch Mateo's hand, the one on his gun, to make sure it doesn't look like he's about to use it.

"Get over here," Mateo says, meeting my gaze.

My good intentions fly right out the window and I hustle my ass over to his side. "Is Adrian here?" I murmur, staying near him.

He shakes his head. "He's busy with something else. Something I'd very much like to pursue the details of, but I'm doing this shit instead."

I flush. "Sorry."

He finally pulls his gaze from Mark long enough to flash me a dry look. "Yes, because this was clearly your fault." Swinging his gaze back to Mark, he demands, "What's this information you have for me?"

"Salvatore doesn't want a war with you. He had no idea his father was going to try to kill you—he never would've supported that."

"Like he never would've framed Meg?"

For a split second, Mark frowns, looking from Mateo to me, then back. "He knew war was coming, he didn't want to get in the middle of it. He needed you distracted."

"I don't take well to that kind of manipulation from *friends*," Mateo says. "And there wouldn't have *been* a war if his father wouldn't have nearly killed my fiancée."

My heart sinks, hearing him call Meg his fiancée. I immediately feel so guilty and horrible about it that I want to die, but I can't deny it happening.

Mark hesitates. "I don't know what you know, and it doesn't seem like you're in the mood for any surprises right now."

"I'm not in the habit of shooting the messenger," Mateo tells him.

"You know Antonio sent Meg?"

My eyes widen in surprise, but Mateo merely nods. "I do."

"Okay. Well... you've taken that better than Sal thought you would," Mark says, looking a bit confused.

"His distraction worked a little too well. I was more focused on the affair," Mateo states. "By the time that came out... bigger fish."

"Okay. Well, considering your usual response to treachery, Sal was prepared for a bigger reaction than that. Anyway, his dad..." Mark pauses, watching Mateo, then says, "He understands that his dad's gonna have to go."

I can't tell if this surprises Mateo. He keeps his expression guarded, but he does drawl, "Really?"

"Salvatore's next in line. He wants to keep the peace, the way you have been until Antonio started screwing it all up. He wants... a marriage, of sorts, between the families. Not even of sorts, actually... he wants to marry your sister."

My jaw falls open, hand flying to my chest. Since Mateo's reaction is far less dramatic, Mark's eyes drift to me. "Francesca?" I ask, floored. "Salvatore and Francesca? Oh my god!" Tugging on Mateo's arm, I say, "You have to let them. Francesca would be so ha—Er, wait, does she want to marry him, or is this a Castellanos version of a Morelli trap?"

Nobody answers me.

"I'll consider it," Mateo says, not even bothering to ask whether or not Francesca's into the idea. "No middle men though. If Salvatore wants to work something out, he needs to come out of hiding and meet with me himself."

"As long as you're open to peace, I'm sure he will."

Mateo nods once.

Mark nods a few times, clearly uneasy. "So… I'm gonna go?"

"I think that's a good idea."

Mark nods, heading for the door, still a little cautious though, keeping an eye on Mateo. "Um, I kinda had to kill a guy in the parking lot of your bakery."

Mateo sighs, tucking his gun away and pulling his phone out of his pocket. "I'll take care of it."

"Awesome." Glancing at me, Mark offers an apologetic look, then he opens the door and slips outside.

"There's no one waiting to kill him outside, right?" I ask, looking toward the window, but I can't see out the dark curtains.

Mateo smirks, tucking his phone back into his pocket and gazing down at me. All the hardness I've sensed from the moment he answered the phone has fallen away, and he grips my hips, turning me to face him. He seems relieved. I stare up at him, certain organs pounding so loudly they can probably be heard in the next room over, other locations on my body inappropriately tingling. It's a jumbled, scarlet-letter-wearing mess over here.

"No, I was going to handle that one myself," he tells me.

"I have a lot of questions about a lot of things," I tell him.

"I can imagine." There's amusement dancing in his eyes again, and this is how I like him best. There's something about his scary side that turns me on, but it's the playful side that stirs my heart.

God, I am a *mess*.

"I can't believe you came for me," I tell him.

"As many times as you've come through for me, I think I owed you one," he informs me.

I roll my eyes lightly. "I don't do you favors so you'll *owe* me," I say. "There's no one keeping track."

"I always keep track," he responds lightly.

I want so badly to wrap my arms around his neck. I can literally feel my insides trying to close the small distance between us, like there's a magnet inside of his body pulling at mine.

And it tears me apart. Because I have *every reason* to stay away. We both do. There are no reasons to close the distance, not one. There are no reasons to keep standing here with his hands on my hips like they belong there, our bodies separated by measly inches, heated memories of our bodies being much closer suddenly flooding my mind.

Then, as if similar thoughts are going through his head, he glances at the bed.

We're in a hotel room. Alone. With a bed.

I'm so terrified—not of him this time, but myself. A little of him. Because if he so much as makes a joke about that bed, I'm going to crumble into a million pieces.

But he doesn't joke. The amusement in his eyes dies, and he looks back at me more solemnly.

I wish I could read his mind, but I don't even think I'd be able to handle it. This is hard enough knowing I'm alone in this torment, but when he looks at me like maybe he feels it, too….

"We should leave," I state, before either of us can act on anything we shouldn't.

"We should," he agrees, but doesn't move.

I can feel my heart beating in my throat. As if they have their own plans, my arms move slowly to his broad shoulders, creeping around his neck. He studies me, and I think I'm going to pass out from the stress. Before he can take it the wrong way—and accept or rebuff me, because I have no idea which one of those would hurt more—I lean in for a hug.

I'm allowed to have a hug, right?

Hugs are harmless. You can hug a family member.

He hugs me back, one of his hands moving up to caress my back.

Everything's thumping. I'm so aroused and guilty and just the worst person in the whole world, but as Mateo holds me, for just a moment, I don't care. I let go of the guilt, of the anguish over my horribly inappropriate feelings, and just enjoy the feeling of his embrace.

I want to stay here with him forever. I never want to leave this crummy hotel room.

God, I am in *so* much trouble.

It lasts far too long for a hug, but before it can morph into anything more, I pull back.

I swallow, but there's a lump in my throat. It's all too much, and I feel like I'm going to dissolve any minute—like the pressure is just too much, and my mind and body can't handle it anymore, so they're just going to give up.

He doesn't let go of my hips. I go to back out of his embrace, to move away from him so I can try to gather the remains of my sanity, but his grip on me tightens, and he tugs me against him.

A noise escapes me that I can't even identify. A whimper? Some helpless sound as the hardness of his cock presses against me, leaving an imprint that I'll still feel long after he withdraws. *Fuck.*

I look up at him, certain he can see the lust in my eyes—it should be oozing out of my pores at this point. My stomach is twisted up in knots, and it's not even Vince this time—I feel bad about Vince, but I haven't recovered from how pissed I am at him.

It's Meg.

I can't do that to Meg.

And neither can he.

But oh, how I want him to.

It feels like he's waiting for me, for some signal he knows I can't give. I can hardly coax the air out of my lungs, and my head is at war with my heart, with my body.

I want him to take away my choice.

The realization kills me, literally slays me, but I want him to pick me up, throw me down on that bed, and fuck me until I forget every reason he shouldn't. I want him to pin me down, I want his kisses on my neck, his cock pushing inside me, relieving this ache I have for him, if only for a stolen moment. I want his brutality. I want the excuse. I can lie to cover his sins, but I can't lie to cover my own.

I can't say yes to the question he isn't asking.

Because Meg said yes to the question he *did* ask.

My brain is a bitch for that reminder, but the bitch I needed. It's not exactly a bucket of ice water dropped on my head, but a slow, chilly trickle dripping through my veins.

I wonder if this is what people mean by *lovesick*.

Only I don't know if this is love. I don't know what this is. Addiction, maybe.

Like I'm not a junkie, I pull away from him.

He could stop me, of course, but he doesn't. He lets me go. He knows it's what's best for both of us. For *all* of us.

I feel literally sick, like the end of a night of hard partying when you know you're going to have one hell of a hangover the next day. I've consumed too much Mateo and now I'm going to crash.

Instead of speaking, I turn toward the door. I still can't breathe properly, and I feel claustrophobic, like if I can just get out of this room and suck in a breath of fresh air, I'll feel a part of the world again, and not stuck in this isolated Mateo bubble where up is down and wrong is right.

I can't let myself be alone with him again.

He's still a threat. Not the same one he was before, but a threat all the same.

"Well, thank you," I say, dragging some semblance of lightness out of myself. "For coming to my rescue," I add, feeling the need to clarify.

Recovering more convincingly, he flashes me a light smile, as if none of that just happened. "Even villains save the day sometimes."

"I wish you were still a villain," I murmur, almost under my breath.

Raising his eyebrows in mild surprise, he asks, "What was that?"

"Nothing," I say innocently, reaching for the doorknob.

He comes up behind me, grabbing my hand, steadying it. Just the sensation of his hand on mine causes my skittering heart to sink. He uses his body to flatten me against the door. Heat from his chest scorches my back. The hardness of his arousal presses against my ass. Every bit of sense I just reclaimed falls out of me and I brace a hand on the door as his other hand skims my side. My body throbs, my mind races, and oh, my god, this man.

"Be careful what you wish for, sweetheart," he murmurs, his warm breath on my ear.

He's so close. *So* close. I'm a little light-headed as his lips float just above my skin. He releases my hand on the knob and pushes my hair back over my shoulder, dropping the lightest kiss on my neck.

The breath rushing in and out of my body right now isn't terribly subtle. He has to know he could hike up my leg and fuck me right here against the door and the only cries he would get out of me would be cries of pleasure.

But this time he pulls back.

I sag, not with relief, but disappointment.

I stumble back as he reaches for the knob this time. He eases the door open and sunshine spills in—a harsh reminder of the world outside. The world we're both a part of.

With one last longing look at the bed, I pull myself together, scoop up what's left of my dignity, and follow Mateo out to his car.

Once Burned

ABOUT THE AUTHOR

Sam Mariano has been writing stories since before she could actually write. In college, she studied psychology and English, because apparently she never wanted to make any money!

Sam lives in Ohio with a fantastic little girl who loves to keep her from writing. She appreciates the opportunity to share her characters with you; they were tired of living and dying in her hard drive. (The Morellis actually *did* die in her old hard drive, but she resurrected them so you guys could meet them! You're welcome, or she's sorry, depending on how you feel right now.)

Feel free to find Sam on Facebook, Goodreads, Twitter, or her blog—she loves hearing from readers! She's also available on Instagram now @sammarianobooks, and you can sign up for her totally-not-spammy newsletter!

If you have the time and inclination to leave a review, however short or long, she would greatly appreciate it! :)

Made in the USA
Middletown, DE
05 June 2023

31840743R00136